A PLUME BOOK

WHY CAN'T I BE YOU

Jeremy Larkin

ALLIE LARKIN lives with her husband, Jeremy, two German Shepherds, Argo and Stella, and a three-legged cat. Her first novel, *Stay*, is an international bestseller. She has never assumed a new identity to attend a high school reunion.

Praise for *Stay*

"Delightful! Both dog lovers and the pooch-free will enjoy this novel of friendship, love, and healing."

—Susan Elizabeth Phillips, *New York Times* bestselling author of *What I Did for Love*

"With humor and exceptional charm, Allie Larkin's story of a heartbroken young woman and the arrival of a clumsy, four-legged friend who brings new meaning to her life is simply wonderful. *Stay* is a treat of a novel that must be shared with every girlfriend who has ever loved and lost."

—Beth Hoffman, *New York Times* bestselling author of *Saving CeeCee Honeycutt*

MAR - - 2013

"I cannot wait to read more from Allie Larkin—an effervescent new voice in fiction. Witty, sweet, and strikingly real, *Stay* is for any woman who has ever experienced heartbreak or loss and needed a friend to lean on. I loved every word!"

—Beth Harbison, *New York Times* bestselling author of *Shoe Addicts Anonymous* and *Hope in a Jar*

"I'm madly in love with this big-hearted, charming keeper of a debut about love in all its forms, including the four-legged kind. Allie Larkin has a special and original voice."

—Melissa Senate, author of *See Jane Date* and *The Secret of Joy*

"Wow! This book blew me away. Sharp. Smart. Observant. Buzzing with romance, friendship, and heart. Most of all, incredibly well written. *Stay* is sure to become the new favorite among Emily Giffin fans. Enjoy!"

—Sarah Strohmeyer, author of *The Cinderella Pact* and *The Penny Pinchers Club*

"*Gilmore Girls* meets *Marley & Me* in this funny and compelling debut."   —*Library Journal*

"A feel-good debut."   —*People*

"Charming . . . Larkin makes writing look easy. . . . *Stay* has everything a summer read needs: humor, heart—and, endearingly, buckets of dog slobber."   —*Miami Herald*

"Enjoyable . . . A pleasing meld of romance and dog tale, with an empowerment theme, making for a gratifying read."

—Bookreporter.com

"Dog lovers will dig this heartfelt tale. . . . If you don't like dogs, you'll relate to this debut novel about finding your way back to life after heartbreak."   —Examiner.com

Why Can't I Be You

Allie Larkin

A PLUME BOOK

PLUME
Published by the Penguin Group
Penguin Group (USA) Inc., 375 Hudson Street, New York, New York 10014, USA •
Penguin Group (Canada), 90 Eglinton Avenue East, Suite 700, Toronto, Ontario
M4P 2Y3, Canada (a division of Pearson Penguin Canada Inc.) • Penguin Books Ltd,
80 Strand, London WC2R 0RL, England • Penguin Ireland, 25 St Stephen's Green,
Dublin 2, Ireland (a division of Penguin Books Ltd) • Penguin Group (Australia),
707 Collins Street, Melbourne, Victoria 3008, Australia (a division of Pearson Australia
Group Pty Ltd) • Penguin Books India Pvt Ltd, 11 Community Centre, Panchsheel Park,
New Delhi – 110 017, India • Penguin Group (NZ), 67 Apollo Drive, Rosedale,
Auckland 0632, New Zealand (a division of Pearson New Zealand Ltd) • Penguin Books,
Rosebank Office Park, 181 Jan Smuts Avenue, Parktown North 2193, South Africa •
Penguin China, B7 Jaiming Center, 27 East Third Ring Road North, Chaoyang District,
Beijing 100020, China

Penguin Books Ltd., Registered Offices: 80 Strand, London WC2R 0RL, England

First published by Plume, a member of Penguin Group (USA) Inc.

First Printing, March 2013
10 9 8 7 6 5 4 3 2 1

Ⓟ REGISTERED TRADEMARK—MARCA REGISTRADA

LIBRARY OF CONGRESS CATALOGING-IN-PUBLICATION DATA

Larkin, Allie.
    Why can't I be you / Allie Larkin.
        p. cm.
    ISBN 978-0-452-29837-8
    1. Young women—Fiction.   2. Class reunions—Fiction.   3. Lookalikes—Fiction.
4. Mistaken identity—Fiction.   1. Title.
    PS3612.A6485W692013
    813'.6—dc23   2012018095

Printed in the United States of America
Set in Goudy Std Regular
Designed by Eve Kirch

PUBLISHER'S NOTE
This is a work of fiction. Names, characters, places, and incidents are either the product
of the author's imagination or are used fictitiously, and any resemblance to actual persons,
living or dead, business establishments, events, or locales is entirely coincidental.

BOOKS ARE AVAILABLE AT QUANTITY DISCOUNTS WHEN USED TO PROMOTE PRODUCTS OR
SERVICES. FOR INFORMATION PLEASE WRITE TO PREMIUM MARKETING DIVISION, PENGUIN
GROUP (USA) INC., 375 HUDSON STREET, NEW YORK, NEW YORK 10014

To my oldest friends. You are superheroes.

Why Can't I Be You

Deagan was jittery on the drive to the airport. I didn't even make the coffee like mud that morning. I made it normal human strength, and I put lots of milk in his. He took forever to drink it, sitting at the rickety kitchen table in the tiny dining area of my sad little apartment, watching me scurry around shoving stray items into my carry-on bag. I couldn't fit anything else in my suitcase. It was packed so full that I had to lie across it to get it to close. My cat, Mr. Snuffleupagus, watched from his perch on top of the dresser and gave me a good swat with his paw every time I passed by.

I'd never been on a business trip before, and while the idea of it had always seemed glamorous and exciting, after spending the previous evening trying to get conditioner into a teeny-tiny bottle and ending up with a big slimy mess all over the bathroom floor, I was beginning to suspect that it was just as much of a hassle as any other kind of travel. The good part was, after the conference ended Deagan would drop Snuffy off at the kitty kennel and meet me in Seattle. We were going to rent a red convertible, road-trip out to Napa, and spend the week at a spa getting massages and drinking champagne in a hot-air balloon. It wasn't a visit to see college friends and crash on their couch or a rent-a-cottage-by-the-ski-slopes-with-sixteen-of-his-work-buddies kind of trip. It was an honest-to-goodness vacation.

Deagan was so busy playing with his cell phone that he didn't do the nudging he usually did to get me out the door whenever we had dinner plans or were trying to catch a movie. And, since I was expecting him to look at his watch and sigh every five minutes when it got close to go time, I wasn't watching the clock on my own. All of a sudden, I realized it was six forty-five and I was already supposed to be at the airport.

"Deags!" I yelled, grabbing a wad of sweaters from a pile at the bottom of my closet, shoving them into the front pocket of my straining suitcase. "We have to leave! Why didn't you tell me?"

"Oh," he said, giving me a dazed look, "yeah." He rubbed his hand over his face like he was trying to snap out of it. "Brendon texted about moving volleyball practice up to five thirty, but Faye can't get out of work in time, so Justin is trying to—"

"Okay, never mind. Tell me in the car!" I yelled, pulling my blazer on frantically.

We made a mad dash to the parking lot. Deagan carried my suitcase and loaded it in the trunk, which was nice, because (1) it was heavy, and (2) while he was loading it, he didn't notice when I slipped on some ice. We'd had a hard rain and an early frost, and the parking lot was like a skating rink.

I caught myself by grabbing the bumper of the nearest car, and set off the alarm. Deagan looked up. I jumped away from the wailing car and shook my head like I didn't know what happened.

"I don't know why people have car alarms," I said, trying to act casual as I got in the passenger seat of his Mazda3. "Everyone just ignores them anyway."

"Uh-huh," he grunted.

Deagan was usually a little quiet in the morning. I told myself it was nothing unusual, but deep down I worried. He hadn't finished his volleyball story. I didn't really want to hear more about the trials and tribulations of scheduling practice, so I didn't ask, but I wished he would say something—maybe tell me he was going to miss me or that he couldn't wait for our vacation. Something.

He fiddled with the heat vents on the dashboard, and I noticed that his hands were shaky. He's just nervous because we're late, and he's driving on icy roads, I thought, but when we stopped at a light, he gave me a look—a really deep, long, soulful look—and my heart got fluttery in a way that was well beyond travel nerves.

My lease was up in two months. We'd talked about it at dinner the other night. That look had to have meaning. That look, the silence, the nerves. He was going to ask me to move in with him.

And it's not like I hadn't thought about it. I knew where I would hang my Jackson Pollock prints, and which corner of his living room would be perfect for the wing chair I'd reupholstered with fabric from an old wool suit. On my first morning living there, I'd wear my black satin bathrobe and make him pancakes and fresh-squeezed orange juice. I already knew I would do everything in my power to keep all bodily functions to myself, no matter what. And I'd decided that someday, when we finally got married, I wasn't going to take his name, but I would consider a hyphenation: Jenny Shaw-Holmes had a good ring to it.

The drive to Greater Rochester International Airport only took fifteen minutes, but by the time we got there I'd thought up five different ways to say, "Yes! I'll move in with you." I'd vetoed three, and was torn between a staid and dignified "Of course I will!" and shouting, "Oh! Deagan!" as I threw my arms around his neck, getting just teary enough to be sweet but not messy enough to embarrass him.

Deagan was a hospital corners kind of guy. He didn't even

have any specks of lint in the leather casing around his gearshift, and all the chrome detailing on his dashboard shone like it had the first day he got his car. Sometimes, I wondered if he even had fingerprints, because he never left smudges anywhere.

He pulled up to the curb at the JetBlue drop-off, put the car in park, hit the hazard-light button with his knuckle, and started fumbling around in his jacket pocket. There was something in there. Something he had his hand around. It had a hard corner.

Holy mother of monkey lovers, I thought. He's got a ring box in his pocket. Maybe it's *the* ring. The one I'd seen in an ad in *Glamour*. We were sitting on the couch drinking coffee. He was reading *Sports Illustrated*. I flipped the page, and there it was: an elegant solitaire with an emerald-cut diamond. I stared at it for a little too long. I pictured it on my finger. I imagined him getting down on one knee and opening the box. By then, we'd been dating for a year, and it seemed about the right amount of time.

"Whatcha reading?" he asked, looking over my shoulder. The page across from it was about new spring makeup colors. There was hardly any text. It was obvious I hadn't been reading about coral lipstick for such a long time. "It's pretty," he said, pointing to the ring. I turned the page quickly, my cheeks flushing.

He asked where it was from, said "hmm" very thoughtfully when I told him Cartier, and never mentioned it again.

Maybe he'd finally gotten the ring and he just couldn't wait. Maybe he'd planned to ask me on our trip, but he was so upset that we'd be apart and the ring was burning a hole in his pocket. Maybe when I got to Seattle, I could post a picture of that ring on my hand. My status would be *Jenny Shaw is getting married!* And all the girls I'd gone to high school with, who were now smugly pregnant and posting about cravings, morning sickness, mucus plugs, and something called a Boppy, could just eat it.

"Jenny," he said, his hazel eyes wide, framed with the kind of dark, thick lashes any woman would die for but only guys seem to have, "I have to tell you something."

"Oh, Deags!" I said, sighing happily.

"I know! I know! You have to go, but I think I need to say this now."

I felt frozen. Like time and air and space and the rotation of the earth had all stopped just to hear what Deagan would say next.

"I just, I have these . . . feelings . . . and I think I owe it to all of us to figure them out."

"All of us?"

He gave me a helpless look, and it clicked into place. "All of us" meant him and Faye—the girl he thought he loved—and me, the one he was pretty sure he didn't.

Faye, from volleyball. For months, I'd tried to ignore the fact that every story about his weekly game seemed to start and end with Faye. I told myself that every story had to include her, because she was a super-amazing volleyball player who carried the team and made every winning shot. But then they made the playoffs, and I went to see the first game. I watched Faye screw up one play after another, and realized Deagan's interest in her had nothing to do with her skills on the court. When I saw her get hit in the ear by a spike because she was too busy making goofy faces at Deagan, it started a twinge in my stomach, a little ball of nerves that bounced around in there and didn't want to go away.

A car behind us beeped, but Deagan didn't even react. He took his hand out of his pocket. He was holding an unwrapped stick of gum. Doublemint. He always bought the value packs that someone might say are about the size of a ring box—if that someone had an overactive imagination and a spatial relationship deficiency. He shoved the gum into his mouth and started chewing.

"It's just, Faye and I, we have so much in common," he said, slowly, pushing the gum from one side of his mouth to the other with his tongue. "And I think if I don't . . . explore that, I think it won't be doing anyone any favors."

"Explore that?" I said, picturing him in bed with Faye, wearing a pith helmet and a headlamp like he was about to go spelunking.

"Don't worry," he said. "I'll still watch your cat while you're gone."

"Thank you," I said automatically, like he was doing me some amazing favor by not starving my cat to death in the face of our breakup.

"But I don't think it's appropriate for us to go to Napa now," he said in a stern voice, as if I'd suggested something completely ridiculous and crass when I'd sent him links to the spa months ago, when we were still, for all intents and purposes, a perfectly happy couple.

I wanted to sob. I wanted to scream. But I just felt numb. Like time and air and space and the rotation of the earth might forget to start again, and I'd just be frozen in his car forever. Finally, I felt one big fat tear drip down my cheek, and then another and another. I wiped my face with the sleeve of my jacket.

An airport-security vehicle with orange flashing lights pulled up next to Deagan's car. The driver honked and made a swooping gesture with his arm.

"I'm sorry, Jenny," Deagan said. "But do you mind?" He hit the button on his door to unlock mine. I grabbed my carry-on bag off the backseat. I didn't look at him. I didn't say anything. I didn't know what to say. I used my damp sleeve to wipe my fingerprints off the chrome door handle as I got out. And then I stood on the curb and watched him pull away, driving fast, like he couldn't wait to start his new life with Faye. Like he couldn't get away from me quickly enough.

I wiped my face with my sleeve again. I could feel the mascara running from my eyelashes, making them stick together, but I didn't have the energy to do anything to fix it. My carry-on felt like it weighed a million pounds. I dragged it across the floor of the airport lobby, even though it didn't have wheels.

"You're cutting it really close," the attendant at the check-in counter said when I handed her my driver's license.

It was only when she asked if I was checking any luggage that I realized my suitcase was still in the trunk of Deagan's car. Even if I wanted to completely humiliate myself by calling and begging him to drive back to bring it to me, it was way too late.

got stuck in the middle seat on the airplane, crammed between a man who looked like a linebacker, with shoulders that pushed into my seat space, and a woman wearing so much perfume I could taste it. The fake, flowery soapiness of her scent made me remember when I was about five or six and I ate a huge mouthful of bubbles in the bathtub because I expected them to taste like candy. They didn't.

I sat between the two of them, trying hard not to cry and failing miserably. The linebacker pretended to ignore me, giving me the side-eye every now and then from behind his *New York Times*, and the woman who smelled like Mr. Bubble kept sighing and clucking every time I sobbed, like she wanted me to talk about it with her. I didn't want to talk about it. I didn't want to be that absurd cliché—crying on a stranger's shoulder on an airplane. But when the attendants came around and gave us all little bags of peanuts, I remembered how much Deagan hated them—he always gave me his bag—and suddenly only having one little bag of stale airline peanuts seemed like the loneliest state of being in the world. I let out a sharp, loud sob that sounded like an angry goose honking.

"Oh, honey," Mrs. Bubble said, patting my arm.

"He used to give me his nuts!" I wailed.

The man in the seat in front of us actually stood up and turned around to stare at me. Mrs. Bubble shooed him away, waving the back of her hand at him.

The linebacker handed me his peanuts, which made me cry even harder. He hurriedly reached for the in-flight magazine in the seat pocket and pretended to be engrossed in an article titled "The Top Tapas in Ten Cities."

Mrs. Bubble fumbled through her purse and handed me a wad of yellow napkins. I didn't want to take some stranger's grubby old Wendy's napkins, but I'd been crying so hard that the front of my shirt was drenched.

"The thing is," I said, mopping tears off my chin with one of the napkins, "she's not even any better than me."

"Of course she isn't," Mrs. Bubble said, with the kind of universal assuredness women who are pros at mothering all seem to have.

But I wasn't looking for reassurance. It was true. Faye wasn't any better than me. She was barely even any different from me. It was insulting. If Deagan had left me for a supermodel or an acrobat, or even someone who played volleyball really, really well, it wouldn't have felt like such an enormous slap in the face. The fact that Faye was average at everything—just as average as me—was maddening. He wasn't even upgrading.

"And why," Mrs. Bubble said, "would you want to be with someone who doesn't know a good thing when he sees it?"

My friend Luanne would have shuddered at anyone calling me a "good thing," regardless of the intention. "You're not an object to be bought and sold by men," she'd say defiantly. Actually, she would have shut Mrs. Bubble down at "oh, honey." No one could ever call Luanne "honey" and get away with it. Same with "sweetie," "deary," "sweetheart," "doll," "baby," or any other term of endearment, no matter who it came from. But Luanne would have agreed with the core of the advice: Why would I even want someone who didn't want me?

Even though I knew I shouldn't still want Deagan, I did. Even after everything he'd said at the airport, I wanted the life we'd planned, and if he called and told me he'd made a mistake, I would have taken him back without question. I would have pretended it never happened and that Faye didn't even exist. We'd planned a life together, and it was going to be a good one.

I hadn't been the only one planning. I hadn't built up our plans for the future alone. It wasn't like the way I became convinced Donatella's was Deagan's favorite restaurant because it was my favorite and I didn't hear him when he said otherwise. For months, our Sunday morning game was to think of baby names while we drank our coffee in bed. And it wasn't just me picking the names; he'd chime in too.

"Luke," I'd say, "if it's a boy."

"Lukas Malcolm," he'd say, "after my father."

"Lukas Malcolm Holmes," I'd say. "Or Lukas Malcolm Shaw-Holmes."

"Don't hyphenate," he said. "It's tacky. Either take my name or don't, but don't make it Luke's problem." And he said it like Luke was already a person, already our son, and we were just waiting for the right time to meet him—after I got promoted to full account executive and he made project manager, after the wedding, when we bought a renovated Victorian in the South Wedge neighborhood in downtown Rochester and stenciled a picture of the Holmes family crest on the nursery wall, just like the room Deagan grew up in. Those were things we'd planned together. We'd even started saving for the house. Not just me. Both of us. Left to my own devices, I would never even dream of painting a big red Celtic lion on any wall in our home, let alone over my baby's crib. Left to my own devices, I would rather move out to the country than buy a house downtown. And, if I was going whole hog on being honest, being an account executive was starting to feel like it might not be tops on my list either.

I told Mrs. Bubble all of this. It was ridiculous, but it felt so good to say it out loud that I couldn't stop myself. She was a really good listener.

The linebacker had exhausted the magazine and thumbed through the SkyMall catalog for a while before he fell asleep. Mrs. Bubble and I giggled as he snored, and it surprised me that I could laugh—that my whole, entire world had fallen apart, but a stranger snoring was still funny.

When we landed in Cleveland, I helped Mrs. Bubble get her travel case from the overhead compartment. "Sounds like you have a lot of thinking to do," she said, as we parted ways at the gate. The linebacker gave me a sheepish wave before heading toward baggage claim.

I decided to buy myself a nice lunch at the airport pub during my stopover. I'd expense it. I'd indulge. It would cheer me up. Instead of feeling sorry for myself, I would celebrate being an intelligent, professional woman off in the world on her very first business trip, company credit card in hand. This trip was a very big deal.

When Monica, my boss, realized her sister's wedding was the same weekend as the seminar she'd already signed up for, she picked me to go instead. Out of ten junior account executives, I was the one she chose, even over Luanne. And it's not like Monica picked my name out of a hat. She actually and purposely chose me. Maybe Deagan dumping me was a sign—the dawn of a new era in the life of Jenny Shaw, power executive. Maybe I needed to flaunt my newfound freedom.

But when the pub was out of the salmon I'd finally decided on, I spilled salad dressing down my brand-new blouse, and I realized a scotch and soda didn't taste as elegant as it sounded, my brave face started to crack. And when my connecting flight to Sea-Tac got delayed, and some snotty kid sitting behind me in the waiting area spit his gum into my hair instead of his mom's waiting napkin, I turned into a complete and total mess. I bought myself a cup of coffee, found an empty row of chairs over in the corner, far away from any and all gum-spitting kids, and called Luanne, while picking sticky strands of what smelled like watermelon bubble gum out of my hair.

"This is why I take Xanax when I fly," Luanne said, sighing, after I told her what had happened.

"Yes, so when your future husband breaks up with you, and you end up with a germ wad of gum in your hair, you're perfectly relaxed about it—exactly."

"I'm just saying air travel is stressful."

"Comfort me, dammit!" I said, and started sobbing all over again.

Things had been a little strained between us since I got picked for the trip and she didn't. When Monica announced it at the weekly meeting, I saw the way Luanne's face fell. She shot a feeble smile in my general direction and excused herself to make a phone call as soon as the meeting ended.

She was still on the phone when I went to see if she wanted to grab lunch. She held her hand over the receiver and whispered, "It's fine, you go," like it was nothing, but I could see the hurt in her eyes, the way she couldn't stand that I'd gotten something she thought she deserved.

I drove to Wegmans and wolfed down a takeout tray of California rolls in the parking lot by myself, because I didn't want anyone to see the hurt in my eyes. It was stupid and selfish, but I really wanted Luanne to be proud of me. If she'd gotten the trip, I'd have whisked her off to lunch at her favorite restaurant to celebrate over midday gimlets and goat-cheese crepes.

That afternoon, I asked Monica if I could take Luanne with me. I just wanted to appease everyone. I wanted things to go back to normal. Monica told me I needed to learn how to take a compliment gracefully.

I watched a plane slowly pull away from the gate.

Luanne sighed. Her breath made static in the phone. "You can do better than Deagan," she said weakly.

"Thank you," I said, just as weakly. Tears dripped between my face and my cell phone. With my luck, the moisture was somehow increasing the phone's radiation, I'd develop a big, inoperable tumor on my face—and then no one would ever love me.

"Deagan always looked like he was bad in bed anyway," Luanne said.

"What do you mean?"

"You know. He's all golf shirts and argyle, like an overgrown preppy frat boy, and I just think that's probably the extent of his skills in bed—frat-boy sex."

"Frat-boy sex?" I said, trying not to laugh. Luanne was doing this on purpose to distract me. It was one of her special skills. Deep conversations weren't her forte, but she could turn any situation into a one-woman stand-up act. It wasn't necessarily comforting, but it was better than sitting in the airport alone, feeling sorry for myself.

"All the grunting and moaning like there's crazy stuff happening, when really it's some kind of modified missionary and he comes if you move even just the slightest little bit."

"Lu!"

"Ha! I'm so right!"

"You're not!"

"'Oh! Ooh! Oh!' That was the extent of your sex life."

"No," I said, wiping my wet cheeks, whispering into the phone. "You forgot to add 'Yesssssss!'"

"See!" Luanne said, laughing. "You're going to be fine. When you come back, we're going on the hunt. We'll get you some hot dentist sex or some steamy science teacher action."

"Dentist sex?"

"Nerds are way better in bed than frat boys," Luanne said. "Trust me. They're grateful *and* creative."

"Are you at work?"

"Yeah."

"You're sitting in your cubicle, moaning and talking about dentist sex right in the middle of the office?"

"That's how much I love you," Luanne said. "Plus, Monica's gone, so it's kind of raucous around here anyway."

"You're the best," I said, looking up at the flight board. "Crap!"

"I'm the best crap? That's so sweet of y—"

"They just moved my flight back another three hours!" I could feel the sobs creeping into my throat again. Delayed flights, like breaking a glass or having the water suddenly run freezing in the shower, always made me cry, even on a good day.

"Go get the gum cut out of your hair," Luanne said. "The last time I got stuck in JFK, I went to a salon on the main concourse and got a pedicure. They have to have something similar in Cleveland. You could use a haircut anyway."

"Thanks," I said flatly. "So my hair is all wrong too?"

"It is full of chewing gum," she said.

Luanne was wrong about the salon. They didn't have anything similar in Cleveland. I ordered a bagel with peanut butter from a coffee shop in Concourse A. In the ladies' room, I stood at the sink scooping globs of peanut butter from tiny white plastic tubs with my fingers, and rubbed it in my hair to try to dissolve the gum. I'd heard peanut butter was a great way to remove something, and I was pretty sure it was gum. I don't know if I was wrong, or if peanut butter doesn't work on gum in hair for some reason, but it all just turned into a huge wad of messy that wouldn't wash out. And there's a reason no one makes peanut butter scented shampoo.

While I was covered in peanut butter, my phone rang. I dug it out of my jacket pocket with sticky fingers. It was my mom. I didn't answer. Ignoring her calls always made things worse later, but I couldn't stand the idea of having to tell her that Deagan had dumped me. I didn't want to hear the lecture—how disappointing it was that she didn't have any grandchildren yet, how she was giving up on the idea once and for all, because it would be easier not to get her hopes up.

I cut the sticky mess out of my hair, strand by strand, with a pair of nail clippers, trying to salvage as much as I could. Luanne was right about my hair. It was such a mess that my butcher job didn't even make it look all that much worse. The adorable layers my hairdresser gave me five months ago were now all ragged and uneven anyway. I'd been working so hard on being the kind of junior account executive that gets sent on business trips in her boss's place, and the kind of girlfriend I thought would make Deagan want to move in with me, that I hadn't even had time to get a decent trim. I'd been hoping to get a life-changing, fantabulous haircut at the spa salon while Deagan and I were away. I'd been hoping for a lot of things.

I slept through most of the flight from Cleveland to Seattle. It was the kind of sleep where you drool a lot and feel even more tired when you wake up, but I was thankful for the break from my thoughts, and that I had a window seat, so I was the only one party to my drool.

I walked to baggage claim and stood with the crowd of passengers waiting for the conveyer belt to start, for a good five minutes before I remembered that my carry-on was the only baggage I had.

The shuttle to the conference center took about thirty minutes. There were only two other passengers on board—a couple, maybe on their honeymoon. They were holding hands and whispering. I did my best not to watch them, and not to think about Deagan.

I busied myself, pretending to look for something in my carry-on bag, so I wouldn't have to exchange pleasantries with them. Seattle was behind me before I even got a chance to look at it. The air was thick and gray and made my hair curl up in all directions, and when I finally did look back, the road behind us was a faint shadow, like a ghost.

Driving into the mountains made me dizzy. Rochester is as flat as flat can be, and this landscape seemed impossible in contrast, like a scene from a movie. The highway was carved into narrow valleys between hills taller than the fog allowed me to see. The walls of rock on either side of the road were covered in metal netting to rein in potential rockslides. In several places rocks had fallen, and the netting was battered and broken. I started getting carsick and spent the rest of the ride trying to look out the front window, focusing on the broken white line on the road ahead of us and nothing else.

The shuttle pulled up to a roundabout in front of the Salish Lodge. It looked familiar, and I thought for a second that maybe I'd been there before. Maybe on a summer vacation, back when my parents were still together, back when I was too young to really remember. But the guy from the couple started humming a familiar song slightly off-key. I shuddered involuntarily and realized we were at the same lodge they used as the Great Northern Hotel on *Twin Peaks*.

I used to stay up late watching *Twin Peaks* by myself on the little color TV my dad bought me for my eighth birthday as a ploy to win my affections after the divorce. My mother said it wasn't good for me, that my television watching should be monitored and I was too young to watch unsupervised. But my dad said, "It's not hooked up to the cable. Honestly, Marie! What's the worst she can watch?"

He helped me set it up in my room, teaching me how to angle the silver arms of the antenna to get good reception, before my mother's dirty looks and heavy sighs drove him out of the house again. I started watching *Twin Peaks* because everyone in my class was talking about it, even though it was on past my bedtime and way over my head. I would sit with my nose almost pressed to the screen, a blanket over me and the TV, so I could keep the volume low and the light from flickering under my door. Face-to-face with dead Laura Palmer and Killer BOB, I held my own hand for comfort, squeezing until my fingers went numb. I slept with the lights on until I turned eleven.

I followed the couple out of the shuttle, averting my eyes when the guy grabbed his wife's butt like I wasn't even there. As I walked up the stone steps to the front door, everything started to feel completely topsy-turvy and sort of surreal. Maybe Deagan wasn't really breaking up with me. Maybe someone had plunked me in the middle of a strange David Lynch experiment. Maybe when I saw my face in the mirror, a creepy wolfish man would be staring back at me. The jet lag and the crying hangover and the thick, dried puddles of mascara on my face made me feel like it wasn't out of the range of possibility.

I knew I had to look absolutely awful, but the woman behind the reception desk gave me a big smile and said, "Welcome to the Salish Lodge," as if she were graciously inviting me into her own home. "Here for the reunion?" she asked. She wore a crisp white shirt and a black sweater with a ruffled front, and her hair was pulled back into a sleek, low ponytail without the slightest hint of a flyaway hair. Her name tag rested perfectly just below her shoulder, so you weren't forced to stare at her boob to learn that her name was Ashley.

"No," I said. "The New Media in Public Relations conference."

"Oh, yes." She took my name and found my file. "Will you be needing help with your luggage?"

I felt my eyes well up again. "They lost my luggage," I said. I turned my head and watched the flames in the big stone fireplace in the lobby while I composed myself.

"Well, I can call the airline and see when they're expecting to deliver it."

"Oh, no," I said, hating to be caught in a lie, even if it was a little one. "It was the car service to the airport. They drove off without leaving it." It wasn't a total lie. "I called, but the best they can do is take it back home for me."

"Then you'll probably be needing a shuttle back into Seattle to do a little shopping before the conference starts tomorrow," she said, with a wink.

"That would be wonderful," I said, feeling worse about the lie. She was so nice. She probably would have been sympathetic if

I'd told her the truth. I just didn't think I could get the words out without turning into an even bigger mess. My ride to the airport did swipe my luggage, and the awful truth of it was that Deagan was nothing more than a car service to me now. I didn't even know what I was going to do after the conference was over. My flight back was a week away, but the idea of taking a romantic wine country vacation by myself seemed slightly more pathetic than booking an early flight home and sitting in my apartment, pretending I was on vacation so I wouldn't have to admit to my entire office that I got dumped at the airport.

Ashley arranged for a shuttle to take me back to the city in an hour, giving me time to "freshen up," which was probably a polite way of saying, "Please go wash your face and pull it together." But she did it in a way that made me feel taken care of, not ashamed.

I took my room key and headed for the elevator. Just as the doors opened and I stepped in, I heard a woman yell out, "Jenny!" Or at least what sounded like "Jenny" from across the lobby, over the sound of a man in a business suit rolling his fancy leather suitcase over the slate floor. I turned around and saw a streak of black hair and a bright blue dress barreling toward me. "Wait, wait! Hold the door," she shouted. I pushed the button to keep the door open, and she charged into the elevator, wrapping her arms around me, knocking my hand off the button. The doors closed.

I've never been a huge fan of elevators, or enclosed spaces in general, or strangers or excessive touching, for that matter, so being in an elevator getting hugged by a stranger with arms that were freakishly strong for her relatively diminutive figure wasn't exactly my favorite thing in the entire world.

"I can't believe it's really you! You're not on the reunion list!" she said, pulling away but keeping a firm hold on both my arms.

She slipped her hands down so we were holding hands, shook hers so mine shook too, and looked me over. "It's me! Myra!" She jumped up and down, taking my hands with her. "You look . . . You look amazing—OHMYGOD! You really did it, didn't you?"

I was about to tell her that I didn't know what was going on. That she probably had me mistaken for someone else, but then she gently ran three fingers down the slope of my nose, and I didn't know what to do. What are you supposed to say to a stranger touching your nose in an elevator? I stared at her with my mouth gaping, like an idiot.

"I liked your old nose," she said, shaking her head at me. "You're the only one who didn't." Her eyes got wide, and I thought she'd realized her mistake. Instead she gushed: "But this one is great too! I thought you looked different when I saw you across the room. It's a flawless job, really."

"Thanks," I said. I knew it was absurd, but I hated the idea of disappointing her. I'll be who she wants me to be until I get off the elevator, I thought. I figured we'd go our separate ways, and I'd just try to avoid her for the rest of my time at the lodge. There would probably be a slew of her old friends at the reunion, and she'd forget about me, or whoever she thought I was, in the shuffle.

She had thick bangs and long straight hair that framed a small, sharp face. She was thin and wiry, maybe a little mousy, but she wore bright red lipstick and looked very pulled together. Her gorgeous, big, dark brown eyes were filling up with tears. Her tears, and the confusion and the hugging and the closeness of the elevator got me crying again.

"Oh, I know!" she said, letting go of one of my hands so she could wipe her eyes. "I've been fighting the mascara battle all day too. I'm such a freaking sap! I mean, thinking about seeing everyone—it just gets me going. But none of us—we didn't know you were coming." She hugged me again, sobbing into my shoulder. "It's amazing!"

For a small lodge, it was turning into the longest elevator ride I'd ever been on, but then I realized that neither of us had pushed a floor button. "What floor are you on?" I asked, breaking away to look at the numbers on the panel.

"Oh no, I'm not staying here," Myra said. "I still live in town. I'm just here setting up for the reunion weekend. And then I saw you. We had no idea!"

"I'm sorry," I said, pushing the button for the fourth floor. "I—"

"No no! Don't worry! It's no trouble! We inflated the numbers a little, just in case. I think, secretly, we were all hoping you'd show up. Did you bring a date?"

"My boyfriend broke up with me at the airport," I blurted out.

The enormity of it hit me. Everything I knew about my life— all my plans, all my goals, everything—revolved around Deagan. Without him, I didn't have anything. I didn't know anything about myself anymore. I felt my knees wobble.

"Oh, Jessie," Myra said, wrapping her arms around me again. And even though this time I was sure she wasn't saying "Jenny," and I was absolutely positive beyond a doubt that I wasn't who she thought I was, I hugged her back, because I needed a hug.

She grabbed the room key out of my hand when the elevator doors opened. "I have so many questions! I mean, what are you doing now? Where do you live? Who's this idiot who broke up with you? And at the airport? Who *does* that?" she said, talking a mile a minute as she shuffled me down the hall. She pushed me into the right room and started the shower for me immediately. "But I'll wait until we get you all cleaned up and feeling better."

She made a beeline for the minibar, grabbed a little bottle of rum, opened it, and handed it to me. "You look like you need this!"

"I don't even have luggage," I wailed, drinking from the bottle like I was taking medicine, even though I almost never drink.

"Then we'll have to go shopping! What a pity!" she said, in fake horror. "How awful that we have an excuse to go shopping together! I have the perfect place to take you. And when we're done, you'll look so fantastic you won't even care that he's gone. Promise." She flopped down on the bed, pulled her phone out of her purse, and flipped it open. I grabbed the hotel robe out of the closet and headed into the bathroom.

Just before I closed the bathroom door, I heard her say, "Oh my God, Heather! You'll never guess who's here!" and then, "No! Better! Jessie Morgan! No, I'm not. She's really, really here."

Before I jumped in the shower, I studied my face in the mirror. I'd never thought much about my nose one way or another, but it really did fit my face perfectly.

"**I can just take** the shuttle to Seattle to go shopping," I called from the bathroom, as I toweled off. I ran my fingers through my hair, trying to create some semblance of an even part, since like an idiot I'd packed my brush in my suitcase. "You must have so much to do for the reunion."

I couldn't bring myself to tell Myra that I wasn't this Jessie person. If I could go into the city to shop by myself and change rooms when I got back, I'd avoid the whole "You know how I hugged you and pretended to be your long-lost friend . . . yeah, I'm not" awkwardness. Maybe I could leave a nice little note from Jessie at the front desk, telling Myra it was great to see her but I had to go. I'd stay away from the banquet room while the reunion was taking place, and everything would be fine.

"Don't be silly," Myra called. "When were you even last in Seattle?"

I froze. I'd never been to Seattle.

Luckily, it was a rhetorical question. "You wouldn't know where to go now!" Myra said gleefully. "I know the perfect place. And I want to spend as much time with you as I can while you're here!" Her phone chimed. "Oh, crap! I have to go check with the chef about something for the reunion menu, but meet me in the lobby when you're dressed and we'll go. Okay?"

I heard the door close before I could even answer. I pulled my salad-dressing-splattered, travel-rumpled clothes on again, and emerged from the bathroom. The room was undoubtedly the nicest hotel room I'd ever been in. A big fluffy bed with a Myra-shaped imprint on the comforter. A wood-burning fireplace stacked with logs and ready to go.

Deagan would have been in heaven. There were few things he loved more than lighting fires. His parents had one of those old-fashioned houses with a fireplace in every bedroom, and he told me once that when he was a kid he used to write his secrets on paper and burn them in his fireplace.

I thought I knew all his secrets. When we lay in bed at night, Deagan would tell me stories about his childhood. His mother always baked oatmeal raisin cookies for after-school snacks. When his father took him fly-fishing in hip waders, he was amazed by the way the cold water rushed past without getting him wet and the feel of the stones at the bottom of the river through the rubber soles. His grandmother taught him how to waltz in the kitchen to Irving Berlin songs when she came to visit for Christmas. The scar on his chin was from falling off his bike, and his mother washed the blood off his face with a wet washcloth. He and his little brother built forts in the living room and bombed each other with throw pillows. When he graduated from college, his dad had his initials engraved into his grandfather's watch and cried as he fastened it around Deagan's wrist. He'd tell me these stories, the things he remembered, and just the fact that they were real made me feel better. Deagan's stories made me believe I could have the things I'd always wanted, that we were going to be a "happily ever after" couple, that when we had kids, one of us would know what a childhood was supposed to be. I needed that to be true.

I threw myself down on the bed, in the Myra-shaped imprint,

burying my head into the comforter. It smelled like Chanel Chance—the perfume Luanne wore. She practically walked around in a cloud of it. It was comforting. Familiar. Like getting a hug when I needed one.

The idea of taking the shuttle and shopping by myself in a city I'd never been to was completely overwhelming. I felt like quitting everything. I could lie in that spot on the bed and do nothing until the cleaning crew came in and had to move me. They could bundle me up with the sheets and whisk me away.

I rolled over on my side. Something stuck me in the face. It was an earring. A tiny filigree teardrop, hanging from a thin gold post. It looked old. The nooks and crannies of the gold were darkened with years of tarnish, even though the rest of it was polished clean. I searched around until I found the earring back, on the floor by the nightstand. I couldn't just leave it there or pretend I hadn't found it. I had to return it to Myra. It reminded me of a pair of earrings Deagan's grandmother had. It was probably an heirloom.

I thought about just leaving it at the front desk with a note for Myra. They probably don't have stationery in here, I thought. Hotels don't really do that anymore, right? But when I searched around, I found a folder with a few pieces of paper and some envelopes in the desk drawer. The discovery disappointed me. I wanted to see Myra again. I wanted to go shopping with a friend and be someone new and forget about Deagan for a while. "I wouldn't want to risk them losing this," I said to myself, out loud, like my lame excuse would somehow make the idea of pretending to be someone I wasn't less crazy or ridiculous.

stood in the lobby, holding the earring gently in my palm, trying not to crush it, while I looked around for Myra. Blue dress. Dark hair. Thick bangs. I couldn't see her anywhere. I walked into a banquet room to look for her.

I'm just going to give her the earring and go, I thought. Without the mess of mascara on my face, she'll realize I'm not really her long-lost friend. No one looks that much like another person.

The room was empty. Across the back wall a big banner read, "Welcome Home Wildcats! Mount Si Class of 1999 Reunion," and posters that looked like blown-up pages of a yearbook hung on every other wall. I'd graduated a year after them, but my class reunion was two years ago. Who has a thirteen-year reunion?

Someone had gone through with thick, bright markers, like the ones that are supposed to smell like berries, but really just smell like toilet cleaner, and drawn doodles on all the posters. Hearts, stars, unicorns, and big red Ws that I supposed were for "Wildcats" littered the pages, and the reunion status of each student was scribbled underneath their name in round, balloon-like high school script: "attending," "not attending," "out of contact."

I found Myra on the first poster. Her last name was Aberly. "Attending! Yay!" was written under her name, along with a goofy smiley face with bangs like hers. There were four Heathers before I even got to the Gs, so I had no idea who Myra called from my room.

Morgan, I thought. That was the name Myra had said on the phone. Jessie Morgan. I followed the posters across the walls, through Collier and Finley, Kapovi and Linden. The pictures could have been from my high school. Flannel shirts and scrunchies, black choker necklaces. Every other girl had Rachel's haircut from *Friends*, and only one or two of them actually had the hair for it.

Finally, I found Jessica Elizabeth Morgan. And she did look like me. It was eerie. Her hair was lighter and slightly orange, and her eyes were a funny color—brown but with a weird greenish tinge. Fake contacts maybe, or bad color balance in the photo. But she had the same smile, the same apple cheeks I'd had in high school, which, thankfully, turned into actual cheekbones as I aged. She even shared the slightly too big ears that I never did quite grow into and had the same light freckles across her nose, which was larger than mine but absolutely adorable. Her nose gave her character, and I hoped, even though I had no idea who she was or where she was, this Jessie Morgan girl never got the nose job she'd so desperately wanted. I hoped, wherever she was, she was happy and had someone to love her and wouldn't ever feel the humiliation of getting dumped at the airport.

She was wearing a black top or dress with spaghetti straps. One of the straps had fallen off her shoulder, and I was thankful that the photo was cropped before it revealed exactly how much cleavage she was showing the camera. Underneath the picture, next to her name, was written "out of contact," with a big pouty face next to it. Someone had crossed that out and written "ATTENDING!!!!" in bright red ink that was still fresh and smelled, indeed, like those big fat fruit markers. Myra must have just written it, and my heart broke for her when I thought about confessing that I wasn't Jessie Morgan. I reached out and touched the picture of Jessie.

"God! Remember us with the Sun-In?" Myra called from across the room as she walked over to me. "We were, like, addicted to that stuff." She put her arm around my shoulder. "Of course, I was scared Grammie would find out, so I just had that one streak you could only see when I wore a ponytail."

I hadn't been allowed to use Sun-In as a kid. My mother would have flipped. But I remembered when Angela Nathans spilled an entire bottle of it on the bus on our seventh-grade overnight trip to Philadelphia. Right at the beginning of the trip. When the bus got hot, it got worse, so every time we left—to see the Liberty Bell or Valley Forge—we came back to a bus full of baked Sun-In.

"I'll never forget that smell," I said.

"I know! Me either," Myra said, laughing. "It still smells the same." She stepped away to smooth down the corner of the poster. "You're going to think I'm a freak, but every once in a while I take a whiff from the bottle when I see it at the drugstore." She looked up and stared at my face. I was positive she would realize that I wasn't Jessie Morgan, but she just smiled. "It reminds me of you and me and Karen." She looked away for a second. "I never thought I'd see you again," she said, and let out a little gasp or a sob or something—I couldn't tell what because her head was turned.

"I found your earring," I said, holding out my hand to her. I couldn't think of anything else to say. I needed to get out of there. I couldn't pretend to be someone Myra had been missing for thirteen years, or however long it had been since Jessie Morgan left.

Myra reached up to her ear. "Oh, thank you!" she said. "That would have sucked! They were Grammie's." She took the earring from me and skillfully stuck it back in her earlobe. "She died last year."

"I'm so sorry," I said.

Myra smiled. "Remember how we used to go over to her house after school, and she'd always have frozen Thin Mints and those little plastic barrel bottles of orange drink?"

I laughed. "I remember those bottles! The stuff inside always tasted the same, no matter what the color was." I don't know why I wasn't telling Myra the truth. It was awful of me. It was fraud. But it felt so familiar to talk with her, to reminisce about things, even if we really weren't talking about the very same memories.

"Your eyes look so different without those green contacts," Myra said, studying my face. I wasn't sure if I wanted her to find me out or not. "No one had the heart to tell you that they didn't make your eyes look green. They just made them look weird."

I remembered how desperately I wanted blue contacts when I was a kid. My mom told me my eyes were too dark for them anyway. Where was Jessie's mom? How come no one told her she couldn't drink sugar water or spray chemicals in her hair or wear colored contacts? I wondered what it must have been like to be Jessie Morgan.

"We should go," Myra said. "Or we'll hit traffic."

I knew it was wrong, but instead of confessing to Myra that I was actually Jenny Shaw, I said, "I guess I don't have to call shotgun if it's just you and me, right?" Back in high school I never bothered to call shotgun—I was usually just happy to be invited along for the ride on the rare occasion that one of our neighbors offered to drive me home from school—but I'd wanted to shout it.

The word always stuck in my throat like a big lump. I'd spent most of my high school social interactions with that same kind of lump in my throat, tears just about to spring up in my eyes.

"Ha!" Myra said. "Remember that? You and Karen used to fight!" She grabbed her purse from behind a plant in the corner of the room. "I'll finish setting things up when we get back."

"I can help," I said automatically, like the part of my brain that was supposed to think before it let me talk had been completely disabled.

"**O**h my God! You know what I have?" Myra said, after we got into her rusty old Honda. She reached up to pull a disk out of the CD sleeve attached to her visor.

"What?" I asked, as I buckled myself in to the passenger seat. The buckle took a few tries, and there were crumbs and little bits of gravel in the upholstery. It felt familiar. Like my car. No matter how hard I tried to keep it clean, my car always ended up filled with random dirt and cereal-bar wrappers.

"This!" She shoved the disc into the CD player. The opening chords of "Bust a Move" thumped through the car's ancient speakers. "Bust it!" Myra shouted, laughing. "Oh, come on! Don't pretend like you don't still love this song!"

"'Love' is kind of a strong word," I said, laughing, "but I do remember most of the words."

Myra bounced around in her seat while she drove, stumbling over the words as she sang along. She was so comfortable with me, and even though I knew it was because she thought I was someone else, her level of comfort made me feel comfortable. When the song got to the part about Harry and his brother Larry, I chimed in with Myra until our singing degraded into a fit of giggles.

The song ended, and we fell into a lull of looking out the window. It must have been a mix CD. The next song was that weird one by Crash Test Dummies. I hadn't heard it in years. The fog had cleared and there was a mountain on the horizon where I hadn't even imagined a mountain would be.

"So, he really dumped you at the airport," Myra said.

"Yeah," I said, watching for more surprise mountains as we got closer to a giant Tully's sign at the edge of the city. "There's someone else."

"But you're Jessie *Effing* Morgan," Myra said, adamantly. "Doesn't he know that?"

"Apparently not," I said. I bit at the tough skin on the side of my fingernail without thinking about it. It was a bad habit, but I almost never did it in front of other people.

"I'm sorry. I won't make you talk about it," Myra said.

"It's fine," I said, sliding my hands under my thighs. "It's not like pretending it didn't happen is going to make it go away." I shouldn't do this, I thought. I shouldn't use this girl to work out my problems. But I couldn't stop myself. "The thing is—I'm not sure I know who I am without Deagan. I never wanted to be one of those girls, you know? The kind who plans her whole life around some guy."

"But you thought he was so much more than some guy," Myra said, waving her right hand around enthusiastically. "I know. I've been there." She sighed. "Remember John Hayes?"

"No," I said, forgetting completely that I was supposed to be Jessie Morgan.

"Yeah, I guess maybe you wouldn't. We didn't really get to be friends with him until after you left. But, oh my God, the summer after graduation, I fell so hard. I gave up a scholarship to the Fashion Institute in New York for that boy. I went to school here instead." She shook her head. "He said all the things I wanted to hear, you know?"

"Yeah," I said. "I do know!"

"He said he wanted to marry me. We got engaged. I had a ring. And then right before junior year, he said he was bored. He decided he was going to transfer to Fairleigh Dickinson, and he moved to New Jersey without me, like he wasn't even leaving anything behind."

"Oh, I'm so sorry," I said.

"I told him I'd try to transfer, so I could move with him. And he said—get this—he said, 'I think things have run their course.'"

"What an ass!" I said. "Run their course? What is it with guys and their stupid breakup statements?" I told her about Deagan and his exploratory mission.

Myra laughed. "Don't they realize that the stupid shit they say when they dump us will live in our heads for all eternity?"

"They must be completely oblivious," I said. She was right too. For the rest of my life, whenever I thought about Deagan, all the memories I had of us would be replaced by the image of him in bed with Faye, wearing a pith helmet, exploring.

"I can practically still hear it. 'I think things have run their course.' Like I was all chewed up and ready to be spat out."

I wondered why Jessie Morgan wouldn't know anything about Myra and John—why she left Mount Si right after graduation. She didn't even stay for the summer. And if they were such good friends, why didn't Myra call to tell Jessie about her heartbreak?

"He's coming to the reunion," Myra said, her voice wobbling. "He's bringing his wife. I mean, I know I should be over it. It was a long time ago now, but whenever I think about having to see him, I just get angry." She wiped the corner of her eye with her sleeve. "I gave up too much for him. And then, of course, he came home for the next two summers, and I was stupid enough to think, both times, that it would last longer than just the summer. Like he'd actually stay for me."

"I'm so sorry," I said. I thought about how I would feel when I got back to Rochester, running into Deagan and Faye at Wegmans. Seeing them out at the Lilac Festival, holding hands and sharing a funnel cake. I felt the dread in my stomach. Everything about me, all my friends except Luanne, revolved around being Deagan's girlfriend, and I felt so incredibly stupid for letting that happen.

"And I can't act like it still stings all this time later," Myra said. "That would be completely pathetic."

"Maybe he's bald," I said. "Or fat. Or smelly."

Myra laughed.

"Maybe his wife is bald and smelly too," I said. "And, hey, she married him. That's far more humiliating than getting dumped by him, right?"

"Thank God you're here." She looked over at me and smiled. She had the nicest smile. Her eyes sparkled and her dark red lipstick framed her perfectly white teeth. One of her incisors was crooked, but even that looked like a stylistic decision on her part. "I'll simply be too busy with my dear old friends to bother with John. Even Fish has promised to completely ignore him."

"Fish?" I wished I had studied the yearbook pictures in the reception room better. Although I was sure I would have remembered seeing a picture of someone named Fish. It had to be a nickname. I tried to remember if I'd seen Fish written in marker or a drawing of a fish next to any of the pictures, but I couldn't.

"Oh my God! He's going to die when he sees you. I'm not telling him you're here. I told Heather, of course, but I think we'll surprise Fish." She had the hugest grin. "Ah! Thank you so much for being here, Jessie. I mean, I know you're not here just for me, just so I have the full group to face John with—but what a relief, you know?"

"It'll be fine. And you look fantastic," I said to her, for lack of anything else to say. "Isn't that the best revenge?"

"Yes," Myra said. "Plus, I still have all my hair." She lifted her arm and sniffed her pit. "And I'm not smelly either."

Myra parked on a side street. "I can't wait for you to see this," she said, beaming from ear to ear as we walked to the corner. "Ta-da!" She held her arms out like a game show hostess when we got to the storefront.

Over the window was a sign that said "Aberly Cadaberly" in big block letters on a plain white background.

"Is this yours?" I asked, thankful that I'd noticed Myra's last name on the reunion posters.

"Yup," Myra said, opening the door with a grand "after you" sweep of her arm. "I have my own boutique line, but then I feature other local designers and some vintage stuff too."

"You have your own store and your own line?"

"I do!" Myra said, lowering her eyes modestly and shoving her hands in her pockets. "Hi, Nancy!"

The girl behind the counter was on the phone and writing something in a notebook, but she smiled, mouthed "hi," and waved at us. She had dark hair and thick bangs like Myra, and a pretty little blue star tattooed at the outside corner of her left eye. It was hard to keep from staring at it.

The store was gorgeous. White walls and thick, warped floorboards painted bright teal. The racks of clothes were grouped by color. Black faded into gray, and blue gave way to green and yellow. The reds and pinks packed a big punch of color in the row across from a rack of white and beige. In the back of the store, big mirrors had borders painted with black curling flourishes like picture frames. A gorgeous old chandelier hung from the ceiling, with necklaces and earrings draped where crystals would have been. Myra's red lipstick was like a carefully chosen accent color in the backdrop of the store. She fit perfectly.

Even though we weren't really dear old friends, I was proud of her, like I was already on her team. We were roughly the same age, and she'd already accomplished so much. It was fascinating. It was wonderful. "Myra, this is gorgeous!" I said, my eyes getting just a little bit misty, as if she actually were my long-lost friend.

"Thank you," she said, blushing. "Okay," she pushed me into a changing room. "Let's get you dressed!"

I heard the click of hangers being scraped across the rack, and then she threw a thick pile of dresses over the top of the dressing room door.

The first one was a gorgeous, bright red dress with a spaghetti strap on one side and a wide strap on the other that continued past the neckline and wrapped across the front of the dress. I tried it on. It had a dangerously low neckline and a flirty, asymmetrical hem.

"Let's see," Myra said.

I opened the dressing room door. Myra squealed. "It's perfect!"

I turned around and looked at the back in the mirror. It made me look thin and curvy at the same time. Daring and sexy and dangerous. I noticed the tag hanging from the seam. A thick piece of white paper with "Jessie by Myra Aberly" written on it in calligraphy pen.

"You designed this for—" I caught myself before I said "her." "For me?"

I flipped the tag over to look at the price, out of habit.

Myra reached over and covered my hand, but before she completely obscured it, I caught a quick glimpse of the price. The dress was a hundred and twenty dollars.

"Don't even look," she said. "It's for you. It's a gift."

I'm not just bending the truth anymore, I thought. I'm conning her.

"I can't take this, Myra," I said, shaking my head. I have to tell her, I thought. I can't take it this far. This is like stealing.

"Please," she said. "Seeing you in this dress, having it look exactly the way I thought it would. It's like magic. It makes me feel like a real designer."

I stared at myself in the mirror, and stood on my tiptoes to see what it would look like if I wore heels. Never in a million years would I have chosen a dress so red, so attention grabbing. I was the girl who wore a tasteful and conservative black dress for every possible occasion. The person in the mirror looked like the me I'd always wished I could be, not the person I really was.

"Myra?" Nancy called from the register. "I have the buyer from Blackberry Boutique in Portland on the phone. I think she wants to carry your winter line."

"Really?"

"Yeah. Can you talk with her?"

"Oh my God!" Myra said, jumping up and down. "Do you mind, Jessie?" She grabbed my arm. "This is huge! I've been sending her lookbooks for the past three seasons."

"Of course I don't mind," I said. "Go for it!"

"I'll take it in my office," she yelled to Nancy before running to the back of the register and disappearing behind a mirrored panel that was actually a door.

I went back to trying on clothes. I needed more than just a

dress, and if Myra wouldn't let me buy the Jessie dress, I could at least buy some clothes for my conference from her.

Of course, everything in the store was flashier and edgier than anything I would normally wear. But it's not like playing it safe had ever really worked for me anyway.

I hadn't bought anything new in such a long time. Deagan and I were saving up for a down payment on a home. Or at least I thought we were. We'd scrimped and pinched and budgeted to work the trip in, but otherwise we were trying to save up to put twenty percent down on a house when we were finally ready to buy. I'd been bringing my lunch to work, wearing my tired old sweaters, and making coffee at home, so I could pull my own weight. My salary was much less than Deagan's, and I hadn't wanted to be a mooch.

I undid months of frugality in about twenty minutes.

"No," Nancy said, when I tried to push the red dress along with a few skirts, a pair of dark jeans, a blazer, a couple of camisoles, a cardigan, and the most adorable beaded vintage sweater I'd ever seen. "I heard Myra. That one's a gift."

"First one's free," I said. "Right? This store is addictive."

Nancy laughed. "You'll have to tell Myra that." She smiled at me, like we were sharing pride in the store. In our friend. "I've never seen anyone work so hard. She's amazing, isn't she?"

"Yeah," I said. "She really is."

Nancy wrapped up my clothes in silver tissue paper and put them in a big teal shopping bag.

I was about to hand her my credit card when I realized the name on it would give me away. That's not how Myra should find out.

"Oh! You know what?" I said, practically shouting. "I'm on

this new financial plan. I need to pay for everything in cash. Is there an ATM nearby?"

"Right across the street," Nancy said, pointing toward the door.

"Right back," I promised.

I dashed across the street and used my card to get a thousand dollars in cash from the machine. I had to take the money out in three transactions, because my bank wouldn't allow me to withdraw the whole amount at once. I wouldn't be able to use my credit card at all in front of Myra, so I needed to have cash. I was going to tell Myra as soon as I could. The money was just in case the right moment didn't present itself immediately.

I ran back across the street with my purse full of cash, trying to avoid thinking about just how crazy all of this was.

"All set," I said, breathlessly handing Nancy a wad of bills to pay for my new clothes.

"I think this call is going to be a really long one," Nancy said. "You just missed Myra. She darted out to tell me that Blackberry is ordering an entire custom-designed line from her."

"Really?" I said. "That's amazing!" It was weird, the way I was so honestly excited for Myra. "And I can fend for myself. I have more shopping I need to do. If you could just point me in the right direction . . ."

"What do you need?" Nancy asked.

"Makeup, shoes, underwear," I said.

Nancy wrote walking directions to Nordstrom on the back of an envelope and gave me a business card for Aberly Cadaberly.

"Call if you get lost."

I gave Nancy my cell phone number so Myra could call me when she finished up, and left my shopping bag behind the counter, but only after swapping my salad-dressing-stained shirt for a brand-new camisole made from recycled silk neckties.

When I got to Nordstrom, I noticed that my cell phone only showed one bar inside the store. If Myra called, there was a good chance she'd go right to voicemail, where my message clearly stated that the caller had reached Jenny Shaw and I was unable to answer. I walked back outside and called my voicemail, changing the message to say my phone number instead of my name. I was going to tell Myra—I promised myself. I'd tell her and give back the dress and stop this whole stupid, crazy charade. I had to. But my voicemail wasn't the right way for her to find out either.

There were four messages from my mother. I didn't listen to any of them. For just a little while, I wanted to forget me.

❧

I bought a fancy, navy blue leather "boarding tote" to bring my new clothes home in. It cost more than a week's worth of groceries, but I did it anyway.

I splurged on makeup. It had been a long time since I'd bought any. My mascara was so old that it probably harbored flesh-eating bacteria, and I'm pretty sure I'd been using the same blush since college. It was gross and embarrassing and as soon as I bought new makeup, I couldn't believe it had been so long since I'd made an effort to do anything nice for myself. I let the woman at the Origins counter remove the remaining smudges of old mascara I was pretending counted as eyeliner and put a brand-new face full of makeup on me. She used products I didn't even know existed. Eye-shadow primer. Lip primer. Cheek color that comes in a tube. And, apparently, as long as the undertones are blue, I can completely and totally pull off red lipstick. Who knew?

When the makeup-counter lady was finished working her magic—smoky eyes, sculpted cheekbones, perfectly lined lips—I actually looked like someone who belonged in Myra's red Jessie dress.

I bought all of it. I handed her my credit card (since she didn't think I was really Jessie Morgan) and didn't even look at the total amount when I signed the slip. It's what Jessie Morgan would do, I told myself. She didn't look like a girl who had ever played it safe.

Then I hit the shoe department and tried on the highest, sexiest black pumps I'd ever seen. They had toe cleavage. I didn't even know that was a thing, but the saleslady told me it was sexy, and I chose to believe her. Jessie Morgan was obviously a toe cleavage kind of girl. They were black, so I rationalized the cost by thinking that maybe when I went back to my everyday life I could still pull them off. Although, as I modeled them in the mirror with my suit pants rolled up so I could get a good view of the way they made my ankles and calves look long and lean, I had a hard time honestly believing I'd ever go back to my old life. What was left for me there? What was the point of being a faithful, loyal girlfriend who put all her time and energy into planning for the future and supporting her boyfriend, only to have him run off with some remedial volleyball player? What was the point in living for tomorrow instead of today, of putting faith in people who would only let me down? Really, what was the point of being Jenny Shaw?

"I will take these shoes," I said to the saleslady, handing her my sensible black loafers to box up. "And I will wear them now."

When I left Nordstrom, I called Aberly Cadaberly to make sure I wasn't holding Myra up. Nancy told me that the phone call with Blackberry had proved to be epic and Myra needed to finish up a few extra sketches before the afternoon FedEx run. "Tell Jessie I'm sorry!" I could hear Myra yell in the background.

"No problem," I told Nancy. "Tell her I said good luck!"

I hung up and stared at the red circle that told me how many voicemail messages I had. It was up to six now. All from my mother.

No matter how much I wanted to ignore them, I had a sick, nagging feeling in my stomach. I called her voicemail number, instead of her home phone, and left a message. It was one of my better tricks. She still hadn't figured out why she never heard the phone ring.

"Oh, hi, Mom," I said. "I guess I must have missed you. Hope everything's going well. I'm on that business trip I told you about. My cell phone isn't getting great service out here, so I'll have to give you a call when I'm home again. Love, love. Bye!"

I hung up and deleted the messages without listening to them. I knew what they would say. Every single one would expand on the great theme of her life: how everyone everywhere, especially me, was letting her down in some colossally crippling way.

I decided to walk back toward Myra's store. Maybe grab a cup of coffee to kill time. But walking in super-sexy, sky-high, toe-cleavage heels proved to be a lot more challenging than just standing still and admiring them in the mirror. The world looked different with an extra four inches, and I couldn't manage to get my bearings. A few blocks from Myra's store, I crossed the street, failed to pick up my foot high enough to clear the curb, and barely caught myself on a lamppost.

My ankle throbbed. I clung to the lamppost for dear life and surveyed my surroundings. Three stores down was a salon beckoning "Walk-ins Welcome." I was in desperate need of a haircut, and a place to sit down, so I took it as a sign.

"Just make it different," I said to the hairdresser, when I sat in the chair. "I don't want to look like me anymore."

I was under the dryer, reading *People* magazine, with some sort of high-gloss chestnut-colored dye marinating in my hair, when the hairdresser came running over with my purse. "Your phone is ringing," she shouted over the noise of the dryer. "Do you want me to answer it?"

"Sure," I said.

She reached in my purse and held the phone up to show me who was calling. It was a 206 number, which I was pretty sure was Seattle. "I didn't catch your name," the hairdresser said.

"Jessie Morgan," I told her, without even a moment of hesitation. It fell out of my mouth so easily.

I felt guilty as she answered, saying, "Jessie Morgan's phone!" But what could it hurt, really? I mean, it's not like I'd ever fly back to Seattle to get my hair cut. I'd pay in cash. I'd tip her well. And she'd never know the difference.

She hung up and dropped the phone back in my purse. Then she shut the dryer off and pulled back the plastic shower cap on my head to check on the dye.

"That was someone named Myra. I gave her the address. She'll be here to pick you up in about twenty minutes." She pulled the plastic cap all the way off. "Which is perfect timing actually. Let's go wash this out."

◆

The floor around me was soon covered in dark brown hair. I went from having limp, lifeless locks that fell past my shoulders, to a short, sexy bob cut just below my chin, with bangs that slid seductively in front of my right eye, so I could push them out of the way.

"Oh my God!" Myra said, when she walked in and saw me, just as the hairdresser spun my chair around so I could see the back of my head in the mirror.

I could see Myra in the mirror too. She held her hand up to her mouth, and I thought for a second that maybe the haircut gave me away. Maybe something about it made it completely obvious that I wasn't Jessie Morgan, but then she said, "God, I always wanted your cheekbones, Jess. Killer."

◆

We left the salon, and I silently promised myself I would tell Myra. I opened my mouth to say the words about six times over, but Myra was so excited about her call with Blackberry, and I didn't want to spoil it.

"So, they were, like, completely worried I wouldn't want to do a line for them." Myra unlocked her car. "Can you believe it?" she said, when we'd both climbed in. "Can you even believe it? They were nervous to talk to me!" She was beaming.

"Well, of course," I said. "You're a brilliant designer."

"Really? You think so? It just means so much to me." She told me all the details of the line she was planning, and I wanted to listen, but my heart was thumping so hard at the thought of telling her. I couldn't quite catch my breath.

I would confess when she dropped me off. Not before then. I wouldn't want to find out I had some stranger in my car while I was driving on the highway with them. It would be scary. I didn't want to scare Myra. I didn't say a word. I tried to listen to her talk about the sketches for Blackberry, how she was thinking navy and pops of color and "like a modern take on forties beach clothes." I watched the scenery and tried to figure out how far we were from the hotel, how much time I had before I needed to come clean. I tried not to imagine her reaction, but I kept picturing her big brown eyes filling with tears, the disgust that would edge into her voice, the panic. My hands shook. I hid them in the sleeves of my blazer.

Maybe it wouldn't be so bad. Maybe if I stayed calm, she would too. I'd just say that I wasn't Jessie and I was so sorry. I'd keep it simple. I would give her the red dress back and then she could drive away or go set up for the reunion and call her friend Heather and tell her about the insane Jessie Morgan impersonator she ran into, and it would be some kind of epic story that they'd all laugh about for years to come.

But even though I only knew Myra, and I didn't know the rest of her friends, the idea of them laughing at me stung. The idea of not getting to go to the reunion made me feel the same way I did when Ronnie McCairn invited every girl in our fourth-grade class except for me and Marta Combs to her roller-skate, pizza birthday party. Everyone knew Marta Combs picked her nose and ate it. Everyone. So it was basically like every girl in the class except for me got invited, because who was going to invite a known nose-picker to her birthday party? That's the way I felt, thinking about not going to the reunion—like I was being left out all over again, which is silly, because I didn't know these people. I didn't know anything about them. I was left out because I didn't belong. If they all decided to laugh at me for years to come, I deserved it. Who pretends to be another person? Like not even to steal their credit card numbers or get a fake passport. Who pretends to be another person just because they're lonely and tired of being themselves?

Me, apparently, because when we got to the parking lot, Myra parked her car and grabbed one of my bags from the backseat and said, "Oh, I can't believe I didn't even see all the clothes you bought! Come on!" There was the promise of girl time and maybe room service and wine and laughing and gossip (even if it was about people I didn't know), and I decided it made more sense to just leave the dress and a note for her at the front desk after she went home. I decided it would be less upsetting for her if she didn't have to hear the words come out of my mouth, if she could just read them and process everything on her own time.

Writing her a note was the kindest way to do this. I'm sure if Dear Prudence ever wrote a column about how to confess to someone that you're not actually a long-lost childhood friend, she would have completely agreed with me on this.

Myra helped me carry my bags up to the room. There was a bottle of champagne on ice waiting for me on the dresser.

"Ooh! Who is this from?" Myra squealed, putting the bags she was carrying down to reach for the card next to the champagne bottle.

I almost jumped over the TV stand to grab it from her. What if it was from Deagan? What if he wanted me back? What if the card said, *To Jenny?* She opened it before I could get it away. I felt like I might vomit.

"Wait," Myra said, looking at the card and then at me. Sweat beaded on my upper lip. The walls felt too close. "Who's Monica?"

"Oh," I said, trying to take a deep breath without it being obvious that I had just been on the verge of hyperventilating. "Monica! My boss. She was supposed to take this trip, but she had to go to a wedding."

"Lucky you!" Myra said. "Should we open it?" She grabbed the bottle and went into the bathroom to grab a hand towel.

"Sure," I said. It was probably fine. It's not like I was going to trek Monica's bottle of champagne back to Rochester with me, and there was no point in it going to waste.

"Do you want to do the honors?" Myra asked.

"Go for it," I said. I'd never opened champagne before and assumed it would be a big messy explosion, like in the movies.

Myra twisted the metal cage off and then held the towel over the cork and twisted it until we heard a pop. She lifted the cork and the towel carefully. A thin mist curled up from the mouth of the bottle. "Perfect," she said, and poured the champagne slowly into the waiting glasses.

"To us," Myra said, handing me a glass and clinking hers against mine.

"To us," I said. I took a careful sip. I wasn't much of a drinker. Plus I was starving and didn't think champagne combined with a fake identity was the best of ideas. I grabbed the room service menu.

"Hungry?" I asked.

"Always," Myra said, laughing. We studied the menu like dinner was the most important decision we would ever make. We settled on smoked duck, beet salad, tuna carpaccio, grilled prawns, and a cheese plate.

I called in the order and didn't even blink when Ashley at the front desk asked me if I'd like to bill it to my room account—the account that went straight to my company. Monica told me to expense my meals, but the old me would have ordered the cheapest thing on the menu and still felt like it was more than I was worth. Jessie Morgan, I was sure, would just order what she wanted to eat. Jessie Morgan wouldn't worry about being an imposition. Myra hadn't spent the past thirteen years missing a friend who tried her best to blend in and never make waves. There was a reason no one I went to high school with missed me.

◆

While we waited for our room service order, Myra pulled all of my purchases out of the shopping bags and laid them across the bed to get a good look.

"Try this," she said, handing me the beaded black sweater and a gray skirt made from recycled wool.

I felt weird changing in front of her. It was another one of those things I'm sure girls who grew up having close girlfriends didn't think twice about. I tried my hardest to act like I was comfortable as I swapped my shirt for the sweater and my pants for the skirt as quickly as possible.

"Okay, you have to wear your hair pulled back with that sweater to show off the boatneck," she said, squinting at me. She snapped a black hair elastic off her wrist and handed it over.

I pulled my newly short hair back into a stubby ponytail with one hand. "This?"

"Yeah," she said, nodding solemnly and straightening out the shoulders on my sweater for me. "Perfect. Kind of a minimalist thing. Let the sweater do the work."

I would have killed for a friend like Myra in high school. Someone to help me pick out things to wear and tell my secrets to. The kind of girlfriend who feels like a sister. I would have given anything I had for her.

Myra stood back and studied me, while I wound her elastic around my ponytail. A thick bunch of bangs wouldn't stay in the elastic and fell over my eye. It looked so much better than when I used to put my hair in a ponytail and little frizzy flyaway strands would sprout up.

"You know what?" Myra said. "That skirt needs a brooch. Like an antique brooch, right at your hip to balance everything out." And then she rummaged through her purse, pulled out an actual antique rhinestone brooch, and pinned it to my skirt in just the right place.

"You just happened to have an antique brooch in your purse?"

"Occupational hazard," she said, shrugging.

"I'm not sure I've even ever actually said the word 'brooch' out loud before this."

She laughed and picked a stray thread off my sweater.

I studied myself in the mirror. The new hair, the new shoes, Myra's perfect outfit—I didn't know I could look so polished.

"You're brilliant, Myra," I said. "I can't wait to see your new line!"

I'm pretty sure I saw her blush, and maybe her eyes teared up a little. They were shiny at least. It must be a funny thing, I thought, seeing an old friend all grown up.

◆

When the food arrived, Myra and I camped out on the bed with the plates in front of us and shared everything.

"Oh my God," Myra said, with a big forkful of smoked duck in her mouth. "This is heaven!" She fell back on the bed dramatically and chewed. "I wish everything I ever ate tasted like this."

"I know," I said, stabbing a prawn with my fork. I waited to lie down until it was safely in my mouth, so I wouldn't get anything on my new sweater. I should have changed back into my salad-dressing-stained blouse, so I wouldn't mess up my new clothes, but it had gotten pretty rank. Plus maybe the new me could be someone who wore nice things without spilling food all over them. Stranger things had happened.

"Good food," Myra said, looking over at me and smiling. "And it's just so good to see you."

"Yeah," I said, "you too."

"Oh my God!" Myra said. "You know what this reminds me of?"

"What?"

"Remember that time you ran away from home and stole your dad's credit card and stayed at the Four Seasons in Seattle and Fish drove us out to see you?"

"Oh my God!"

"I know! God you had balls. Like an iron pair. You, me, Fish, Karen, Heather, and Robbie all camped out in your suite, daring each other to eat escargots. Remember?"

"That was crazy," I said. I couldn't imagine ever doing something like that. I would have spent the whole time worrying about what would happen to me when I got caught.

"Oh, your dad was so mad!" Myra said. "There was, like, almost actual smoke coming out of his ears."

"Well, I deserved it, I guess. That's not even just pushing the limits. That's like—blatant rebellion." I was such a Goody Two-Shoes as a kid. For everything they put me through, my parents had it easy. My biggest indiscretion was hiding a failed math quiz or watching TV past my bedtime. Once, when I was really acting up, I told my mom I was going to my dad's house after school, so I could go to the library and read Judy Blume books. Maybe that's what this is, I thought. Maybe pretending to be Jessie is my blatant rebellion. I missed that stage when I was younger and now I'm playing with fire to make up for lost time. Maybe everyone needs to rebel.

"Oh man, it wasn't even you at your best," Myra said, taking a big bite of tuna. "Mmm. Not even close. But your dad just had to swallow it and move on. You had him wrapped around your little finger."

"I can't believe I got away with that."

"Well, I mean, since you knew about his affair and all, and

your mom didn't . . . ," Myra said. "We all wished for that kind of leverage. I mean, not for the affair part, because that was awful. To walk in on them . . ." She shuddered. "It's not like you'll ever be able to un-see that. But to get away with everything you did . . . I was always in awe."

She grabbed a piece of cheese. "Oh my God," she said, with her mouth full. "Try this. What is this?" She shoved the rest of the piece into my mouth.

"I think it's Gruyère," I said awkwardly, covering my mouth while I chewed.

She was so at ease with me. I felt like an alien, and it wasn't even because of the whole Jessie Morgan thing. I didn't quite know what to say or how to act or how to just be in the moment the way Myra did. I wanted sleepover-party, hair-braiding, trying-on-clothes-together girlfriends so desperately when I was in high school. But I didn't know how to be that kind of friend. Those girls were a different breed of people. Those kinds of girls, the ones who called each other girlfriends and talked on the phone to plan outfits, they had a different lineage, like they were created and raised to be friends with other girls. Their moms had girlfriends too, and knew how to raise them to be that way.

I almost had girlfriends the summer before high school. We could all walk to each other's houses. We stopped over unannounced, helped ourselves to food from each other's fridges without asking, and told silly secrets, like which boy we thought was cute, or where we were when we got our first period.

My mom was doing well then. There weren't wine bottles around. She played happy mom when they came over and served

teenager food like ridged potato chips and onion dip. When I
told her that Rachel K. had a nut allergy, she called her mother to
make sure we didn't have any unsafe foods in our house. And my
mom and I made a special batch of Toll House cookies minus the
walnuts, just for Rachel K., singing along to Carly Simon while we
baked.

When it was my turn to have everyone over, me and Shelia
and the Rachels camped out in the living room, poring over issues
of US Weekly, Teen, and Seventeen that I'd saved my allowance to
buy because Sheila's mother wouldn't let her read "trash." My
mother brought us snacks on the fancy serving dishes from her
wedding registry that had never really been used. We had soda in
cans—diet and regular—and we each got our own, even though
Regular Rachel never finished hers. My mother acted like it was
nothing for us to have food in the house. Like it wasn't strange
that she was playing the perfect mom all of a sudden. And by
August I had finally let my guard down. I believed that this was
our new normal. I was happy.

But then a week before school started, my mom called my dad
when his alimony check was late, and a woman picked up the
phone. My mom stopped grocery shopping. She ran to the store
every couple of days but came back with paper bags that clinked
when she carried them up the stairs to her bedroom.

She left money on the counter and expected me to order dinner every night. I ate cold Chinese food for breakfast. I tried to
rotate our takeout orders so she wouldn't get mad at me for ordering pizza too many times or not enough or, worse, decide that she
didn't want what I'd ordered and get in the car to go pick something else up. I'd been both the passenger on those car rides and
the one sitting by the phone, waiting to hear her car in the garage,

my breathing getting shallow if I happened to hear sirens off in the distance. So I kept a calendar in my room, taped to the underside of my desk blotter, and used color-coded dots to remind me what we'd already ordered that week. Red for Chinese, green for Italian, blue for salads from the pizza place, yellow for chicken wings.

She didn't eat much anyway. Like she was on a hunger strike or trying to out-skinny whoever my dad might start dating next. Like she was trying to disappear. When I took the garbage out on Sunday nights, I bagged all her bottles in opaque black plastic so no one would see them in the recycling bin.

I had to make excuses for why Sheila and the Rachels couldn't come over anymore. When Sheila said, "Did you see Johnny Depp on the cover of *US Weekly*? I can't wait to come over and read it!" I told her that my mom was redecorating and there were paint fumes. That only worked for about two weeks, and then it just compounded the lie, because not only did my mom spend all day in her room, watching soap operas in her nightgown, but we didn't have freshly painted walls and new slipcovers on the couch cushions. We had a big stack of mail on the kitchen table, newspapers piled in the hallway, and dirty dishes all over the house. For a few weeks, I smuggled the magazines to Sheila at school, hoping that being her supplier of Johnny and Kate gossip would count for something, but it wasn't the same. I was weird. I was lying. They shared their secrets, and I wasn't sharing mine. I felt like they could tell.

Eventually, I stopped getting invited to their houses. They made plans without me. I could never get my mom to take me to the store to buy me the right kind of sneakers or hair clips. One day in October, they sat at a lunch table that only had three open seats. They didn't even look back apologetically or anything. They just sat there and went on with their perfect little teenage lives, and I didn't exist anymore. They didn't skip a beat.

It's not like it really mattered. Between schoolwork and trying to keep the house clean and our bills paid with alimony and child support so the electricity wouldn't get shut off again, I didn't have time to have friends anymore anyway.

Sometimes I couldn't help but think, if only my dad had sent the check on time. If only he'd had the good sense to tell Cheryl not to pick up the phone at his place, if only he'd walked on egg-shells like we were supposed to, I'd have been wearing a pink scrunchie and Tretorns with a matching pink stripe, sitting with the rest of the Four Amigos, laughing when Rachel K. snarfed Diet Coke out of her nose right in front of Trent Wilner. I wouldn't have gotten stuck sitting at the loser table, where no one talked to anyone and we all averted our eyes to hide the embarrassment we felt for not having anywhere else to sit, for even existing.

Sometimes I still believed the person my mother was that summer before high school was the person she most wanted to be. Sometimes I still missed her.

Myra and I finished every little last bit of our room service order.

"Oh," Myra said, holding her stomach. "That was amazing! I've been so busy with the store. It's been a while since I've had a real meal! Thank you, Jess!"

"No problem," I said, picking up the tray and carrying it to the hallway.

Myra got up and opened the doors to the balcony. The sound of water rushing over the falls behind the lodge filled the room. "Wow, Jess! Have you been out here yet?"

I put the tray outside the door and met her on the balcony. The air was damp and smelled like pine trees. And if you stood on the left side of the balcony and looked out to the right, you could see Snoqualmie Falls.

"This room is amazing," she said.

There was a citronella candle and a book of matches on the little cast-iron table next to the balcony chairs. Myra lit it, and I ran inside to make coffee in the mini coffeemaker on the dresser.

We sat out on the balcony, clutching our mugs for warmth. It wasn't freezing, but it wasn't exactly balmy.

"When we were kids, did you ever think we'd be here?" Myra asked.

"No," I said. It was truthful at least.

"So, who are you now?" she asked. "You seem different. You're not as frantic. You listen." She waved her arms around. "You're not bouncing off the walls. What changed?"

"Everything." The cool air made goose bumps on my arms.

"Where were you?" Myra asked, leaning back in her chair and putting her feet up on the railing.

"Just living life, I guess," I said. It was lame, but I couldn't think of what else to say. I didn't know where everything left off for her and Jessie.

There were a few stars peeking out from behind the clouds.

"Where did you end up going to college?"

"Ithaca," I said, because if she didn't know where Jessie had gone, I might as well be honest about all the other details of my life. "The college, not Cornell."

"Well, yeah," she said, laughing. "There's no way you had the grades for Cornell."

For some stupid reason, I was offended. I wanted to tell her that I had gotten good grades in high school. I'd even gotten a scholarship. But she wasn't talking about me. She was talking about Jessie Morgan's grades.

"So where do you live now?" she asked. "I can't believe I don't even know."

"Rochester," I said.

"Minnesota?"

"New York."

"But not like New York, New York," Myra said. "Right?"

"More like south of Toronto, New York."

"Is it freezing cold all the time?"

"Yeah. In the winter. But you get used to it." Of course, I'd lived in Rochester my whole life. I was born used to it. But it was something to say. Something benign.

"I didn't even know you applied to Ithaca. We checked everywhere we could think of. Me and Fish. We even e-mailed some girl named Jessica Morgan at Florida State, and a J. Morgan at the U of O. We thought maybe one of them was you, but neither of them wrote back."

She looked at me, and the way her forehead wrinkled and her eyes looked so sad made me wish I could have somehow pretended to be Jessie then too. I would have written back, said something kind, ended the wonder.

"Why did you leave us?" Myra said. "I mean, if it's okay to ask."

"Of course it's okay to ask," I said. "But I don't know if I have a good answer."

"Was it everything with your parents?" Myra said softly.

"Yeah," I said. I thought about everything with my parents. If I'd had the guts and the chance to disappear from everything they were, from all the weight they dumped on me—cleaning up after my drunk mom, pretending my dad didn't have a new girlfriend every weekend—I might have left. I might have never told anyone where I was going. "It was just too much, you know?"

Myra put her arm around me and leaned her head on my shoulder. "You didn't have to leave me, you know. You could have told me. Any secret in the world, I would have kept for you."

"I'm really sorry," I said.

"Don't be. You know the thing I've learned the most? That everything looks different when you're a kid. It's like Alice in Wonderland. Nothing is as it seems, and then you get older and get to decide if you want to go back and see everything the way it really is or if you just want to move on."

"So which is it?" I asked. "What are you supposed to decide?"

"I'm not sure," Myra said. "Remains to be seen, I guess. If you poke at a sore spot, do you stop feeling the hurt or does it get worse?"

"What's your sore spot?" I asked, eager to steer the conversation away from me. The less I talked about myself, the less likely I was to screw up and say something that would give me away.

"That I didn't go to FIT. That I stayed behind for John." She sighed and grabbed her mug. "I think I overcompensate for it now. I live like a monk. All I do is work. Like I need to prove to the world that I'm not the kind of girl who gives up everything for a boy. Now I'm, like, romantically impaired. I don't know if I know how to be in a relationship. I don't know if I've left room for one."

"Sometimes," I said, "maybe we do things for the wrong reason, but we end up with the right result. At least I hope it works that way."

Myra shook her head like she didn't want to think about herself anymore. "What's your sore spot?"

"I think maybe I try so hard to be who everyone wants me to be, I don't know who I want to be."

"But you're Jessie *Fucking* Morgan."

I reached for my coffee mug and clinked it against Myra's instead of answering. "To falling down the rabbit hole," I said.

"Drink me," Myra said, wiggling her mug back and forth like it was talking to her.

◆

If I could make up a dream friend to have gone through high school with, she would end up being exactly like Myra. Actually, if I could make up a dream friend to go through adulthood with, it would be Myra too.

We stayed up talking until three a.m., fell asleep on the big king-sized bed, and had room service breakfast on the balcony. We spent every waking moment talking about life and jobs, who we are now, how we were both still waiting to feel like grown-ups, and this hot guy who owns the coffee shop next to Myra's store. And I didn't feel self-conscious. I didn't feel like I had to pretend I never get morning breath or sleep in my eyes. I didn't feel like everything that came out of my mouth had to be funny or clever. Even though I knew it was completely bizarre, I felt like it was okay to just be me when I hung out with Myra.

My life didn't really start until college.

I got to go away to school. My mom was going to make me live at home and go someplace local, but my dad said that Ithaca wasn't far and it would be good for me to have a little bit of distance. His proclamation was, of course, followed by my mother shouting, "What the hell is that supposed to mean?" and then yelling and screaming until my dad finally said, "Thank God I don't have to listen to this shit anymore," and slammed the door behind him hard enough to make the windows rattle.

For weeks after that, I was the enemy and I had to tread lightly. I'd learned to read every single smidge of a warning sign. There were clues in her tone, in the subtle movements at the corners of her lips when she talked. She had a twitch that sprung from her left eyebrow when the tide was about to turn. A simple conversation would devolve into a lecture about how selfish I was, what a hardship sending me away to school was going to be, how no one ever thought about her needs. I was ungrateful. I didn't know how much she'd given up for me. I made things hard for her with my father. She wondered sometimes if her life would have been better if she hadn't had a child. Her words smelled like bourbon.

But in the end I got to go away to school. If my mother hadn't let me, she'd be proving my father right on some level, and she couldn't let that happen.

My roommate, Yarah, was from Brazil and used to tell me that she felt like an eight-legged sea creature around American college kids. I never told her that I felt that way too.

The first time it snowed, Yarah and two girls from California who lived on the third floor ran outside in their pajamas and stared in amazement. I did too, even though Rochester is one of the snowiest cities in the country. The snow in Ithaca felt different, exciting. We twirled around on the quad and tipped our heads back to catch flakes on our tongues.

After they went to bed, I sat in the TV lounge and watched the way the snow stuck to the tree in front of our dorm. It felt like the first time I'd ever really seen snow. I snuck back into my room and grabbed my coat and walked around campus alone, taking in the silence the snow brought with it, the big clumpy flakes falling in the streetlight, and the fact that I had the freedom to watch the snow any way I wanted.

I was shy and quiet. I watched people more than I was a part of anything. But for the first time, I was starting to live. I worked at the college art gallery and sketched in my notebook while I monitored the sign-in sheet. I took the bus into town and read about the Maasai in Tanzania over steaming cups of espresso in a small dark coffee shop in the Commons. I had freedom.

In my spare time, I mostly hung out with Yarah. She was a violin major, and she practiced as much as I did homework. Late at night, when we were done working, we'd eat ice cream in the TV lounge and watch *Welcome Back, Kotter* reruns on Nick at Nite. Yarah was never drunk. She never had harsh words for me. We were polite to each other, careful, and our room was a safe, simple, happy place. It was the first teeny-tiny little hint that life didn't always have to be what it had been.

Luanne lived down the hall from me junior year. She was this loud girl from Larchmont whose mom sent her care packages filled with fancy perfume and cigarettes. We were in most of the same comm. classes, but we weren't friends. When her mom came to visit, she'd take half the dorm to Joe's for dinner. I was never invited. I was never one of the girls who came home with a Styrofoam box of eggplant parm to eat in the TV lounge the next day.

My mom never sent me care packages. She never came to visit either. A two-hour drive may as well be a trek across the Sahara on a camel to a mom who's always drunk or hungover. She never came to visit me and I didn't have a car, so for four years, in between major holidays and her obsessively needy, almost daily phone calls, I got to be someone other than Marie Shaw's daughter. Second semester freshman year, I decided I needed to pursue a double major: communications and anthropology. Sophomore year, I picked up the studio art minor. It meant I got to spend my summers at school too.

Sometimes on Sundays, when Yarah had to put in time at the practice rooms, I'd go with her. I'd sit on the floor in the hallway, turning my knees into an easel, drawing while I listened to Yarah's violin mix with all the other music pouring into the hallway. I made vows to myself about what my life would be.

I was going to find a job at a big PR firm in New York City after I graduated. I'd have a little loft, work on my paintings on the side. Take slides to galleries on my days off. It was a practical plan, but it left room for dreaming.

But by the time I graduated, the economy was in the toilet. I couldn't even get interviews with New York firms. I did, however, get an interview at Levi & Plato. So did Luanne. It was my only offer, and I took it. I think Luanne had a choice between Levi & Plato and an unpaid internship in Yonkers, so she took the job too.

Luanne didn't know anyone in Rochester, so suddenly we were "old friends from college." Yarah moved back to São Paulo after graduation, and even though I had my own apartment, I was sucked back into the vortex of taking care of my mother when I wasn't working, so I was more than happy to be Luanne's dear old friend. Having Luanne drag me out for drinks at Pearl on Thursday nights was easier than trying to set up some vague semblance of the life I'd wanted for myself. I forgot all over again that I had choices. I got good at being my mother's daughter and Luanne's friend. I still painted on Sunday afternoons—it was a vestige of who I'd wanted to be. But then I met Deagan, my paints went to storage, and I spent Sundays on the sidelines at the indoor beach volleyball courts, breathing in the smell of too many bare feet, playing the good girlfriend to the best of my abilities. I didn't even complain when he tracked sand through my apartment after the game.

So many years later, I still wished I'd told Yarah that I felt like an eight-legged sea creature around all the other college kids too. I wished I could have let myself be better friends with her, instead of carefully keeping a little bit of distance between us. I told myself it was the language barrier, but it was my barrier. Yarah's English was perfect.

Myra left to go to work, and I had about twenty minutes before I had to be at the conference. I used the shower cap from the toiletry kit to keep my hair dry, since it was still looking direct-from-the-hairdresser fabulous. It gave me time to call Luanne while I did my makeup.

"Great timing," Luanne said, when she picked up the phone. "I'm about to pull the trigger on these plane tickets. I'll meet you at the hotel on Sunday, and we can rent a car and drive out to the spa on Monday. I can crash in your room, right? I found a place that rents classics, because what, we want to get stuck in an economy car? No. I'm thinking something with fins. Is a Bel Air too obvious? Maybe an MG?"

"Hi, Lu. How are you this morning?" I dipped the flat-tipped brush into a tiny smudge pot of charcoal eyeliner and drew a thin line along my top lashes, flaring it up just the slightest bit at the very end. I was better at it than I thought I'd be. It was just like painting, but on my face instead of canvas.

"Whatever, pleasantries, blah, blah, blah, et cetera," Luanne said. "So is Sunday good? Because I have to order these tickets and get back to work. You guys are three hours lazy over there. I have a lunch in a few, and my client has been on my ass all morning about the Context account."

It's not like Luanne was a bad person, but after staying up all night pouring my heart out to Myra, Luanne kind of seemed like a caricature of a friend. The loud sidekick in a romantic comedy. And when I thought of her that way, all of a sudden, I kind of wanted to high-five myself. I usually felt like the sidekick in my friendship with Luanne. When it comes down to it, you probably aren't supposed to feel like the sidekick in your own life.

I had to make a choice. Luanne was a big old monkey wrench in the plan. I couldn't tell her the truth. There was no way she'd ever understand. How would I even start that conversation? And I couldn't have her showing up at the hotel and risk her running into Myra. These kinds of things always end badly in movies. If Myra did find out I wasn't Jessie, and Luanne wasn't there to bear witness, at least when I went home I could pretend none of it had ever happened. And if Luanne didn't show up, the chances of Myra finding out dropped dramatically.

So instead of saying, "No, Lu, I'm pretending to be this other girl, and if you show up here, you'll out me," I said, "You know, I think this is something I need to do by myself, Lu. I mean, no offense or anything. I think I really need to *process*, you know? To sit with myself or something." And it wasn't even a lie.

"Sit with yourself?" Luanne said, with a snotty little cough. "Do you have a split personality all of a sudden?"

"You know what I mean. If you come, I'll have a fantastic time."

"And that's a bad thing?"

"That's a wonderful thing, but then I won't be processing. I won't be getting over Deagan. I'll just be putting everything off until later. And I'll get home and it'll all hit me, and I'll be stuck running into him and Faye at Wegmans and hiding in the cereal aisle."

"So you need alone time now."

"Cap'n Crunch can't save me if I don't man up and save myself."

"Woman up," Luanne said.

"Exactly."

"I get it," she said softly, and suddenly I felt awful about the way I'd been feeling about her. "I'll even take care of your cat."

"You hate my cat."

"That's how awesome a friend I am. But I'm watching him at your place. I'm not driving him to the kitty kennel. The puking beast does not enter my car."

"Lu."

"Yeah?"

"Thank you for understanding."

"You owe me a spa day. You, me. Ithaca. Wine. Hot stones and a masseur named Sven."

"Deal," I said.

We said good-bye, and I hung up the phone. I felt bad for lying, but in reality, I was processing, and if I spent a week at a spa with Luanne, I'd probably need three weeks to recover.

It's not that I didn't love Luanne. She saved me from the adult version of the loser table. But she wore me out. And even though I could never quite put my finger on anything she said that was directly hurtful or mean, I always kind of felt like I needed to curl up in the fetal position and cry for a few hours after I spent any significant amount of time with her. Little, seemingly benign comments like "You know, I admire how you wear colors that clash with your skin tone—you're such a rebel!" or "You look so much better when you pack on a few extra pounds!" all added up to a big feeling of ick.

It was just easier this way. I was sparing Luanne's feelings and my own. I was sparing Myra's feelings too.

I brushed my teeth, watching myself in the mirror. I wasn't used to the hair or the makeup. It was eerie, like watching a stranger copy my movements. I kept expecting the girl in the mirror to stop brushing or spit before I did.

I'd like to say the lying was a new thing, but it wasn't. When you spend your whole life trying to be good enough to appease your drunk mother, you get really good at telling people the things that will make your life easier. Suddenly it's less like lying and more like a million tiny accommodations to keep everyone happy.

Of course, nothing I ever did really made my mother happy. But the idea of what could have happened if I didn't at least try was always completely overwhelming. If my mother got so angry over a C on a science quiz that she slammed the dishwasher closed with enough force to break every glass in the top rack, what would she have done if she found out the truth, that it had actually been a D and I'd cried my way up to a C? I can still remember the exact sound of the glasses when they broke, and how when I cut myself picking the broken shards out of the dishwasher my blood was so red it looked fake. I can remember the way she screamed so loud it made my heart rattle in my chest. But I can't remember a time when I ever really felt completely and totally like myself. It was easier than it should have been to be Jessie Morgan, because I wasn't ever really Jenny Shaw either. I never had the luxury of just being me.

I swished some water in my mouth and spit in the sink. The girl in the mirror did too. Then we added a dab of gloss to my lips in unison, and I felt like maybe this mirror person could actually be me. I wanted her to be.

And then, of course, I looked at the clock and realized I was already five minutes late to the conference and had to finish getting dressed so fast that when I raced to the elevator I realized I'd forgotten to do the little hook at the top of my skirt, and the zipper was slipping. I almost lost my skirt right in the middle of the hallway. I held on to it with one hand, reached out with my briefcase to stop the elevator door from closing, and slipped into the elevator. It wasn't empty. There was a gorgeous guy in a gorgeous suit standing there smiling at me.

"In a hurry?" he said.

"Yeah. Lobby, please?" I hoped that when he hit the button for the lobby I could discreetly hook and re-zip my skirt. But he was going to the lobby and the button had already been pressed. I mean, of course he was. Who isn't going to the lobby in a hotel elevator headed down? It's just the way it works.

I thought about dropping my briefcase to see if I could get him to pick it up and to buy myself some zipper time, but with my luck, he wouldn't pick it up, and I'd have to and would probably manage to drop my skirt in the process.

Luanne was a fierce advocate for picking wedgies when wedgies occurred. She always said that life is too short to walk around with underwear bunched up your crack. I'm sure she'd express similar sentiments about unzipped skirts, but I just couldn't muster the courage to go for it. Jessie Morgan, I'm sure, would have just zipped. She would have found a way to be cute and sexy about it. But I wasn't Jessie Morgan that morning. I had to go back to being Jenny Shaw. I held my hand on my hip and tried to make it look like it was just a comfortable and casual way to stand.

"Coming?" Suit Guy said, when we got to the lobby. He stepped out of the elevator and held the door open for me from the outside.

"Oh, I forgot something upstairs," I said, and pressed the Door

Close button with the corner of my briefcase as soon as he let go. I zipped and hooked my skirt, smoothed my hair, took a deep breath, and pressed the Door Open button. I rushed to the doors of the conference room, only to end up standing right behind Suit Guy in the line to sign in.

"What are you, Clark Kent or something?" he said, smiling, when he noticed me standing next to him. "Did you fly back to your room?" He found his name tag on the table and pinned it to his suit lapel. Kyle Scott. Good name.

"Um, no," I said, looking over the rows of tags for my name. It wasn't there. "I thought I left my phone upstairs but turns out it was in my bag." I picked up the tag for Monica Levi.

"I'm Kyle," he said, offering his hand. He had a great smile and firm handshake. Like Deagan. If you made a spreadsheet of guy types, Kyle and Deagan would end up in the same column. "Monica." He pointed to my tag. "Nice to meet you."

"Oh, no," I said, shaking my head. "I'm not Monica. I'm just filling in for her."

"I guess I'll see you in there, Not Monica," he said, running his hand over his head. He had a buzz cut, not because he was losing his hair—you could see his healthy hairline of blond fuzz— he had a buzz cut, I think, because his face was so gorgeous it would have been stupid to take any attention away from those clear blue eyes and that bright white smile.

"Yeah," I said. "See you in there."

I turned to the woman behind the table. "Is there a way I can get a new tag?" She took the name tag from me, pulled the paper with Monica's name on it out of the plastic sleeve, crossed out Monica's name, and handed me the pen so I could write my own.

"You might not want to pin that on your sweater," the woman

said, as I put the tag back together again. "It'll snag. Maybe pin it to your skirt instead."

I carefully pinned the tag at the waistband of my skirt so my sweater fell over it and no one could read it. Just in case. And when everyone was introducing themselves at the meet and greet, my name caught in my throat every time I introduced myself as Jenny Shaw. Like somehow I was the lie, and Jessie Morgan was the truth.

When the meeting started, Kyle was the one running the first session. He stood up at the head of the table and ran a PowerPoint presentation on the impact of new media.

It was really a conference for managers. Anyone who worked on the front lines and got stuck tweeting for a client who didn't understand Twitter etiquette, or tried to convince a company that their idea for a blog on whatever widget they were pushing needed to have a personal touch, already knew everything Kyle was talking about. Monica didn't, but that's why she had a team of lowly account execs like me.

My eyelids were getting heavy. I made thumbnail sketches of the people in the room, to keep myself awake. Kyle wasn't bad to look at, but he talked about social media in a very corporate way. He was linear and overly precise. It was all about metrics and numbers and staying on point, like the PR textbook version of social media. Drawing the angle of his eyebrows was far more interesting.

"So here's the thing," Kyle said. "There's a lot of random conversation on Twitter, but if you've got a copywriter tweeting for a brand, you have tell them to be specific. Don't let them take a picture of their lunch and call it a tweet."

I shook my head and sighed.

"Excuse me?" Kyle said, eyes wide. I guess I'd been more obvious than I'd thought.

"It's just that—I disagree." I'm not sure where my sudden outspokenness came from, other than the fact that I was possibly too tired to be self-conscious. "If you have a brand that needs to work on being approachable, maybe you do need to focus on a more personal side. Maybe you set up Twitter accounts for a few key players, get them to tweet about their lives, and throw in details about work from time to time."

Kyle didn't say anything. Everyone was staring at me, so I did that nervous thing I always do and kept talking when an uncomfortable silence would have been far more merciful. "Say Jill from product development is working through lunch on a project she's really excited about. She's R & D and it's prelaunch, so she can't talk about the actual product, but she can tweet a picture of last night's leftovers on her desk. Maybe there's a company logo somewhere in the background. She can tweet something like 'So excited about this new project, I don't even mind eating leftover meatloaf at my desk.' Then people will want to know what the project is. They'll be curious. It's not a sales pitch. It's voyeurism. When that project launches, her followers will be interested because it's something Jill cares about, and they've come to care about Jill. She's commented on their car troubles and bad breakups. She's not a salesman. She's their friend."

Once, in tenth grade, I was so into reading My Antonia in my lap, under the desk, during math class that I forgot where I was and burped really loud. The whole classroom stared at me. Nervous laughs erupted around the room, and I wished I could shrink up small enough to crawl inside my desk.

That's pretty much what it felt like when I told Kyle I disagreed with his Twitter philosophy. Someone giggled. I felt my face getting hot. But then I thought, Jessie Morgan would have done that. She would have challenged anyone who was wrong, without worrying about what they thought of her. I was right. I had a good point. I wasn't going to be embarrassed by that.

"I mean, the metrics are good," I said, holding my own hand under the table, "but you can't measure warm feelings about a brand. Five loyal customers who care about Jill might get you a lot further than thousands of followers who have already muted you. It's more of an art than a science, I guess, is what I'm saying."

There were actually some people in the room nodding in approval, a few even seemed to be taking notes on what I'd said.

"Interesting," Kyle said, his eyes narrowing into slits as he gave me a sly smile. He clapped his hands together. "Well, you're still going to have to report back with numbers. Twitter followers may like pictures of lunches, but I can guarantee you that your client is going to want cold, hard numbers." He hit the button on his clicker and went right back to his PowerPoint, but he called out items on his charts with greater intensity. Jessie Morgan, I thought, wouldn't even notice that she'd made him angry. I decided to pretend I didn't notice either.

All day I'd been choreographing in my head what needed to happen after the conference let out for the evening. I thought about going to the pre-reunion cocktail hour. I thought about not going. Confessing. Not confessing. I played out every possible scenario in my head, instead of listening to Kyle talk about social media metrics.

In the elevator on the way back to my floor, I decided I would go to the front desk and leave the Jessie dress for Myra, with a note explaining that I wasn't Jessie Morgan. I'd ask for a room change—say there was a draft that kept me from sleeping or the couple next door was loud or something like that. Draft probably. That was less embarrassing to explain. Or maybe if I went with the more embarrassing choice, I'd have to say less. I read once that people are more likely to get caught lying when they say too much. They over explain. Maybe if I implied there was crazy sex going on next door, and didn't say much else, they'd rush to fix the situation and the less I said the better. Any which way, I decided that I wasn't going to the Mount Si Class of 1999 Pre-reunion Cocktail Hour. It was absurd that I'd even considered it.

When I got back to my room, I put the Jessie dress on, because it was the most perfect thing I'd ever worn, and I wanted to see myself in it one last time, to feel like someone who could pull off a dress like that for one more moment. I turned from side to side, admiring the way the dress swished across my body as I moved, and I couldn't help but think about Myra, designing the perfect dress for a friend she'd lost. She'd be so hurt and confused when the front desk returned it to her with my note, and then she'd have to put on a smile and steel herself to see her ass-face of an ex-boyfriend and his wife. Or maybe she wouldn't even go. Maybe she'd be so freaked out that she'd spent the previous night pouring out her heart to someone who was only pretending to be her long-lost friend that she'd just go home and give up the chance to show John what he was missing out on. Maybe she'd cry and have weird mascara tracks on her face and be humiliated. And I couldn't do that to her. I liked Myra too much.

So instead of dropping the dress off and switching rooms, I called Myra.

"What are you wearing to the cocktail hour tonight?" I asked when she answered.

"Did you see that little black dress in the window at the store?" she asked, not missing a beat.

"Yes," I said. "The one with the silver thread sewn in? Right?"

"Yeah, I snagged it."

"John's not going to know what hit him!"

"Are you getting a cold? You sound funny."

"Oh," I said nervously. "You know, airplane air. I always catch something."

"So, what are you wearing?"

"I was just trying on the red dress."

"No! Wear that tomorrow!" She snapped into full-on designer mode. "Gray wool skirt, keep the brooch on it. But wear it with the recycled-tie silk camisole. Bring your black sweater, the one you had on yesterday, but only wear it if you absolutely get too cold to go without it."

"Okay," I said. "Thanks, Myra!"

"It's what I do."

"See you downstairs in twenty minutes."

"I'm already here, setting up. Come down whenever."

We hung up, and a second later she called back to tell me I should wear my hair pinned back on the left side and she had bobby pins in her purse so she'd pop up and do it for me.

⬥

"Oh my God, I'm so nervous," she said, running into my room. "Do I look okay?" She was wearing the gorgeous dress from the shop window and black pumps with silver polka dots and crazy flared heels. She had perfect black winged eyeliner on her top lash line and her lips were shining with a pale pink gloss. Her hair was pulled back in a very high, sixties-style ponytail, and her bangs were brushed to the side.

"You look like a movie star," I said.

"Thank you! I'm so glad you're here," she said, hugging me. "I couldn't face him otherwise. I just couldn't. You know, Karen is in Florida and Heather—you know how Heather is."

"Mmhmm," I said, standing in front of the mirror and pulling my hair back on the opposite side of my swooshy bangs. "Like this?"

"Almost," Myra said, digging two bobby pins out of her purse. "I'll do it."

I had to take my heels off again, so I was close enough in height for her to reach. She twisted my hair behind my ear and secured it with two crisscrossed bobby pins.

"Crap," she said, looking in the mirror. "I forgot my necklace."

"Here." I unhooked the clasp of my Tiffany bean necklace. I hadn't taken it off since Deagan gave it to me for my birthday last year. I handed it to Myra.

"Really?"

"Yeah, this top has enough happening to stand on its own," I said, co-opting language Myra had used the night before when we were going through my purchases.

She put it on and looked at herself critically for a moment, turning just a little from one side to another before nodding. "Thank you. That works really well." She gave me a nervous smile.

"You look amazing," I said. "You're going to be fine."

"Okay," she said. "You know what I need?"

"What?"

"Some bounce time."

"Huh?"

"Oh, come on! You can't tell me you don't remember the bounce!"

"Oh my God," I said, pretending it was dawning on me, even though I didn't have the slightest idea what she could be talking about.

"Yes!" Myra said, heading over to the clock radio. She plugged her iPod into the dock.

"Really?" I still had no idea what she was talking about.

She kicked her heels off, so I did the same. She scrolled through her iPod until she found the right song. The opening bars of "Why Can't I Be You?" played, and I recognized it immediately.

My mom thought a guy wearing eyeliner was disgusting, so I had to hide my Cure CDs under my mattress like a boy hides

porno mags. I bought them because this guy, Kevin, in my art class
wore a Cure shirt at least once a week. He also did these amazing paintings of bones. You could look at them and know what he
was feeling when he painted them. I wanted to talk to him so
badly, but I didn't know what to say, so I did that thing where you
could get ten CDs for a penny through the mail and ordered every
Cure CD they had.

I never got up the nerve to talk to Kevin, but all through high
school I listened to *Kiss Me, Kiss Me, Kiss Me* every single night
before I went to bed. I'd wake up with headphone cord marks on
my face. So when Myra started jumping around and singing, it was
easy to join her and pretend that this was some kind of old girlfriend tradition, something we'd always done.

We bounced around the room, flailing our arms like Robert
Smith and smiling at each other as we sang along.

"Okay," Myra said, flopping down on the bed, breathless,
when the song ended. "Now I can do this."

"Good bounce," I said, holding my side and trying to catch my
breath.

"Great bounce." She laughed. "God, like thirteen years since
we've done that, huh?"

"Too long," I said, smiling.

"I'll say."

"Man, we're old!" I said. "How can it be so long since high
school, when I still feel like an awkward kid all the time?"

"Oh!" She shook her head. "Crazy talk! You were never awkward. I'm the one who had those braces and the Lisa Loeb glasses."

"Lisa Loeb! I had a green dress kind of like the one she wore
in that video. I thought it was so cool." I panicked for a second,
worrying that maybe Jessie Morgan hadn't dressed like that, that

maybe I'd just given myself away with one stupid comment. But Myra was busy putting her shoes back on and didn't seem to notice my misstep.

We checked ourselves in the mirror before we left. We were flushed and a little rumpled, but in a good way. We looked vibrant, wild, happy. The hair and the clothes and the makeup made me feel like someone new, but the happy is what made me unrecognizable.

As we walked through the lobby and up the stairs to the bar, Myra squeezed my arm like we were headed into a haunted house.

"You'll be fine," I told her. "You're going to be the most gorgeous person in there. I promise." The bar was dimly lit, with candles flickering against polished wood and brass.

"Swear?" Myra asked.

"Shit!" I said, smiling, feeling bold like Jessie would.

"Oh my God! What?"

"I was swearing." I laughed.

"Ha-ha. Not funny, Jess."

"He's not a shark or a zombie, My. He won't jump out and get you."

"Yeah, but I'm worried that when I see him my heart will break all over again. Is that stupid? That's stupid, right?"

"No," I said. "It's not stupid. I understand."

"You rock, Jessers. I don't know how I've survive—"

All of a sudden a hyperactive blond blur charged at us. "No way!" the blur screeched in the cutest little chipmunk voice. She was only a little bit taller than Myra and had her arms wrapped around me before I could see anything other than a giant mass of yellow curls. "Jessie *Fucking* Morgan!" It was like hearing a cartoon character curse.

"Oh my God," I said.

"You don't even recognize me!" she said, and instead of it being an accusation, she seemed thrilled. "I know! Right?" She was
wearing a strappy little royal blue dress that swished out as she
turned from side to side to show off her figure. She put her hands
on her hips. She had the tiniest little waist. "Can't believe it, can
you? It's me! Heather! Well, like half of Heather. I lost eighty-five
pounds, which is basically an entire supermodel."

"You look fantastic!" I said. I didn't know what she'd looked
like before, but she was undeniably beautiful.

"Robbie is parking the car. He's going to die when he sees you!"

She covered her mouth and nose with her hands for a second, like she couldn't quite handle the shock. Then she shook her
head.

I stiffened, waiting for her verdict on me.

"Okay, and I know it's rude to say, but that nose is incredible." Heather touched my nose cautiously with her index finger,
like she expected it to be a mirage or a hologram.

"Thanks," I said, feeling every muscle in my body let go just a
little. In her mind I was Jessie Morgan. She had no doubt. Then it
hit me: Why would she doubt it? Who would pretend to be some
random girl they'd gone to high school with? Why would that be
in anyone's mind as something to suspect in the first place? Myra
had already validated me. Heather was expecting Jessie Morgan,
so she saw Jessie. Everyone else would too. I just had to make sure
I didn't say anything ridiculous.

"My roommate in college . . . ," Heather said. "Well, I only
went to college for a week, but that's a whole other long story.
But my roommate, she got a nose job the summer before college,
and they did a really bad job, and if you got too close to her you
could, like, see the chisel marks down the ridge of her nose. Like

here." She pointed to her own nose. "Like these little dents. And it freaked me out. But your nose is really smooth! It's perfect." She stared at my face as if I were a medical marvel. Then she gasped. "That's not why I only lasted a week—her nose. That's not why I left. Of course, it didn't help that when I was lying in bed every night, I kept thinking about how she was there in the next bed with a nose full of chisel marks, wondering what it must have sounded like when the doctor hacked away at her face." She wrapped one of her curls around her thumb and let it unravel again. "I left because I missed Robbie too bad, you know? And then he came up and proposed and that was it. I mean, I was never going to be a rocket scientist or anything. And there he was at my dorm room in the middle of the night with this ring." She flashed her left hand at me quickly, and there was the small flicker of a diamond in the candlelight. "And I thought, what am I even doing here? And . . . Oh my God! I can't believe how much we have to catch up on."

"Yeah," Myra said, herding us over to the bar. "You're going to have to take some breaths from time to time or you're going to pass out trying to tell Jessie everything."

"I know, right?" Heather said, laughing. And she was actually a little breathless.

Myra ordered a pitcher of mojitos for us.

At the far end of the bar there was a wall of windows, and I could see the greenish glow from the falls all lit up. I wanted to go look, but Myra and Heather didn't seem at all interested in the view. They'd probably seen it a million times.

While we were standing at the bar, waiting for our drinks, a guy in a navy peacoat snuck up behind Heather. He wasn't very tall, but he was striking. He had broad shoulders, bright blue eyes, a mess of brown hair, and a five o'clock shadow that outlined his jaw. He smiled at Myra and slipped his arms around Heather's waist. I almost yelled, "Robbie, how are you?" because I thought it would be good to pretend to recognize him. But I wimped out. Or possibly I had suddenly become the luckiest person alive, because Heather turned around and screamed, "Fish! You have to stop doing that! One of these days I'm going to grab your package or something."

"Do you usually grab Robbie's package in public?" Fish asked, smiling. He had a really great mouth. His lips curled up at the corners like he was up to something or he had a secret he might tell you if you asked the right questions.

"No," Heather said, giving him a quick hug and a peck on the cheek, "but, you know. Old married people get frisky sometimes." Even in the dim bar lights it was obvious she was turning red.

I hopped off my barstool, thinking I'd get to hug him, and not hating the idea of having him wrap his arms around me.

He saw me, suddenly, and did a quick double take. There was a flash of recognition in his eyes, but then he focused completely on Heather and acted like he hadn't seen me. I worried I wasn't passing for Jessie as well as I'd thought.

"I'm totally telling Robbie that I grabbed your package," Heather said, smiling.

"It's your funeral," Fish said. Then he laughed and shook his head. "No, that would really be my funeral, wouldn't it?"

"Yeah, it would," Heather said, laughing.

"So," Myra said, grinning, "I can't believe you haven't noticed who's here."

Fish shot me a pointed look, like a warning, and it made the hairs on the back of my neck stand up. He looked away for a second, and I wanted so desperately to meet his eyes again. I'd never felt that kind of electricity before. Deagan made me a little nervous when I first met him, but this was different. This was more than butterflies. It was like all of a sudden everything everyone in movies and songs and sitcoms and books said about chemistry made sense. My chemicals desperately wanted to get closer to his chemicals.

"God," Fish said, rubbing his chin with his hand, looking at Myra's brooch on my skirt. "You look different, Jess." There was something flat about the way he said it.

"Thanks," I said, trying hard to smile.

"Yeah." He gave me a bewildered look, meeting my eyes again for a split second. "Take it as a compliment." He shook his head and reached over to give Myra a kiss on the cheek.

From what I'd put together from my conversations with Myra, Fish was Jessie's ex-boyfriend. But Myra seemed so excited to surprise him, so I didn't think there was any bad blood. I thought he'd be happy to see Jessie. I wanted him to be happy to see me.

Our pitcher of mojitos showed up and so did Robbie. He towered over everyone. He wore ripped jeans, work boots, and a Carhartt jacket. He was completely underdressed for the bar, but he had a sweet round face, like a teddy bear, and adorable deep dimples that made me think most people would be willing to forgive his faux pas. "Jessinator!" he said, in what was absolutely not an indoor voice. He gave me a hug, lifting me off my barstool and leaving me gasping for breath. His jacket smelled like cold air and engine grease. "Holy crap! You're really here! We missed you around these parts." He kissed me on both cheeks and then my forehead before he pulled away and looked at me. "I missed you like crazy. No one to wreak havoc with me." His face looked strained, like he might be fighting tears. He took his jacket off and hung it over the back of the barstool next to mine. "I had to settle down and get boring." He patted his slight beer gut. "It's all your fault!" He laughed and it was so loud that the people around us stared. He didn't notice, or if he did, he didn't care. It made me laugh too.

Myra poured drinks. She handed one to Robbie, but he handed it right to me.

"What's with this shit, My Oh My?" Robbie said, looking into my glass and making a face like a kid staring at plate full of brussels sprouts. "It has grass in it." He kissed Heather hello, even though he'd presumably just seen her when he dropped her off at the front door. She wrapped her arms around his neck and kissed him back.

"It's mint," Myra said, even though Robbie wasn't listening. She waved her hand to get the bartender's attention. When he came over, Myra stood on the rung of one of the stools, leaned over the bar, and shouted, "You see these two here?" She pointed to Fish and Robbie. "They're too prissy for mojitos. You need to get them some beers."

"Pike," Fish shouted to Myra.

"Stout?" she asked.

"Yeah."

"Pale for me," Robbie said, his eyes sparkling. "Stout is like *eating* beer. You're supposed to drink it, dumb ass." Robbie grabbed Fish's shoulder and slapped hands with him. "Hey, man!"

"Hey," Fish said to Robbie, his eyes so much softer than when he looked at me, "so I know this guy who's looking for a new clutch shaft for his Farmall."

"Oh. Cool! What year is it?" Robbie asked.

"It's a fifty-two Cub."

"Ew!" Heather said, putting her drink on the bar so she'd have both hands free to herd Robbie and Fish over to some empty chairs by the fireplace. "If you guys are going to talk tractor parts, do it somewhere else and leave us to our girl talk, okay?"

"All day with the tractor talk. I need a break, you know?" she said to me, rolling her eyes when she came back.

"I can imagine," I said, taking a small sip of my drink. I knew I had to be careful.

Myra was quiet. She watched the door and sipped her drink through a pair of red stirrer straws. The bar wasn't too crowded. Most of the people coming for the reunion would probably just show up the next day, for the main event. I got the feeling that Jessie's friends cared more about hanging out together than catching up with the few random meatheads and former cheerleaders at a table in the corner.

"Robbie took over his uncle's shop," Heather said. "I do all the books and stuff." She shook her head and her pretty blond ringlets trembled around her face. "God, Jess. It's so weird that you don't even know this, right? I mean, I used to tell you everything and now there's like thirteen years of stuff you don't even know."

I tried really hard to listen, to pick up any clues that might be useful later, but over Heather's shoulder, I saw Kyle, from the conference, at the other end of the bar, raising his hand to get the bartender's attention. I watched from across the bar, wondering if he'd be there all night. He couldn't be a part of the reunion too. What would the chances of that be? Two of us from the conference at the reunion? And I was pretty sure he was older than Jessie's friends. Late thirties.

"Uh-huh. Totally," I said, nodding my head at Heather.

The bartender poured a shot of tequila for Kyle, who kicked it back immediately, smacked some bills on the bar, and got up. He caught me watching him and smiled.

Heather was still talking. "Um, you know . . . ," I said, interrupting her. "I'm sorry. I have to go get this thing . . . in my room. My . . . inhaler. I need my inhaler."

"You have asthma now? I told you not to smoke in high school. God, you and Robbie! I finally got him to quit three years ago, but I told you guys not to start in the first place! Didn't I? Remember, Jess?"

"Yes, you did, Heather," I said quickly. "And I didn't listen, and I need to go upstairs to get my inhaler. I'll be right back, okay?"

"Okay. Do you need help?" she asked, looking me over with concern.

"No, I'm good. You stay here." Kyle was getting closer, so I just started walking.

I ran down the stairs and got as far as the big stone fireplace before Kyle yelled, "Jenny!" across the lobby. Luckily no one else was there to hear it. I contemplated running for the elevator, pretending I hadn't heard him, but he called out, "Hey, Jenny!" again, and I worried about being rude and then having to see him at the conference in the morning. More importantly, I worried if he yelled again, someone else might hear him do it. So I turned around and said, "Oh, hey!" like maybe I hadn't heard him the first time.

"Wow," he said, "You look . . ."

"Thanks," I said, before he could even say how I looked. I watched the door to the bar nervously, hoping that none of Jessie's friends would come out to the lobby.

"Hey, I just stopped up for a drink, but a bunch of us are grabbing dinner over in the dining room." He pointed across the lobby. "And then we're going to hit the city and head to a club. Come with?"

"I can't," I said, "but thanks."

"Come on. I'll even let you take the piss out of my bar stories like you did with my PowerPoint." He rubbed his head and gave me a smile—the kind that was meant to look shy and awkward but wasn't. There was nothing shy about him.

I fell for this kind of act with Deagan. Fool me once: shame on the smiling guy. Fool me twice: not going to happen. I gestured back to the door of the bar. "I'm having drinks with some friends."

"Are you from around here?"

"Sort of," I said. "Something like that. There's a . . . history." I willed myself to shut up. The fewer the details, the more believable the lie—the words cycled in my head like a mantra.

The door to the bar opened. I held my breath and tilted my chin down so my hair fell to cover my face.

"History was always my worst subject," Kyle said, smiling again. Some guy who looked like a total meathead walked out of the bar and headed outside, pulling a pack of cigarettes from his jacket pocket. I'm sure he was there for the reunion, but he looked like he'd probably been a jock in high school. Jessie Morgan's friends were not jocks. They were the kind of motley group that can only form when people become friends way before puberty sets in. Their history is stronger than high school cliques. Without that, Jessie would have probably gone to the mean girls, Myra to the art-room kids, Heather to the nerdy girls who liked horses, Robbie to the out-back smokers, and Fish—I couldn't figure out where Fish would have fit. But none of them would have hung out with the jock in the lobby.

"Well, uh . . ." I breathed a sigh of relief.

"Are you okay?"

"Yeah, I'm fine. I just . . ." I met Kyle's eyes. He had really nice eyes. And even if the shy smile thing was an act, for a split second I thought about just going with him. Hanging out with the PR people. Going into Seattle. It would be easier. I would know what to expect. I wouldn't be lying. Or at least I'd be lying to myself, which is inherently easier than lying to other people. But I really wanted to be there when Myra's ex showed up. I wanted to hear what Heather and Robbie had been doing since high school, because they were sweet and funny. And Fish. I had guys like Kyle figured out, but I didn't get Fish at all, and I wanted to. "Yeah, you know, I'm good here tonight. But maybe tomorrow?"

"Well, then," Kyle said, smiling, "I'll ask you again tomorrow."

"Good," I said, smiling back, and watched him walk into the restaurant before I climbed the stairs to the bar, just to be sure the coast was clear.

When I got back, Robbie was up at the bar with the girls, waiting on beers. Fish was talking to some guy across the room. He looked at me when I walked in. He stopped talking, but when I made eye contact, he looked away. I could see him stumbling on his words, wrinkling up his forehead like he'd forgotten what he was saying.

"I mean, thirteen years since high school, but a bag full of Pixy Stix and a stack of John Hughes movies is still my favorite way to spend a Friday night," Myra said, poking at the mint in her glass. She used her red straws like chopsticks to pick up a sprig so she could nibble at it. "Tonight excluded." She grabbed my arm. "If you lived here again and this was what Friday night could be . . . Nope," she said, shaking her head. "I'd still choose Pixy Stix and John Bender." She took a sip of her drink. "But you'd be invited, of course."

"You'll have to fight me for Judd Nelson," I said. "He's totally mine."

"Ew!" Robbie said. "You guys are perverts!"

The bartender looked like he wanted to shush us.

Myra punched Robbie's arm. "Shut up!"

"No," Robbie said, "think about it! So you had a crush on Judd Nelson playing a high school kid when you were in high school."

"So?" Myra said. "I'm failing to see your point."

"I haven't made my point yet," Robbie said, laughing. "Now, you still have a crush on Judd Nelson in his role as a high school kid, but you're thirty-one. That's totally creepy. You're getting all hot and bothered over a high school kid."

"Judd Nelson is in his fifties now!" Myra said.

"But that's not what we're talking about. We're talking about your crush on Judd Nelson in *The Breakfast Club*, where he's only, like, seventeen."

"One," Myra said, "I won't be thirty-one for three more months."

"How is that better?" Robbie asked, shaking his head but smiling wide.

"It just is! And two, when I watch it, it's like my high school self still has a crush on Judd Nelson playing a high school kid. It's nostalgic. I'm remembering how I felt about him when I was sixteen."

"I don't know," Robbie said, laughing. "I still think it's a little pervy." The bartender handed Robbie his beers. Robbie left some wrinkled bills on the bar.

"Three," I said, picking up where Myra left off, "Judd Nelson was twenty-six when he was in *The Breakfast Club*. It wouldn't be weird at all if Myra dated a twenty-six-year-old."

"Okay, so you're not a perv, My," Robbie said, smiling. "You're just a cougar."

"Robbie!" Heather said, and tried to cover his mouth with her hand. He pushed it away.

"Really, Robert," Myra said, raising an eyebrow at him. "Really? If I dated a guy four years younger than me, you'd call me a cougar?"

"If the tail fits," Robbie said, smirking. "Plus it's almost five years, because you're going to be thirty-one in three months."

"Well," Myra said, dragging the word out like she was searching for a comeback, "well, maybe my imaginary younger man is going to be twenty-*seven* in two months."

"Oh! Oh! You're reaching," Robbie said, stretching his arm out like he was trying to grab something just past his fingertips.

"Go drink your beer, Robert. Fish is thirsty. Go away," Myra said, shooing him with her hands, laughing.

Robbie kissed the top of her head before he walked away. "Love you, My!" he said, in a patronizing voice.

"Piss off, Robbers," Myra said, but she was smiling. She reached for the pitcher and poured herself another drink.

"Oh," Heather said, "I wish Karen was here. Then we'd all be together!"

Myra caught my eye and smiled nervously, and I got the idea that there was something about Karen. Did Karen hate Jessie too?

"She's stuck in Florida until Dylan's okay to fly again," Heather said, tucking her hair behind her ear.

"I heard! She left me a message. That's awful," Myra said.

"I know," Heather said. "He's going to have to get tubes when she can get him back here. That's like the third ear infection in two months."

"So," I said, working with the context clues, "does Karen just have Dylan?"

"No," Heather said, pulling out her phone. "She has Paige too." She scrolled through pictures on her phone, found the one she was looking for, and passed it over to me. The picture was of a little girl with long brown hair and gorgeous big brown eyes. She was sitting on a tractor with Robbie, and he was letting her steer. They were both laughing. The next picture was of Heather holding a little boy, a toddler, on her lap and they were both clapping their hands.

"That's Dylan," Heather said. "We babysit a lot. Karen's husband left right before Christmas last year. He was a total douchewad." She rolled her eyes. "She's better off without him. And he's lucky he left. I was ready to castrate him in his sleep."

Myra whispered loudly, "Couldn't keep it in his pants." She'd taken care of most of the second pitcher of mojitos by herself.

"So Dylan is sick?" I asked.

"Yeah," Heather said. "Karen took the kids to Disney. The divorce has been really hard on Paige and Karen wanted to cheer them up, but then Dylan's ears got so bad that the doctor she took him to said she can't fly back until he's better."

"That's awful!" I said.

"Yeah, I feel so bad for them. Karen is all stressed out, because she's stuck there and missing this and missing work and spending more money on a hotel than she had in the budget. Paige is bored out of her mind. Poor Dylan keeps asking for his dad. It all sucks."

"Do you and Robbie have kids?" I asked, and then realized it was probably a rude question. I already knew the answer. If Heather and Robbie had kids, I'd have seen a full slide show.

Heather sighed. "No, we've been trying. For a really long time. No luck yet. But Dylan calls me Aunt H. now. It makes my heart feel like it's a trillion times bigger, you know? If we can't be parents, I am determined to be the greatest fake aunt there ever was."

"You guys?" Myra said, looking at us gravely, like she was about to say something madly important. "Too many mojitos. Too little food."

So we grabbed menus. I ordered Myra a Coke, and Heather discreetly handed the pitcher back to the bartender, even though there were probably two drinks left in it.

"Wait," Robbie called from across the room. "You guys are getting food?" He and Fish came back over.

"You can't order food without us!" Fish yelled to Heather. "They have the best burgers here."

Fish made every effort to stay as far away from me as he could, waiting to sit down until the last possible moment, trying to tell Robbie he should sit next to his wife. But since I was sitting between Robbie and Myra, and Heather was at the end of the bar on the other side of Myra, the farthest Fish could get from me was the other side of Robbie.

And before we knew it, we were all sitting in a row at the bar, drinking Cokes and eating burgers like overgrown teenagers in some upscale version of a village soda shop. I loved it.

Fish pretended to be so into his burger that he couldn't be

bothered to look my way, but every so often I caught him staring. One time he even smiled. Just a little bit.

"Hey," Robbie said, holding his burger in front of his mouth and pointing across the bar with his index finger, "is that Justin Finkel?" There was a guy wearing a gray wool suit and a flashy silver watch signaling the bartender smoothly, with two fingers, like he was hailing a cab.

"Yeah," Fish said, "I think it is."

"I mean, that's who he would turn into, right?" Robbie said, aggressively taking another bite of his burger.

"Fuck him," Fish said. He looked over at me, but I turned my head and pretended to be paying attention to whatever Heather and Myra were talking about. I didn't want to push my luck and have to pretend I knew who Justin Finkel was, but I kept listening.

"Yeah, I know," Robbie said. "It's just . . . You know how you have some things that are, like, on replay in your brain?"

"Yeah," Fish said.

"Sometimes when I screw something up or I feel like I'm in over my head, I can still hear him calling me a fucking retard when I had that panic attack in the middle of the SATs. Like, I still remember the way my pencil smelled and the stupid loud clock and then Justin's voice over and over."

"He's such an asshole," Fish said. Out of the corner of my eye, I saw him lean over to gently bump his shoulder into Robbie's.

"He looks like he's a rich, successful asshole," Robbie said.

"You're successful. You guys are in the black at the shop. That's no small thing."

"Yeah, but I've got dirty fingernails and a house with a leaky roof, you know. And I know Heather doesn't care, but—"

"Heather's proud of you, man. You gotta do what you love. What else is there? You want to be that guy? In that shirt? You want to sell meaningless shit for a living? You fix things. You've got dirt under your fingernails to prove that you do something. You don't just push widgets around."

Robbie punched Fish in the shoulder lightly. "Thanks."

"Joke's on him, man, because he still looks like a douchebag. And you," Fish said, gesturing to Robbie, "are just a whole lotta fabulous, my friend."

I couldn't help myself, I looked over. Robbie had a mouth full of milkshake, and he was in danger of spitting it across the bar. He managed to swallow it before he started laughing, but his eyes teared.

"He is fabulous, right, Jess?" Fish said, catching my eye and smiling, like he'd forgotten he was avoiding me. Or maybe, in the face of making Robbie feel better, the way he felt about me didn't even matter.

"Robbie," I said, "you are exquisite."

"Aw," Robbie said, putting his arm around me. "I love you, Jess."

While we were eating, Kyle walked back in. He went to the other end of the bar and ordered another shot. He held it up and nodded his head toward me before he downed it. He flipped a twenty on the bar, said something to the bartender, and walked away.

This is it, I thought. My cover is blown. I started thinking about my escape plan. It would go better if I took my shoes off before I ran out.

"One for the road, you know?" Kyle said, patting my shoulder as he walked past. "See you tomorrow, Not Monica."

"Who's that?" Heather asked, smiling at me like maybe there was a secret to be found out.

Fish slurped at the ice at the bottom of his glass with his straw. Loudly.

"Oh," Myra said, "Jessie's here for a conference too."

"So you didn't really come to see us," Fish said, staring me down.

"Well, I did." I hedged. "I mean, it just—it all worked out nicely, you know?"

"Whatever," he said, and wiped his hands on his napkin. "I gotta go see a man about a horse."

"Charming," I said, before I could stop myself.

Fish gave me that look again, the warning one that made my pulse charge through my veins. It wasn't a bad feeling.

"You guys," Myra said, wadding up her napkin and tossing it on her empty plate. "One, I don't think John's coming tonight." She took a sip of her soda. "And *b* I have to go finish setting up for the reunion tomorrow."

I thought she was really drunk, but then Robbie pointed at me and said, "Oh my God! Ha! Remember, you always used to do that? 'One' and *b*, or *a* and 'two,' whenever you had a list of things. Like you couldn't remember which you were using."

"One, totally. And *b* I'm sure it was intentional," I said, defending myself or Jessie or I don't even know who.

"Yeah," Robbie said, getting up and putting his arms around me and Heather. "Keep telling yourself that, Jesseroo." He grabbed my face with his hand and smushed my cheeks. "Look at this face," he said to Heather. "Just precious!"

"Look at this face," Heather said, smushing Robbie's cheeks while he was still holding mine. "You guys are goons."

We all piled into the reunion banquet room to help Myra finish getting ready.

Fish grabbed a wound-up wad of twinkle lights from Myra's decorations box and sat on a table in the corner by himself to untangle them.

Myra put Heather and Robbie to work blowing up red and white balloons with a helium tank. Robbie blew them up, and Heather tied ribbons on the ends. They were a well-oiled machine. Robbie sang, "Ninety-nine red balloons, ninety-nine red balloons, ninety-nine red balloons, ninety-nine red balloons."

Myra and I laughed.

"Oh my God!" Heather said. "That song does have other words."

"Yeah," Robbie said, holding up a finished balloon and hitting it across the room like he was serving a volleyball, "but I don't know what they are."

I kicked my heels off and stood on a table while Myra handed me a cascade of streamers to hang over the DJ booth. "A little bit this way," she said, and I moved them toward her. "No, to the left now."

"Ninety-nine . . ." Robbie stopped. We heard him suck helium from one of the balloons. "Red balloons." His voice had gone munchkin. "Ninety-nine red balloons."

Myra turned her back to Robbie. "Oh my God!" she mouthed to me, laughing so hard her face turned red.

Her laugh made me laugh harder. I tried to keep my head down so Robbie wouldn't see.

"We can't encourage him," she whispered, shaking her head. "He'll never stop."

"Robert!" Heather yelled. "You're killing brain cells."

"I didn't have that many to begin with," Robbie said, his voice slipping from cartoon character back to normal.

"That's why we have to be extra careful, sweetheart," Heather said, kissing him. "You're such a dork."

"Oh my God," Myra said, taking a deep breath. "Okay, a little to the left." Her voice wobbled on the edge of giggles. I stepped to the far corner of the table, but I couldn't quite reach the right spot.

"Fish!" Myra yelled. "Get over here!"

"What?" Fish said, making no effort to get up.

"Help Jessie."

Fish gave her a pained look.

"Oh, grow a pair," Myra said, and walked away.

Fish sighed and jumped up on the table next to me.

"Hi," I said. "Just a little bit farther over . . ." I stretched my arm out as far as I could. He grabbed the bunch of streamers from me and smacked them up without really looking at where they were supposed to go.

He jumped down from the table. "I'm going to head home," he yelled to Myra. He kissed her on the cheek, whispered something to her, and then walked to the door without even saying good-bye to me.

"Hey," Robbie said. "Don't leave me here, man! They'll make me glue glitter on doilies or something. Drop me off on your way."

"Fine," Fish said, without looking back.

Robbie ran over and handed his keys to Heather. "Drive Myra home."

"I'm sobered up," Myra said.

"Drive Myra home," Robbie said again, loudly.

"Love you, *Dad*," Myra yelled after Robbie, as he jogged out of the room to catch up with Fish.

"Love you, ladies! Behave yourselves!" he yelled over his shoulder as he left.

"Thanks for staying with me, girls," Myra said. She sat down and started making loops out of red, white, and gray streamers. "You're saving my ass." Her hands moved so fast, and then all of a sudden there was a perfect bow in front of her. She started in on another one.

"No problem," I said. I tried to copy Myra's loops, but I kept stretching the crepe paper out too much, and the resulting bow looked floppy and pathetic.

"Of course! I wouldn't miss this," Heather said.

"Actually." Myra raised an eyebrow. "I think technically we're saving your big fraud of an ass."

"What do you mean?" I said. My heart didn't pound as hard this time. There are only so many times you can deal with about-to-be-found-out shock before you either die or adapt.

"Ms. Class President," Myra said, smirking at me.

Thankfully, I bit my tongue before I said, "Really?" From what I knew of Jessie Morgan, she didn't seem like the class-president type. I didn't say anything. I just smiled.

"Just think," Heather said. "If Robert Pierce had done his platform speech while wearing a spandex miniskirt and a tube top, he'd be here making crepe-paper bows instead." She finished a bow that was only slightly better than mine. "Remember your red patent-leather stilettos? I still don't know how you could walk in those things."

"God," I said, cringing at the idea of some little tart winning a high school election that way. "I can't believe—I can't believe I did that!"

"Yeah," Myra said. "And you got all the glory while I did all the grunt work. That's why we're having a thirteen-year reunion, by the way. It's your fault. Everyone waited for you to emerge from the ether to plan the ten-year, and it never happened."

"I'm so sorry," I said.

"Hey," Myra said, "homecoming dance, winter formal, and prom. I learned how to make a mean crepe-paper bow." She seemed a little annoyed, but then she looked at me and her face softened. "And, you know, we don't love you because you've always been a straight arrow. Plus I'm sure we're all way more interesting now than we were three years ago anyway." She scrunched up her face like she was being super serious and handed me a bow. "Go hang it somewhere. Do your job, Madam President." She laughed.

I hung bows around the stage with rolled-up strips of tape. I watched Myra and Heather as I worked. Myra stuck a bow in Heather's hair. Heather crossed her eyes and stuck her tongue out.

"You look lovely, darling, don't you?" Myra said, in a terrible British accent.

"Yes, yes," Heather said, sticking a bow on Myra's head too.

"And you look simply smashing. Jessie, do be a dear and come look ridiculous with us, will you?"

"But of course," I said, and jogged across the room to join them.

When we finished the bows, we moved on to name tags. Myra had cards made up with everyone's high school yearbook pictures on them, but we had to get them in plastic sleeves and set them up in alphabetical order on the table by the door.

Myra handed me a card for Jessie. "I made this one on my computer this morning. I figure if we have to wear dorky name tags, you do too."

"Ha!" Heather said, holding one of the cards to her chest to hide it from us. "Brad Wilson. Do you remember how cool we thought he was?"

I smiled and nodded.

Myra held the back of her hand to her forehead, like she was swooning.

"And, here it is," Heather said, turning the tag out to face us.

Brad Wilson was a scrawny little baby of a kid with hockey hair.

Myra laughed so hard that actual tears rolled down her cheeks. "We wasted our youth mooning over a guy with a mullet!"

We stayed up way later than we should have, playing "cool or not cool?" with the name tags until well after midnight.

Myra yawned, and then Heather and I followed. "You know," Heather said, "if I stay any later, I'm going to be too tired to drive."

"Yeah," Myra said, stretching out her arms and yawning again. "We should get going."

"I'm just going to run to the ladies' and then I'm good to go," Heather said, and did a quick little jog for the door.

"You know," Myra said, laying her head on her arm to look at me. "You could stay with me next week."

"Oh," I said. "I don't—"

"You told me you were going to spend next week with Deagan. You already have the time off."

"I mean, I should really—"

"Seriously, Jess," she said, sitting up and reaching for her purse. "You should really stay."

"I'm not sure everyone's happy to have me here."

"Fish, you mean?"

"Yeah," I said, running my hand through my hair. I still wasn't used to how short it was.

"I think he'll warm up. He just needs a little time. You broke his heart."

"Really?"

"God, Jess! Sometimes you can be so dense!" She laughed and smacked her palm to her forehead. "He told you he loved you after graduation, and you ran into the bathroom and then basically disappeared forever. You think maybe that might bruise a guy's ego a little? Maybe? Possibly?"

I leaned on my elbows and covered my face with my hands. I didn't know what to say, and I was feeling overwhelmed.

"Hey," Myra said. She patted my arm. "He has to get it out of his system, you know? Make sure you know that he was hurt. He'll warm up. I've watched him watching you when you're not looking."

"Really?"

"It's Fish," Myra said. "He has to watch you. It's like what he was put on earth to do. Stay. Make up with him. After everything you guys went through, don't leave without patching things up."

"I have the trip all booked," I said. "I'm not sure if it's refundable." I wasn't going to stay at Myra's house. That was a line too crazy to cross.

"Well, the offer is there," she said, reaching across the table to squeeze my hand.

After Myra and Heather left, I wandered around the room, looking for Fish's picture on the yearbook page posters. I didn't even know what his real name was. Myra or Heather must have gotten his name tag.

I started at the beginning of the yearbook pictures and worked my way around the room until I found a picture I was sure was Fish. Gilbert Warren Foster. He was wearing a plaid shirt, open, over a Pearl Jam T-shirt, and even though he was blinking funny in the picture, I would have thought he was cool when I was in high school. I would have bought a Pearl Jam CD for an excuse to talk to him, and I might have even worked up the nerve to actually say something.

I found Robbie, who had massive aviator eyeglasses sliding halfway down his nose, a big warm smile, and the same deep dimples. I wouldn't have recognized Heather if she'd had a nickname like Fish, but I could pick her out from the narrowed-down sea of Heathers. She was pudgy with mud-colored frizzy hair pulled into a side ponytail and fastened in place with a big white scrunchie. She wasn't what anyone in high school would have thought of as pretty, but she had a hopeful smile and an awkward sweetness.

I'm sure if my face had been up there with everyone else's, it would have had that same raw promise. We can't see how beautiful it is when we're young and nervous and think everyone else knows just how awful we feel about ourselves. I wasn't that different from them. But what I never had is what was most beautiful about Fish and Heather and Myra and Robbie—they were people who were cared about. You could see it in their faces. You could still see it. They were secure in knowing they had friends. They were loved, and they always would be. I choked back tears.

I looked at Jessie Morgan's picture again and wondered what kind of person would ever leave friends like these.

So, it turns out that you can't just type "Jessica Elizabeth Morgan" into Google and expect to get the Jessica Elizabeth Morgan you're looking for right up top, or even expect to find her in the first five hundred results. I know this, because instead of going to bed after a long night of mojitos and meeting Fish and decorating, I stayed up until the wee hours of the morning convinced that the next link I clicked would lead to her. And every time it didn't, I'd say, "Okay, one more," and hold out hope that the next one I clicked would show a picture of someone who looked like me, but with a bigger nose, or race stats from a 5K fundraiser and the woman mentioned would be exactly Jessie Morgan's age.

I knew she hadn't gone to Florida State or the U of O, which I assumed meant Oregon. I wracked my brain to try to remember if Myra had mentioned any of the other schools Jessie applied to, but I didn't think she had. And it's not like I could have asked her, "Hey, so where did I apply to college?"

I looked on Facebook for Jessica Morgans who had gone to party schools. Someplace like Arizona or Southern California. Bikinis and sun and cute boys—a place to wear her tube top. But there wasn't a single thirty-one-year-old Jessica Morgan who looked the slightest bit like me anywhere.

Then it occurred to me that maybe she wasn't even Jessie Morgan anymore. Maybe she had a married name. Maybe she changed her name. Maybe there was a real reason Jessie left Mount Si and never came back. She dashed into a bathroom and then she disappeared. Maybe she was in the witness-protection program. The FBI or the CIA or whoever relocates witnesses let her walk at graduation and then swooped her away to be a dry cleaner in Lansing or a bartender in Kansas City. Maybe there was a good reason Myra had never been able to find her.

At around 4:00 a.m., the sheer stupidity and awfulness of what I was doing hit me. I started to sweat. My hands shook, and I couldn't get enough air. I grabbed my inhaler and went outside to sit on the balcony, with the comforter wrapped around me, and listened to the rush of the falls as I tried to calm myself down.

I woke up a few hours later, in one of the patio chairs, with a crick in my neck and dew on my face, and was generally damp and creaky all around.

Thankfully when I got down to the conference, most of the other attendees looked like they'd had a pretty rough night. Kyle's face was pale, and when he turned the projector on to do another PowerPoint, he winced as the light hit his face.

While Kyle talked about creating the right voice for a blog, I wrote down everything I knew about Jessie Morgan in my notebook, hoping that something would give me a clue about why she left and what I should do.

- Boyfriend: Fish
- Best friend: Myra
- Class president—tube top?
- Smoker
- Slutty dresser
- Fake green contact lenses
- Got into trouble with Robbie all the time. What kind of trouble?
- Went to the bathroom, never came back. Alligators in the sewer?

I made myself laugh out loud. Kyle looked in my direction. I covered my mouth and pretended to cough. When he looked away, I drew a big, toothy alligator on the page, and then a sewer pipe, and then the entire plumbing system of a high school and the route the alligator would take to grab Jessie Morgan and bring her down to his underground sewer-pipe lair, like a crocodilian Phantom of the Opera. Then I drew Jessie Morgan wearing a tube top and sitting in a gondola with an alligator dressed in a white half mask and a cape pushing them along the sewer with a pole.

I can't say I heard a single word Kyle or Michael, the next presenter, said. In fact, I hadn't even noticed when Michael switched places with Kyle, but at least it looked like I was taking notes.

When I finally did look up, the PowerPoint slide read, "Mistakes to avoid" in big letters across the screen. I had to bite my tongue to keep from asking Michael, who had hair like a salt-and-pepper helmet, which mistakes we should embrace.

The longer I stayed in PR, the less faith I had in the abilities of PR execs to actually communicate, and the less I wanted to be one. The main focus of my job was preparing for the launch of a forty-proof alcoholic energy drink called Ivolushun, which was being marketed specifically to college kids, steroid-happy gym rats, and hipsters who would hopefully find something ironic about it.

The week before I left for Seattle, we had a meeting with the Ivolushun brand coordinator, who came into the office wearing a slim-cut maroon suit and about three bottles of drugstore cologne, and said, with a straight face, "We're not legally allowed to call it an energy drink, so the campaign needs to convey energy with-

out actually using the words 'energy,' 'energetic,' or 'energified,'"
as if he actually believed "energified" was a word.

It was easier to think about Jessie Morgan than it was to question my entire career path, so I went back to my notebook and
listed things I needed to learn about Jessie.

- Find out where Jessie applied to college.
- What would she have majored in?
- How long did she date Fish?
- WHY DID SHE LEAVE?

At lunch, when I should have been mingling and making
great corporate connections, I grabbed a sandwich and snuck out
to the reunion room to look at Jessie Morgan's picture again. I
hoped I'd find some clue about who she might be now, but there
was nothing. Her senior quote was, "The only thing we have to
fear is . . . spiders." She was voted most likely to rob a bank. And
she was supposedly in the photography club, but she wasn't in the
photography club picture.

I sat on the table, ate my sandwich, and stared at all the faces.
I tried to come up with the equivalents from my high school. Roy
Dillard would have been Michael St. James. Katie Lewis was a
dead ringer for Mary Colby. Jake Wooster was—

"Hiding out?" I hadn't even heard Kyle come in, but there he
was. I blushed, hoping he hadn't been there long. When I get
caught up in my thoughts, I tend to make faces as if I were having
a conversation with someone, even though it's just me and I'm not
saying anything out loud. Not an attractive habit.

"Taking a break," I said, wiping my mouth to make sure I
didn't have any crumbs or mayo stuck to my lips.

"Rough night?

"Long one, at least," I said.

"So did you go to high school here?"

"Wouldn't you like to know?" I said, for lack of a better answer. My brain was slow and fuzzy from staying up so late two nights in a row.

"Well, that's why I asked."

"Mmm." I raised my eyebrows and smiled.

He stared at me like he wasn't quite sure what to say next.

"How about you," I said. "Did you have a rough night?"

"Oh," he said, rubbing his head, "it was a great night. It's the morning that got rough."

"That's usually how it goes," I said, even though I was the kind of girl who was in bed by eleven more often than not. He didn't have to know.

"So," Kyle said, pointing at all the pictures on the walls. "If I look, will I find you up here?"

I shrugged.

He walked over and leaned against the table where I was sitting and flashed me that purposefully shy smile again. "Think you'll come out with us tonight?"

"That remains to be seen," I said, and picked a slice of onion out of my sandwich.

It's funny, because I pretty much threw myself at Deagan. Once he showed the slightest bit of interest in me, I jumped in and did all the rest of the work. I invited him places and schemed and tried so hard to get him to like me. But withholding the most inconsequential bits of information from Kyle seemed to be driving him crazy.

"You know," he said, "it's good team building. Going out with the group. You'll make some connections."

"Huh," I said, laughing, "is that what they're calling it these days?"

"Oh," he said, holding his hand to his chest, in a gesture of mock seriousness. "You think I'm hitting on you?"

"You are," I said. "Don't worry. I've got you figured out." I don't know where the confidence was coming from. It was like Jessie Morgan had taken over my brain in some kind of bad body-swap movie. Or maybe I was too tired or too caught up in the Jessie drama to care.

"You do?" Kyle said.

"Maybe." It was stupid, the way I was playing with him. I wasn't really interested. I liked feeling like I had power. Like if I wanted to, I could get a guy like Deagan to throw himself all over me. It didn't fix anything, but it made me feel better.

"Well, if we don't catch you in the lobby tonight, we're headed to a place called Finaghty's in Snoqualmie."

"I'll keep that in mind," I said.

"Just say yes," he said. "Come with us."

"We'll see."

He smiled and shook his head at me. "Well, I should head back in. Michael is starting up again in five minutes. Don't be late. I'll give you detention."

"If I'm late," I called after him, "I'll make sure I have a hall pass."

I was the last one back to the conference room, and a girl named Stacy, from San Diego, had taken my seat up front, across from Kyle. Mostly, I think, she sat there so she could force Kyle to pay attention to the way her boobs erupted from a black satin pushup bra, straining the buttons of her thin white shirt.

I sat at the far end of the table, opened my notebook, and wrote.

- Afraid of spiders
- Photography club

When I looked up, Kyle was watching me. He smiled when my eyes met his.

I added some torches to my alligator drawing.

❖

"So, I'll see you later," Kyle said, when the lecture ended and everyone was filing out of the conference room.

He was so cocky. Like he knew he could have me if he wanted me. And I hated to admit it, but if I went out with them, he probably could. Because I liked feeling chosen. I liked that even though Stacy had her cleavage on full display, Kyle was looking at me. Kyle was asking me to come out with him, and that was exactly why I couldn't go. I couldn't be that girl anymore—the one who waited to be chosen. I was sure Jessie Morgan never waited around for anyone to choose her.

I went to my ten-year high school reunion. It was about two months before I met Deagan. I got brave and asked this guy, Noah, who I worked with, to go with me. Kind of like a friend thing, except I liked him and I guess he didn't know that. He met some girl at a nightclub the weekend before, and they did that annoying thing where they started acting like they were totally in love immediately. He told me she was jealous of me, "Even though we're just friends." So at the last minute I ended up dateless.

In high school the closest friend I had was this guy named Mark Reed, who sat at the same lunch table with me, mostly because we weren't wanted anywhere else. He had thick glasses that made his eyes look bigger than they were and orange freckles across his cheeks. Sometimes we'd do our chem homework together, and I'd share my pretzels with him.

He asked me out once. We'd been letting our legs touch under the table at lunch for, like, two weeks, when he finally asked me to go to the movies with him. But my mom was on a bad streak. I worried that if she found out I had a date, she'd go ballistic and call me a slut, like she did when some guy from the swim team prank called our house, pretending to be my boyfriend, during freshman year. Or she'd get manic and want to micromanage every single thing about the situation. Either way, I worried Mark would somehow end up getting hurt, and I liked him too much to let that happen.

I told Mark that I only liked him as a friend. "I just don't like you that way," I said. It was probably true. I didn't have any burning desire to kiss Mark or be his girlfriend, but I was sad to pass up the chance to secure him as my friend. To lock it down.

He moved his knee away from mine. "Oh," he said softly, blinking. "I'm sorry." His glasses magnified the red creeping into his eyes. "To put you on the spot like that."

"No," I said. "It was nice of you."

Even his freckles looked sad.

We still did our chem homework at lunch together for all of sophomore year, but he kept his legs directly in front of his chair, and if my knee happened to knock into his knee, he moved his leg away immediately. Junior year, we had different lunch periods and drifted apart. I ate alone in the library, hiding my baggie of pretzels in my lap and popping one in my mouth when the librarian wasn't looking. Instead of real friends, I had Jane Austen and Willa Cather. I read my way through at least a third of the alphabet by the time I graduated. I took notes on the characters as I read, and at night, after I finished my homework, I painted them. My bedroom walls were covered with watercolors of Antonia, Emma, Anne with an *e*, Jo March, Jane Eyre, Scout, and Pip, the way other girls taped up torn pages from magazines and made photo collages of their friends.

Still, I thought, the one person it would be nice to see, the one reason for going to my high school reunion, was Mark Reed. He was always nice to me. He was probably doing interesting things now.

Plus my braces were long gone, my hair wasn't as frizzy, and my skin had cleared up. I bought myself a new dress, and I felt like it would be nice to go and feel all grown-up. To feel like I'd moved on from all the bad stuff. To feel different. But when I got there, on a big board in the lobby with photos of people who weren't able to attend, there was a picture of Mark Reed. Filled out and acne-free, wearing a tuxedo, walking on the beach at sunset with his beautiful bride.

It wasn't like I'd hoped Mark and I would somehow fall madly in love or anything, but the fact that he had moved on and grown up so much that he didn't even feel the need to go to the reunion so everyone could see how different and handsome and successful he was made me feel lonely and left behind.

Carla Carrigan talked to me for twenty minutes about her home-based cosmetic-sales business, until she realized that I wasn't the girl who sat behind her in senior year social studies. "Oh no. Wait, that was Jenny Mulligan," she said, smiling at me like I was some kind of freak who wasn't worthy of hearing her new lip-gloss sales pitch. "Oh, you know, I think that's Julia and . . ." She didn't even finish her sentence. She just walked away.

I stared at people I'd barely known reuniting with people they'd actually cared about. I stood around listening to Ace of Base, drinking ginger ale, and eating cheap cheese on stale crackers, until the pathetic reality of my high school existence made me so overwhelmingly sad, so overtly aware of what I had missed, what was normal, what my mother never let me have, that I couldn't stand it anymore. I worried I might scream or burst into flames or, worse, start crying. So I left. I decided there was no point in standing around waiting for someone to recognize me. No one knew who I was. No one cared.

On my way out, I ran into the Four Amigos. There were still four of them without me, because Rachel, Sheila, and Rachel K.

adopted Jodie Moorehouse when she moved to our district from California, and they were all dying to learn how she got her hair so sun streaked and straight. Plus I think they realized that if they were friends with Jodie, when all the boys watched her, they would also be looking in the general direction of Sheila and the Rachels. Even when my mom was on a good streak, I had never brought that much attention to the table.

Jodie held her camera gingerly in her perfectly manicured hands, trying to get the other three to pose for a picture.

"Jenny Shaw?" Sheila said, as I walked past them.

"Hi, Sheila."

"Jenny. You look fantastic. I almost didn't recognize you."

"Thanks," I said, because I had never learned the right way to address a backhanded compliment.

"Come on, girls," Jodie said. "Do the thing."

Sheila and the Rachels put their arms around each other and kicked their legs up like they were Rockettes.

"Oh, wait," Sheila said. "Jenny . . ."

And for a split second I thought maybe they wanted me in the picture with them. The original Four Amigos. Maybe that summer we all spent together actually meant something to them too.

"Jodie," Sheila said, "Jenny can take the picture. Get in here!"

"Do you mind, Jenny?" Jodie asked. It was one of those questions that wasn't really a question. "We haven't all been together like this in, what? Six months? It's crazy!"

So I took the picture. I didn't even do anything snotty like cut Rachel K. out of it or wait until Sheila was doing that funky "the flash is coming any second" kind of blink. I took a nice picture of them. It's not like their friendship was there to hurt me. It's not like I'd earned a place in their picture. I hadn't been there to get ready for prom together. I hadn't helped them nurse breakups with ice cream. I wasn't a part of their group, and I'm not even sure if I wanted to be. I didn't think they were the people I would choose as friends now, if I could, but feeling excluded made my throat tighten and my eyes water, even though maybe I was supposed to be too mature for those kinds of feelings.

"Great! Let's get one more!" Regular Rachel said. "How about one where we're all Charlie's Angels?" She clasped her hands together with her index fingers out like she was holding a gun.

"That's cheesy," Rachel K. said.

"Oh," Sheila said, "let's just get a nice normal picture."

Then Jodie said something, but I don't know what, because I'd rested her camera on the table behind me and walked away before any of them noticed.

When the conference was done for the day, I went back to my room to relax. I showered in the big bathtub-shower combo. Before I got in, I opened the doors to the balcony and slid the Japanese screen to the bathtub open. The cool, fresh air and the hot water was the perfect combo. I filled the room with steam.

After my shower, I made a pot of coffee and drank two cups while sitting out on the balcony in my big fluffy white hotel robe, taking in the view, trying my hardest to just be. But then I realized I should probably change my spa stay to just one person. There were appointments booked, and I didn't want to get billed for Deagan's massages and mud baths. I paced around my hotel room while I waited for someone to pick up the phone.

"Hi," I said, "I have reservations booked for next week, with my boyfriend, but now it looks like I'll be coming alone. Under Jenny Shaw."

"Hmm," the woman on the other end of the phone said. "I don't see anything here."

"Maybe it's under Deagan Holmes?"

"Okay . . . ," she said, and I could hear her typing. "It looks like that reservation was canceled."

"Canceled?"

"Yes, there's a note here in the system that the reservation was canceled last month."

"Last month?" My heart pounded. So not only had Deagan dumped me to "explore" Faye, but he'd planned on doing it for at least a month.

We'd been a couple in that month. Things had been pretty normal. We went to dinner. We watched movies on the couch. We had sex. And that whole time he was already planning to break up with me. He was pretending like everything was fine, and he already had one foot out the door.

I hung up the phone and sat on the floor. The cool, fresh air was starting to get too cool, but I couldn't bring myself to go shut the door, so I just sat there, crying and shivering like a pathetic mess.

There was a knock at the door, so I picked myself up off the floor and wiped my face on the sleeve of my robe.

"It's Myra," I heard her yell, before I even got to the door.

"You're not ready yet," she said, when I let her in. "What's going on?"

"I just . . . ," I said, and then I broke down again.

"Oh, honey," Myra said, and handed me a pack of tissues from her purse.

"A whole month," I said. "He was planning to dump me for a whole month! He canceled the spa reservations a month ago!"

"Oh no!" Myra said, wrapping her arms around me. "I'm so sorry, J."

"How could he? How could he pretend that everything was normal while he was planning to break up with me the whole time? He's such a liar." Of course, as soon as I said it, I realized what a big fat double standard it was to call Deagan a liar, and that made me cry harder.

"I think you dodged a bullet," Myra said. "He showed you who he really is, and, thankfully, he did that before you got married or bought a house or had a kid."

"He didn't even want any of those things with me."

"Which just goes to show you how stupid he is," Myra said. "So you dodged a bullet." She sat down on the bed.

I crashed on the floor again, wrapping my robe around myself tightly and hugging my legs to my chest. "I guess I'm just finding it hard to feel lucky," I said.

"Well, of course. When someone shows you their true colors like that, you still get to be sad that they aren't who you wanted them to be. You miss who you thought they were, even if who they really are completely sucks."

She looked at me. It was a hard, heavy look, and it made me wonder if this wisdom she was sharing with me was something she'd learned the hard way when her best friend disappeared right after high school. If it was, I guessed Myra was way too polite to ever say so.

I felt guilty in the strangest way, as if I'd been the one to hurt her all those years ago. Of course, I was pretty much feeling all-round awful, so it was hard to separate misplaced Jessie guilt from just plain misery.

"Hey, you're still coming to the reunion, right?"

I sighed and shook my head. I knew I shouldn't go. I knew I needed to end the charade. When I thought my life was simple, it was a big mess. Now that it was actually a mess, how would I fare?

"Come on," Myra said. "I won't take no for an answer."

"No," I said, smiling weakly.

"See, I'm not going to accept that," she said, grabbing my hands and pulling me up off the floor. "Do you want me to wait while you get ready?"

"No," I said, wiping my eyes. "I'm sure you have stuff to take care of, Madam Better President Than I Ever Was."

"I can come back, and we can walk down together."

"I'm a big girl," I said. "I can manage. I'll meet you down there."

Myra left. I stood in the bathroom, drying my hair with the fat round brush I'd bought from the hairdresser. I thought about bailing. Myra would probably be busy with all the people and the last-minute details. Maybe she'd forget about me. I had an excuse. I got dumped. I got worse than dumped. I was cheated on and canceled on and lied to and humiliated.

I couldn't stop picturing Deagan and Faye lying in bed together, talking about how he was going to dump me. Did they have discussions about how stupidly oblivious I was? Other people had to know. Had I missed the pitying looks when I'd gone to the Old Toad for beers with the volleyball team after a game? Was everyone talking about clueless, ridiculous me behind my back? I thought about it while I put my makeup on, while I found my shoes and shimmied into my red dress and grabbed the name tag I'd swiped the night before. I thought about it when I left my room and took the elevator downstairs. What I didn't think about was what I was about to do, and then I was at the door to the reunion, with all the streamers and glitter and a DJ playing Depeche Mode, and I just stood there, like a deer caught in the disco-ball lights.

Then I had a horrible, horrible thought: What if Jessie Morgan did show up?

I scanned the room in a panic, looking for someone who looked like me. But I couldn't see faces in the dim light. She could be lurking and I wouldn't even know it. I couldn't even check to see if she'd picked up her name tag, because I had it.

I decided I needed to just go back to my room, wash my face and go to bed, catch an early flight home in the morning, and pretend none of this ever happened.

"Well, you sure clean up nice, Jessie," some guy said, as I walked past him on my way back to the elevator. His name tag read "Marshall Hetfield." In the high school picture next to his name, he was a younger, smiling guy with slightly more hair. He wore a letter jacket and held a football up by his ear like he was about to make a pass. The high school version of Marshall Hetfield was the kind of guy who never had acne or got picked last in gym, who was prom king and dated the head cheerleader.

Adult Marshall was still attractive, but he wasn't what he had been.

He put his hand on my shoulder, like he was holding me in place.

"Hi, Marshall," I said, smiling. There was something thrilling about getting away with being Jessie, and it snapped me out of my panic.

"You heading in?"

"Yeah," I said. "Sure." The adrenaline kicked in. It was good to feel something other than hurt.

"I'm just running out for a smoke, but it's really good to see you." He slipped his hand around my waist and kissed my cheek. I could practically taste his cologne. "What do you say, when I get back we head over to the high school and meet up under the bleachers like old times?" he whispered into my ear.

"I'm good for now," I said, smiling enough to seem at least a little bit flirty. "But thanks." While I was in bed by ten on Friday nights in high school, wondering what it felt like to be actually, honest-to-goodness kissed, Jessie Morgan was hooking up with guys in dark corners.

From across the room, by the door, Fish was watching us, glaring. He looked away when he caught me watching him back.

"Find me if you change your mind," Marshall said, his face still very close to mine. His breath was hot. "I dream about you." I saw a flash of gold on his finger. When he walked away, I could still smell his cologne and the whiskey on his breath, like it had soaked into my hair and my dress.

"Hey," Myra said, running across the lobby to me. "I have a surprise for you."

"Uh-oh," I said.

"Don't kill me." She held her hands over her face and peered at me between her fingers.

"Are you giving me a reason to?" I looked for Fish, but he had disappeared into the darkened reception room.

"Okay, so yesterday," she said, grabbing my hand and leading me across the room, "Robbie and I talked the DJ into bringing his karaoke machine."

"I don't like where this is going."

I had never sung karaoke in my life. Not even when Luanne dragged me out to some dive bar on the west side because she had

an urge to belt out "I Will Survive" to a room full of strangers after a bad breakup. I hid in the bathroom until it was over. Luanne
was too drunk to notice I wasn't singing backup.

"Come on, Jess!" Myra said. "It'll make Robbie's day."

"What song?" I asked, cringing. Not that any answer would be
a good one.

"Do you even have to ask?" She pushed me up the stairs to
the stage.

Robbie was already standing there with a mic in his hand.

"Hey, guys," he said to the crowd. "Do you remember Jessie
Morgan?" The guys in the class yelled and whooped and hollered.
I think a couple of the girls may have booed. My heart was pound-
ing so hard—I felt like the whole room lurched with every beat.

What was the song? What if I didn't know the song? And
even if I did, I'd never sung alone in public before. I was in cham-
ber choir in high school, so I had an excuse to stay late after
school. I loved adding my voice to the Fauré Requiem or old English madrigals. I liked feeling a part of something, pretending the
people in choir were my friends. But it was one thing to be a tiny
little voice in the alto section. There was safety in that. It is another thing entirely to be up on stage singing karaoke in front of
a class full of strangers. There were at least three hundred people
in the room.

Everyone stared at the well-lit stage. I made note of the exit
signs, but they seemed so far away. If I didn't go through with it,
I'd have to push though a sea of people to escape. There wasn't a
good way out.

Part of me wanted to do it, to know if I could. Everybody has
rock-star dreams sometimes. Everyone wants an excuse to let go.
I had mine in front me. All I had to do was take it.

The music started, and I knew the song. It was "Paradise by the Dashboard Light." My dad was a huge Meat Loaf fan. I grew up listening to that record. I didn't know all the words, but I knew enough to get by if I followed along with the karaoke screen.

I walked toward Robbie. There were people. So many people. And the light was bright, and my stomach was churning.

Robbie jumped down from the stage, grabbed Heather's scarf from her neck, and ran back up, waving it around. He flipped his head like he had long Meat Loaf hair, even though he had a buzz cut, and when he sang, he even kind of sounded like Meat Loaf.

Everyone watching was going to expect me to go for it like that. Jessie Morgan had to have been amazing. She had to have given it everything. She was a girl who wore tube tops and stole her dad's credit card. She had no inhibitions. If I was going to be her, I had to get rid of mine.

The DJ had a shot and a beer waiting for him on the deck. I stole his shot. He saw me do it and was about to say something, but I mouthed, "Thank you," and gave him a big smile, and he smiled back. It's amazing what a little red dress can do. I would not, in my usual clothes, with my old haircut, have gotten the same reaction. In my usual clothes, I would never have grabbed the mic, but me in that red dress was another story.

I missed chiming in on the first chorus. When my solo came around, every single inch of me was shaking, but I could feel the burn of tequila all the way down to my stomach. I took a deep breath. I was terrified that when I opened my mouth, I would throw up in the middle of the stage. I looked at Robbie and pretended it was just him and me. I could sing in front of Robbie. When he smiled, I felt like he was looking out for me. I opened my mouth and belted out the words and tried my best to not look like I was terrified. My voice shook at first, but two lines in it started to sound strong.

Robbie watched me, slack-jawed and shocked. I worried that I wasn't nearly as good of a singer as Jessie, but when my first part was over, he gave me the thumbs-up. I kept my eyes strictly on him or the screen and pretended no one else even existed. The words took over, and it was like I was singing to Deagan, asking him to love me forever, knowing that he wouldn't.

I danced with Robbie. I stole the scarf and then wrapped it around his neck. I sang into the mic with the kind of rock-star moves I'd practiced with my hairbrush in front of the mirror as a kid. By the end of the song I was just letting it all out and I didn't care who heard me. I looked at the audience. I didn't know them. I didn't care if they judged me. It didn't matter. I jumped up and down and sang as loud as I possibly could. And when it was over, there was this awful, horrible silence in the room, like I had quite possibly just embarrassed myself worse than all the tiny humiliations of my life balled up together, and I realized I didn't even care. And then Robbie gave me a big sweaty hug, and everyone was clapping and cheering. Heather threw her strapless bra up on stage, and Robbie caught it. Even Fish was clapping.

When I jumped off the stage, they crowded around me.

"God, Jess," Robbie said, handing me another shot. "When did you learn to sing? In high school, you couldn't carry a tune if your life depended on it."

"But you and I did karaoke all the time."

"When you were tanked," he said, laughing. "Good God! You were awful!"

"Yeah," I said, forcing a laugh. I thought of Yarah and sketching in the hallway outside the practice rooms at Ithaca. "I took voice lessons in college."

"Whatever your teacher got paid, it wasn't nearly enough," he said. He planted a big sloppy kiss on my forehead. "That was so much fun." He clinked his shot glass with mine. "Cheers, Jesseroo."

"Cheers, Robbers," I said, and we threw the shots back in unison.

Apparently once the karaoke floodgates have been opened, they cannot be closed. A group of girls who had probably been the cheerleading squad got up on stage to sing "Man! I Feel Like a Woman." I'm guessing they'd also done the number in the senior talent show or something, because they had vaguely coordinated dance moves.

"Oh my God," Myra said, when she worked her way through the crowd with her clipboard and her drink. "You guys were awesome." She gave me a big hug. "Sorry to put you on the spot."

"No, thank you," I said. "I don't do stuff like that . . . anymore." I felt like if I could do that, I could do anything. I wanted to do all the things I'd always been afraid to. I wanted to talk to strangers and dance like no one was watching and all those other clichéd, greeting card, inspirational things.

"I can't believe you can sing so well when you aren't trashed! Who knew?" Myra said, smiling. And then she froze. I turned around and saw a gorgeous man in a suit walk in with a woman wearing a short silver-sequined dress.

"Holy shit," Myra said, trying to put her drink down on the edge of a cocktail table. She missed and the glass crashed to the floor, splattering soda on our legs. "Crap!" she said, reaching frantically for a stack of cocktail napkins. She looked like she was going to cry.

"What?"

"John's here."

"It's okay, My. It'll be fine. You can handle this."

"His wife is wearing one of my dresses."

"What?"

"Yeah. Nancy must have sold it to her. I don't remember seeing her." She shook her head. "It's such a weird feeling."

"Come on," I said, grabbing her hand.

"What?"

"We're going to dance." I took her clipboard and handed it to Fish. "Can you tell the bar back that a glass broke over there?"

He stared at me.

"Please," I said. "For Myra."

He nodded.

I dragged Myra out on the dance floor, and we danced to off-key former cheerleaders singing Shania Twain like it was the best music we'd ever heard.

"Do you think he did it on purpose?" she yelled over the music.

"The dress?"

She nodded.

"You know what I think?" I shouted. I grabbed her hand and held it up to twirl her around. "I think we should dance like we don't give a fuck."

She clasped her hand to mine, and we did a sloppy tango across the dance floor. When Heather returned from the bathroom, bra back in place, we made a Myra sandwich and tangoed

across the floor the other way, all three of our hands knotted together. Fish sat at a table, nursing a beer and twisting a piece of
streamer around his fingers. Robbie tied Heather's scarf around his
forehead like a warrior and joined us on the dance floor, doing the
running man with his tongue hanging out of his mouth and his
eyes crossed. We danced our way through the football players singing "Livin' on a Prayer" and a couple of really drunk girls stumbling through the words to "Tubthumping." We were sweaty and
breathless and laughing, and I didn't care if we looked stupid. I was
having fun.

Then the DJ came back and played "Name" by the Goo Goo
Dolls. Heather went to get us more drinks. Robbie asked Myra to
dance.

"Come on, Fish," I said, running over and grabbing his arm.
"Dance with me."

He stood up and followed me for a second, but then he pulled
his arm away. I figured he must be one of those guys who didn't
dance under any circumstances. But I also figured Jessie Morgan
wasn't the kind of girl who took no for an answer, so I tried to put
my arms around his neck.

He raised his hands to break my arms away.

"Come on, grumpy. Dance!" I said, trying to reach for his
hand again.

"You know what? Don't even touch me," he said. "Don't
even."

"Oh my God!" I blurted out. "What is your problem?"

"You!" he yelled. "You are my problem, Jessie." And even
though the music was loud, everyone heard. People stopped talking to watch us. "You disappear completely for thirteen years. And

then you just come back like nothing happened and act like you always did. Like we're the most important people, until something better comes along. That's my problem, Jess. You left. You don't have a right to come back anymore. Everyone else might be fine pretending it's okay, but I'm not. You left. That's all you get."

He walked out, leaving me standing there in the middle of the dance floor with everyone staring at me. And even though he was really yelling at Jessie, even though he wasn't actually mad at me, standing there with all those eyes on me was awful. The tequila was catching up with me. I started crying. I took one deep breath after another, but I couldn't pull it together.

I grabbed my purse and ran out the door. I wasn't running after Fish. I was just running. I needed air. I needed to confess. I needed to leave. I needed to be done with Jessie Morgan. I'd pushed it too far.

I ran through the lobby and tripped down the stairs to the parking lot. I pulled my heels off and kept running. It was drizzling. The pavement was freezing and my feet picked up bits of gravel as I ran, but it felt good to move, to put distance between me and all those people. It felt like if I ran fast enough, I might get away from myself. I dashed through the parking lot and down the stairs to the falls.

My face was wet with tears and rain, my arms were full of goose bumps, and my toes were numb. Snoqualmie Falls was lit with green lights, but the path was dark. It didn't seem like the smart way to go, but I needed the air, the freedom. I needed to be Jenny again for a moment so I could catch my breath. The water rushing over the falls was loud and disorienting.

I got all the way to the end of the observation deck before I realized that someone else was out there—a dark figure walking toward me. He reached out his hand, and I tried to scream but my voice wasn't working. It came out like a squeak.

He grabbed my wrist. His face was so close.

It was Fish.

Before I could say anything, he wrapped his arms around me and kissed me with more intensity than I'd ever been kissed in my entire life.

I should have stopped him, but I didn't. It was the most romantic thing that had ever happened to me, so it was easy to ignore the fact that it wasn't actually happening to me. Fish was kissing Jessie. But I let myself believe that Fish was kissing me, because I really wanted to be kissed.

He pulled away and hugged me hard. "Don't disappear this time," he whispered. "Please."

And I didn't know what to say, so I just hugged him and reached for his face in the dark and let my mouth find his.

He didn't have his jacket, and I didn't have my sweater, so it wasn't long before we started shivering. His body shook under his thin dress shirt, teeth chattering, even though he clenched them tight to get them to stop.

"Shit," he said, patting his pants pocket. "Robbie took my keys. Asshole."

"Because you shouldn't be driving and he doesn't want you to die?"

"Oh my God!" He laughed. "Who are you?"

"The safety police."

"I think that's redundant."

"I think you're redundant."

"How so?"

"I don't know. I'm just talking." I laughed. I never just said stuff. With Deagan, I always looked at everything from every angle and tried hard to consider the best thing to say and the best way to say it.

"If I had my keys, we could sit in the car and warm up."

"We could just go back in."

He hugged me close. "I don't want to," he said. "I don't want to share you right now." He breathed deeply. My face was pressed into his chest. He may have been crying. I couldn't tell.

"We could go up to my room," I said.

"You know we're going to run into everyone."

"Not if we're stealthy," I said. I pulled away from him and dug my extra room key out of my purse. "If we get separated, I'll meet you in room four-thirteen."

I grabbed his hand, and we ran up the stairs and across the parking lot, my bare feet smacking against the asphalt. We giggled like kids when we ducked behind a pillar to avoid the "Tubthumping" girls, who were stepping outside to smoke. They didn't see us, or if they did, they didn't care, but that didn't stop Fish and me from pantomiming our plan. "You first," Fish mouthed, pointing at me, waving his key with the other hand. I took a deep breath and tiptoed out from behind the pillar.

Heather was in the lobby on her cell phone. "Hey!" she said, covering the phone with her hand when she saw me. "It's Karen! Do you want to say hi?"

I coughed. "I have to get my inhaler again. Emergency!"

"Oh! Oh! Okay! We can always call her back later," Heather said.

I took the elevator up to my room, and my whole body buzzed with the idea of meeting up with Fish. Of what we were about to do. But by the time I got to my floor, I started to panic. I couldn't sleep with Jessie Morgan's ex-boyfriend and I couldn't pretend we were meeting in my room to do anything else. This was where I had to draw the line.

But when the elevator door opened, Fish was standing there, out of breath from running up the stairs. Without saying anything, he grabbed my hand and we ran down the hall to my room.

He opened the door with the key I'd given him.

We didn't say anything. He kissed my neck. I unbuttoned his pants. He pushed the straps of my dress off my shoulders, and it was suddenly less about erasing Deagan or erasing myself than about the crazy animal attraction I had for him. I wriggled out of my dress. We fell onto the big fluffy bed together.

"I can't believe you're here," he said. And in that moment, I completely forgot he wasn't really talking to me.

'd never had a one-night stand. I had a couple of short, sad, two-week relationships when I first moved back to Rochester. Luanne would drag me out to bars and I'd meet a guy and think, okay, he could be someone. We'd go on a few dates, then he'd spend the night, and I'd wake up before he did and he'd just be there, in my bed, breathing, and I'd get overwhelmed by the idea of having someone else to take care of in my life. And then, because Rochester is like living in a small town even though it's a city, I'd see him out at the bars with some other girl a few weeks later, and all I could feel was relief. Not jealousy. Jealousy would have been normal. I felt like "Good, she can take care of him. Better her than me."

Deagan was different. He wasn't needy. I never felt like I'd have to take care of him, but he didn't take care of me either. I tried, really hard, to be warm. To do things for him. But because he didn't need me, he also didn't notice when I made the effort to go to his games or make him a nice dinner. It was all very civilized—the opposite of romantic.

So, with Fish, after the initial explosion of passion, I expected an "oh crap, what have we done?" moment. But it didn't happen. I didn't want to run screaming. I didn't want to run at all.

We lay in bed, tangled up in the sheets, and talked like old friends, snippets of conversation punctuated by sex and sleep, a steamy scented bath, late-night room service. All I wanted was to be in the same space with him. Being near him made me feel better than I'd ever felt.

◆

"When did your hands get so bony?" he asked, threading his fingers through my fingers and holding our hands up to kiss mine. "You have these, like, bird hands. I don't remember that."

"Bird hands?" I said, laughing. "You have these, like, eel legs." I wrapped my leg around his.

"You know what I mean."

"You have, like, elephant antlers and lizard wings. Oh! And monkey gills."

"You!" he said, rolling over on top of me. "Are crazy. I don't have a single monkey gill."

"What about here?" I asked, grabbing his ribs. He twitched. "Oh! Does that tickle? What about here?" I reached down and grabbed at his knee.

"What about here?" Fish said, and tickled me back.

"Fish!" I yelled. "Wait!"

"What?" he said, letting go of me.

"Nothing," I said, and went right back to tickling him.

"Cheater!"

◆

"I can't believe I slept with Jessie Morgan," Fish murmured. "My sixteen-year-old self would die."

"Really?" I asked.

"Jessica," he said, sighing as he wrapped his arm around me and pulled me close.

"Gilbert," I said, running my fingers along his arm. He had beautiful biceps.

"I had the biggest crush ever on you. And you knew that the whole time. Stop pretending you didn't."

I'd been so sure that Fish was Jessie's boyfriend. If this were one of those *Back to the Future* time-travel things, I would totally end up fading from the picture or accidentally running over my own grandfather or something. It's a good thing that the only consequence of all this was that I ended up in bed with an incredibly hot guy. At least that was the only consequence I wanted to think about. In one more day I'd be back in Rochester and Fish would be happily daydreaming about how he finally got his high school crush in the sack. No harm, no foul. I was sure people hooked up at reunions like this all the time. Just a one-night thing to get the long-term yearning out of their system. I was helping Fish make his childhood dream come true and getting over Deagan at the same time. It was win-win.

"I know it now," I said.

"Everything's easier in hindsight, huh?"

"Yeah."

"Like now," he said. "With more perspective. I'm guessing that you didn't leave at graduation just because I told you I loved you."

"I'm so sorry," I said, picturing him holding that horrible thought in his mind for years.

"I mean," he let out a funny laugh, "you didn't say it back, and then you disappeared. But you didn't leave because of me, right?"

"No," I said. "I didn't."

He sat up and looked at me. "Why did you leave?"

"Because," I said, sitting up and wrapping my legs around him, "I was a stupid, stupid girl."

❖

I ran the bathwater and added bubbles while Fish poured wine. We shed our robes at the edge of the tub and climbed in, resting our heads across from each other.

"Ew!" Fish said.

"What?"

"Your feet are disgusting."

"What do you mean?"

"They're black on the bottom from running around without shoes on." He grabbed my foot and scrubbed hard with a washcloth.

I splashed water at him.

He splashed me back. "I can't believe," he said, "I'm taking a bath with Jessie Morgan."

"I can't believe," I said, "I'm taking a bath with you." And as soon as I said it, it made me sad. I couldn't pretend to be Jessie forever, but when I stopped, what would I be left with? What would I be leaving Fish with?

"You're missing the reunion," I said, worried that I was taking something important from him.

"I'm not missing anything."

I should have insisted that we go back to the party, but he drifted over to kiss me, and I didn't have the willpower to stop him.

❖

"So does everyone in your grown-up life call you Fish?" We were wrapped in the fluffy hotel bathrobes, sitting on the floor, with the room service tray balanced between our laps.

"Nah," he said. "It's mostly just Robbie and those goons."

"I love the name Gilbert. Like Gilbert Blythe," I said, shoveling artichoke dip into my mouth with a crusty piece of bread.

"Huh?"

"Gilbert Blythe from *Anne of Green Gables*. It's one of my favorite books."

"Who are you, and what have you done with Jessie?"

My heart stopped. "What do you mean?"

"You don't read."

"Well," I said, trying my hardest to keep the panic from showing up in my face, "I had an image to protect and all. Once I got to college, I felt free to, you know, read books."

"You were a wild child in high school, so you had to go to college to be a rebellious reader?"

"What did you go to college for?" I asked, eager to change the subject.

"Premed. As planned," Fish said. "My rebellions came later."

"When you went to college, did people call you Gilbert?"

"Mostly," he said, rearranging the plates on the tray so the french fries were closer.

"Good."

"You're the one who started calling me Fish!" he said, making sure to cover every inch of his fry in ketchup. "In second grade."

"Really?" I said, placing my hand dramatically on my chest. "Me?"

"You don't remember?"

"It was such a long time ago."

"I wanted people to start calling me Gil instead of Gilbert, and you said, 'Ew! Like a fish gill,' and then everyone called me Fish for ever and ever."

"Amen."

"What?"

"It just seemed like there should be an 'amen' at the end of that."

"Are you drunk?"

"Terribly."

"Ha," Fish said. "Me too." He grabbed the bottle of wine we'd ordered and poured us each another glass.

◆

Later Fish fell asleep before I did, and the sound of his slow, steady breath made me want to hold him tightly.

woke up with my head on Fish's chest and his arm around me. I didn't feel like I wanted to run screaming. I just wanted to stay.

"Hey, you," he said, when I yawned. "I've been trying so hard not to wake you."

"I don't think you did," I said, sitting up so I could look at him. "I'm pretty sure I woke of my own volition."

"Whoa," Fish said. "SAT words first thing in the morning?"

"It's never too early for grandiloquence," I said, smiling.

"You," Fish said, touching his finger to my bottom lip, "are even better than my memories of you."

I didn't know what to say, so I kissed him. I loved that I was a better Jessie than the actual Jessie, that I was a better fit for Fish.

Fish's phone beeped. He got out of bed and reached for his pants, retrieving his phone from the front pocket. He was naked, and gorgeous. He had the most perfect ass.

"Breakfast?" Fish said, putting on his boxer briefs. "Robbie just texted to say they're all going to Twede's for hangover food."

"I have the closing session for my conference."

"So," he said, climbing back on the bed, "I shouldn't be a bad influence and tell you to blow it off."

"No," I said, wrapping my arms around his neck. "You shouldn't."

But with the two choices in front of me—going to the last

meeting of a conference that had only served to teach me that I was completely and totally bored with my choice of careers, or one last moment with Fish, Myra, Robbie, and Heather—I couldn't make a good case for sitting in a conference room watching yet another uninspired PowerPoint presentation.

"Although," I said, "I could really go for some pancakes."

"Really?" Fish's whole face lit up.

We showered together, and got dressed and walked through the lobby holding hands, and I felt the kind of nervous excitement that I think you're supposed to feel about meeting someone new. I didn't feel the crushing weight of everything I was responsible for; it had been shoved to some small, dark, out-of-the-way place in my brain.

When we got to his truck, Fish opened the passenger door for me. It wasn't locked. It was a Ford pickup in the same avocado green as my grandmother's refrigerator. It was probably just as old, but the chrome was shiny and there wasn't a spot of rust anywhere. Before he got in, he lifted the floor mat and held up his car key triumphantly. "Yes!" he said. "Robbie remembered to leave it." He smiled. "I worried about payback for leaving him stranded at the campground last month. Drove all the way home from Dungeness before I realized I still had his keys."

"Oh no."

"Heather was so pissed," Fish said, laughing. "She'll get me back one of these days." He started the truck and gave the dashboard a pat. "Can you believe Robbie has kept this thing going for me all this time?"

"It's in really good shape," I said, running my hand along the seat. The vinyl was spotless and uncracked.

"I was going to get a new truck last year, but the look on Robbie's face when I talked about it killed me." He clutched his chest. "I felt like I was cheating on him every time I went car shopping."

"That's so sweet," I said.

"Yeah," Fish said, laughing. "I guess all the time he spent hot-wiring cars in high school was its own kind of education."

We drove on the same road the hotel shuttle had taken to get to the lodge. It was mostly wooded and so green, with a mountain that I guessed was the actual Mount Si looming in the background. I wondered if Fish and Myra and Robbie and Heather even noticed the mountains anymore, the way I had stopped noticing the abandoned restaurant next to my apartment complex. When you grow up with mountains, does every place else feel like it's missing something? I wanted to ask, but I couldn't. I was supposed to have grown up with mountains too.

At the edge of the town was a white diner with a big red neon T and very familiar white-and-yellow café sign out front. I felt like I was in *Twin Peaks* all over again.

When we got to the diner, Fish parked the truck and asked, "Are you ready for Robbie?"

"Um, I guess," I said. "Is he going to tease us about driving together?"

"You don't remember? Robbie in the morning is a whole lot of Robbie."

I laughed. "I guess I forgot that part."

As soon as Fish opened the door to the diner, Robbie shouted, "Jessers! Fishy!" from a booth in the corner. The inside of the restaurant didn't look like the *Twin Peaks* diner, but there were photos from the show on one of the walls. The booths were shiny blue and the floor clean white.

Myra had her head in both hands. She moaned when Robbie dragged an extra chair across the floor and it squeaked.

Heather looked a little tired, but not much worse for wear. She slipped out of the booth to give me a hug while Robbie was still standing.

"So," she whispered, "Fish is wearing the same clothes he had on yesterday."

I blushed.

"Never you mind," Fish said. "For all you know, I picked her up on my way here."

"Ooh!" Robbie said, loud enough for everyone in the diner to hear. "Sure you did." He winked at us.

"Why . . . ," Myra said, when Robbie sat down again. "Why must you be so . . . ?" She raised her hand toward him and flopped it around.

"Tablespoon of honey before you go to bed," Robbie said. "You never listen to me! Honey chases the drunk away."

"No," Myra said, staring at him. She wasn't wearing any makeup and her face was very pale. "That's not a thing, Robert. Stop trying to make it a thing." She dropped her head into her arms.

"It's not a thing? How come I'm not hungover?"

"Because you're evil," Myra said, her voice muffled by the inside of her elbow.

"Someone's cranky," Robbie said, laughing.

"I'm not a morning person," Myra said. "Not everyone gets up at dawn crowing like a rooster."

"Are you calling me a cock?" Robbie still wasn't using his inside voice.

"If the beak fits," Myra said.

"You're not really a night person either, My." Fish said.

"I'm a four o'clock in the afternoon person!" Myra shot Fish a dirty look over the crook of her arm. "Four o'clock. That's my time."

Thankfully, the waitress showed up with a thermos of coffee and mugs all around. Robbie poured three sugar packets into one of the mugs, filled it with coffee and enough cream to make it the color of a manila envelope. He slid it slowly across to Myra like he was worried she might bite him if he startled her.

"I love you," Myra said, in a small, soft voice, lifting her head up so she could drink it.

After we ordered, Robbie started drumming on the table with his fork.

I laughed. "You can't sit still, can you?"

"Every other day of the week," Robbie said, "I'm up at five, working on tractors. My hands need to move."

"I," Heather said, "am back in bed for an extra two hours of sleep at five."

"You're not a morning person like Robbie?"

She shook her head. "No one is a morning person like Robbie." She gave his arm an affectionate squeeze.

The waitress brought us a huge tray of plates piled with eggs, potatoes, pancakes, and sausage. Myra perked up a bit. Everyone settled into their food, and chewing took the place of conversation until we'd made a dent in our breakfasts. Then they were back to teasing each other and laughing, sharing stories about their week, and eating off each other's plates without asking. Fish's knee rested against mine under the table.

Myra absentmindedly drew dresses on her place mat with the crayons from the kids' pack. Heather pointed at the drawings and said, "I want that one but with those sleeves." Robbie ordered an extra plate of pancakes "for the table" and ate them all himself. Fish picked up the coffee thermos and everyone handed their mugs to him for a refill. I looked around the table and all I could think was, I want this.

We paid the bill and piled out into the parking lot. Robbie kicked at gravel as we walked. "So," Myra said, having perked up considerably, "I made the bed in the guest room."

"You're staying?" Fish asked. His whole face lit up.

"Jessie and Fishy sitting in a tree," Robbie sang.

Fish blushed, but he didn't say anything. My hand was right next to his, but he didn't reach out to hold it. I wondered if he didn't want them to know that we'd hooked up.

"I don't know," I said.

"Come on," Myra said. "It's like fate. Your trip was canceled. You've got the week off from work."

"I have tomorrow afternoon off," Fish said. "Myra doesn't work on Mondays. We can go hiking." And the way he smiled made me honestly believe it was a good idea to stay.

wasn't scheduled to check out of the hotel until the next morning. I had to e-mail Monica a report about the conference. Myra had to go to the store to do some work. Heather and Robbie had errands to run, and Fish said he had to get through some paperwork. So Myra arranged to pick me up in the morning. Fish drove me back to the lodge. He leaned across the front seat to kiss me when he dropped me off at the front door.

"I'm so glad you're staying," he said, resting his hand on my cheek. I felt flush with happiness, even though I wasn't sure I was going to stay. I still hoped maybe I'd find the willpower to take an early flight back to Rochester.

"See you tomorrow," I said, and let myself kiss him one more time.

I spent the afternoon writing up a report of the seminar. I don't know why I felt the need to cover for the presenters, but I embellished, adding my own knowledge and information to the report, as if the conference had been more than a regurgitation of basic social-media common sense. I guess when you're raised to be an enabler, it's hard to know when to shut it off.

I e-mailed the report to Monica, flopped down on the big fluffy bed, and flipped through channels on the television. But even though I was completely exhausted, I couldn't relax. I

couldn't decide if I should book a ticket home for the next morning. Or maybe check myself into a mental institution. Home
makeovers and crab fishermen and reruns of *Boy Meets World*
could not take my mind off what I had done and whether I should
stay. I pulled out my laptop again and started looking for flights
home. I compared layover times and tried to decide if I'd rather
spend two hours stuck in the Cleveland airport or four hours at
O'Hare. I couldn't make a decision. I just kept thinking about
kissing Fish good-bye and how I didn't want it to be the last time
I kissed him.

So as soon as the dining room opened, I put on one of my
new skirts and wandered down to the lobby. The idea of eating
dinner in a fancy restaurant by myself was a little uncomfortable,
but the idea of staying in my room alone with my thoughts was far
worse. At least I could people watch and eat good food.

❧

The dining room was gorgeous. Wood beams and a roaring fireplace. Since dinner hours had just started, the room was sparsely
populated. I asked for a table by the fire and studied the menu as
if it were the most all-consuming task in the world. The room
filled up fast. Mostly couples.

The honeymooners from the shuttle were there. He was in a
suit, and she wore a beautiful royal blue dress that she must have
chosen just for this. I thought about how their life would go. They
were married now. They'd buy a house. Maybe they'd have two
children. She'd stay home with the kids for a few years, and he'd
work late. Over the years, they'd drift apart, but then they'd drift
back together again, and it would be okay, because they loved
each other enough. Because they could trust in love. They were

ready to say yes to the life ahead. At least that's what I imagined for them.

Wanting to marry Deagan had nothing to do with being ready to settle down into the life ahead of me. Planning a wedding, buying a house, picking out dresses for our honeymoon—I'd wanted all of that, not because I loved Deagan so much and wanted to spend my life with him, but because I needed the distraction. If I was busy planning, I didn't have to look too carefully at the things that weren't what I really wanted them to be. I could believe I was working toward security. The most terrifying thing about pretending to be Jessie was that I could finally see what was missing.

"Are they famous?"

I looked up and there was Kyle, sitting down at the next table. We were both facing the same direction.

"Excuse me?" I said.

"Well, you seem so intent on watching that couple over there. I wondered if they were from a reality show I haven't seen."

"No," I said, shaking my head. "At least not that I know of. I was just thinking. My head was somewhere else."

"Ah," Kyle said. "Is it because the seminar this weekend was so inspiring?"

"Actually, it's partly because it wasn't." I was shocked by my own honesty.

"Ouch."

"Not you," I said. "You were fine. I just feel like everyone else was throwing catchphrases around without actually saying anything."

"I hear you." Kyle opened the menu and started reading. "Wait," he said, looking up again. "I was only fine?"

I laughed. "You were spectacular. My heart was in my throat the entire time, just waiting for your next brilliant proclamation."

"All right," Kyle said, smiling. "Enough of you."

"Would you like to sit with me?" I asked. It seemed less awkward than sitting next to him and pretending he wasn't there. And I guess I wanted to give myself one last shot at being Jenny Shaw before I decided to spend the week at Myra's house. Maybe dinner with Kyle would snap me out of it.

"I don't know," Kyle said, tapping his fingers on the table. "You rejected me all weekend. Now you're making fun of me." He pursed his lips in mock disapproval. "I think maybe I'm better off eating right here."

"Suit yourself," I said, smiling. I pulled my napkin off the table and draped it across my lap.

"All right, fine." He stood up and took his menu with him. "You twisted my arm."

He sat across from me and unfolded his napkin.

"Have you ordered?" he asked.

"No," I said.

"Red or white?"

"Red."

He called the waiter over and ordered a bottle of cabernet without any further consultation. It bugged me. Not that I was particularly picky, but it was the kind of thing Deagan did. It made me feel like an accessory.

"The salmon is amazing," he said. "I had it my first night here. It has a vanilla glaze."

When the waiter came back, I ordered quail, not because I particularly wanted quail, but because I wanted to exercise my right not to appease people. Kyle raised his eyebrows, like he had expected me to take his advice on the salmon.

The rest of our dinner was pleasant. Kyle, when he dropped the salesman bravado, was actually a pretty nice guy. He told me a story about how one of the other presenters got his tie stuck in his briefcase about twenty minutes before his presentation started.

"He slammed it shut and it locked, but then the lock was stuck. I had to help him open it, but he didn't want to tell me his lock code. Like I really want to break into that guy's briefcase."

I laughed.

"See," he said, pointing his fork at me. "You're having a good time."

"I am," I said.

He shook his head. "You had a whole weekend and you blew it."

"Eat your salmon," I told him.

"You're so bossy."

"Actually, usually I'm, like, the opposite of bossy. You bring out the worst in me."

"Worst or best?" He wiped his mouth with his napkin. "Because it's kind of working for me."

"You're impossible," I said.

"Actually, I'm really quite possible."

"You did not just say that!" I laughed.

Kyle laughed too. "No, of course not."

We finished the wine and ordered dessert. Kyle tried to pick up the check, but I had the waiter charge my half to my room.

Kyle walked me back to my door. "So, are you headed home tomorrow?" He rubbed his hand over his head.

"Yeah," I said, and the way he looked at me made me blush. I thought about how much less complicated everything would be if I had gone out with Kyle instead of going to the reunion.

"Well," he said, giving me his fake shy smile again. He leaned in and tried to kiss me. It would have been so easy to just let him. To go back to being the same old Jenny Shaw, making the same old safe choices. But I didn't want to. At the last second, I turned my head.

"Oh," he said.

I grabbed his hand and shook it. "It was really nice to meet you." I slipped into my room and shut the door behind me before I could make any more mistakes.

I washed my face, trying to focus on the sound of the water running, the calming scent of rosemary-mint soap, and the way the lush loops of the cotton hand towel felt against my skin. I brushed my teeth and counted tiles on the floor. Anything to keep from thinking.

When I checked my phone, there was a message from Deagan, saying, simply, "I thought maybe we should talk." I didn't call him back.

Before I climbed into bed, I set the alarm clock, so I'd be packed and ready to meet Myra when she came to pick me up.

Myra pulled up to the front door of the Salish Lodge at nine on the dot. I was already waiting with my carry-on bag and travel tote.

"I'm so glad you're staying," she said, as she took my bags from me and loaded them into the back of her car. She wore dark, widely cuffed blue jeans, a tailored teal, plaid flannel shirt, and her hair was tied back into two low pigtails, like she had perfectly styled herself to look casual.

"Me too," I said.

"Okay, so here's another one," she said, cranking up the car stereo as we drove through downtown Snoqualmie. "En Vogue!"

The song was "You're Never Gonna Get It." I didn't know the words well, but Myra knew them all. I mostly just joined in on the chorus, because it was easy, and Myra didn't seem the wiser.

Myra was singing her heart out, so she didn't notice a man who looked exactly like Fish walking down the sidewalk with a gorgeous blond woman wearing movie-star sunglasses. They had a gorgeous blond dog by their side, and both their hands were on the leash, like they were so in love they needed to share every little experience. They were walking in front of a cute little gazebo, and I wondered if they were going to sit there and canoodle. My heart pounded. My palms started sweating. I'd lied to Fish, but Fish was lying to me and to that woman.

I could sort of manage being Jessie, but I couldn't handle being the Faye in this situation. Maybe I was a liar, but I was not the other woman, not under any circumstances. I couldn't believe I'd agreed to stay for a week so I could see more of Fish. I felt sick.

I didn't say anything to Myra. I took deep breaths and tried to sing harmony on the chorus, so she wouldn't notice how upset I was. I felt like I was choking.

◆

Myra's house was not at all what I expected. Her store was impossibly chic and flawlessly designed, but her house was like the inside of a bag lady's bag.

"Oh my God, it hasn't changed!" I said, taking a not-so-wild guess.

"Well, a little bit," Myra said, her face turning red. "The living room curtains used to be in the dining room. And I had to get new dishes. Grammie's had that gold edging on them. It sparked in the microwave." She used her sleeve to wipe some dust off the top of the coffee table. "And I got a microwave. Grammie was always scared of them. Said they cooked your insides." Myra laughed. "You know how she was."

"Yeah," I said. It sounded like something my own grandmother would have said. Back when I still saw her, before the divorce. Before she stopped talking to my dad because she hadn't raised him to leave his family like that.

"It must be hard to think about changing anything," I said, even though I really wanted to ask her about Fish. Did she know Fish had a girlfriend or a wife? Did he have kids? How big of a home wrecker was I?

"It is hard," Myra said, walking into the kitchen. "Part of me wants to leave it all exactly the way it is. And then there's the part of me that lives on microwave enchiladas." She opened up the fridge. "I have PB and J and"—she pushed a pickle jar out of the way—"PB without J. And half a pickle that I haven't eaten because I don't want to deal with dumping out all the pickle juice."

"PB and J works," I said. "Hold the pickles."

"We need to call Heather and beg her to feed us tonight."

I laughed.

"No, seriously. That's our best plan."

"I don't want to put her out or anything."

"Are you kidding? That girl is like the Iron Chef. Remember how she used to bake cookies all the time? Now she's moved on to high-level spa cuisine. It's crazy! And Robbie is so meat and potatoes. He doesn't appreciate it. So Heather is just as nuts about cooking for me as I am about eating what she cooks. When I actually have time to eat, I keep her in groceries and she keeps me fed."

"It's nice," I said, "the way you guys are like family."

"They're my everything," Myra said. Her eyes welled up.

My eyes did too.

Myra pulled out every photo album and yearbook she owned, and we sat on the couch, eating our sandwiches while we flipped through the pages.

In a series of Halloween pictures from high school, Myra was dressed as a robot in a big cardboard box painted silver, and the girl I assumed was Karen wore a Raggedy Ann costume that was fairly modest. Heather was a chubby Edward Scissorhands, with a white face and aluminum-foil talons on every finger. Robbie and Fish were dressed like Scully and Mulder. Robbie, in a red wig and unflattering pantsuit, towered over Fish.

"Oh my God!" I said, pointing to a picture of Jessie in the shortest, tightest French maid's costume I had ever seen. Her butt cheeks peeked out past the hemline. "That doesn't even qualify as a dress! Who lets their kid out of the house like that?"

"I don't think your parents were really paying much attention," Myra said.

In the picture Jessie had a big smile on her face, but her eyes looked sad and dull. I didn't understand the outfit, but I understood that kind of unhappiness.

"Where are your parents now?" she asked.

"I don't know," I said, deciding it was better to be vague. "We don't exactly keep in touch."

"I figured," Myra said. "I mean, you left and then there was a For Sale sign at your house. Your mom wouldn't talk to me, you know."

"I'm sorry," I said.

"I had a box of your leftover portfolio photos. You left them here, and I thought you might want them, so I went by your house to get your new address. She said she wasn't your keeper anymore."

"Really?"

"It's not like she was ever a particularly warm person," Myra said, laughing. "Remember when she told us not to bother trying out for the school play because no one would pay to hear us sing?"

"Geez!" I said. It sounded like something my mother would say.

"It's amazing that you're not in the loony bin, Jess."

I wondered if that's where Jessie had actually ended up.

"I think I have those photos in the basement somewhere. I should remember to look while you're here," Myra said.

I flipped the album page and there was a picture of Myra,

Jessie, Heather, and Karen sitting, cross-legged in a row, on the same couch we were sitting on now, wearing pastel flannel pajamas with crackly green mud masks on their faces.

"We were such babies with our pudgy faces!" Myra said, squishing her cheeks with both hands. She studied the picture and looked at me. The look in her eyes made me worry.

The phone rang and Myra jumped up to get it. "Hey," I heard her say from the kitchen. I grabbed another photo album and flipped the pages quickly. "That sounds perfect!"

Toward the end of the album was a photo of Jessie, Myra, Karen, and Heather dressed in black, wearing matching military caps that were way too big for their tiny little heads. They couldn't have been more than nine or ten. There was a ripped ticket stub from Janet Jackson's *Rhythm Nation* tour next to the picture. I wondered whose parent had taken them. Neither of my parents would ever have taken me to a concert when I was that young. Or at all.

"Great," Myra said. "We'll see you then!"

I put the photo album back on the coffee table, as close as possible to where it had been. When Myra came back in the room, I pretended to be consumed by the sleepover party pictures.

"That was Fish," Myra said. "He's on his way over."

I wondered if his girlfriend was coming. Or his wife. Or whoever that gorgeous woman with the dog was. I didn't want Myra to know I slept with him. Maybe they'd all really thought Fish had picked me up on the way to breakfast, that he hadn't spent the night. Maybe they assumed he'd been at his girlfriend's house. Maybe they didn't know about his girlfriend. I didn't want Myra to think I was the kind of girl who would sleep with a taken man.

I didn't want to leave her friendship with Fish in ruins by telling her he'd turned me into the other woman without my knowledge. So I just smiled and said, "That's nice. Hey, remember when we went to see Janet Jackson?"

"Oh my God!" she said. "I think the pictures are right here!" She reached for the photo album I'd just searched through and showed me the photo and the ticket stub. "Our first concert! Remember how grown up we thought we were?"

"Yeah," I said, running my fingers over Jessie's face in the picture.

Myra jumped up and plugged her iPod into the stereo. "This calls for a bounce!"

She scrolled through until she found "Rhythm Nation." "Do you still remember when we did the dance for the talent show?" she asked, over Janet's pledge about color lines.

I had never even been in a talent show at all. But I did dance to the video on MTV on the big TV in the living room, trying to copy Janet's moves, with the sound turned down low so I wouldn't bother my mom. So when the robot voice counted down—"five, four, three, two, one"—I was ready. Myra and I hopped around the living room doing our best with Janet's hand movements. I didn't remember all the moves perfectly, and I wasn't the world's greatest dancer, but neither was Myra. During the dance breakdown at the end of the song, Myra and I were jumping high and giving it everything we had. Grammie's Norman Rockwell collector plates shook on the walls. Hummel figurines rattled in the china cabinet. We were breathless and laughing and we must have looked like complete idiots. When the song ended, we heard clapping. Myra screamed.

"Oh my God, Fish!" she said, holding her hand over her heart like she needed help to keep it in her chest. "You scared the crap out of me."

"Can you do it again?" Fish asked, smiling. "I only caught the last minute or so."

"Screw you," Myra said, giving him the finger.

It's kind of what I felt like saying to him too.

"The truck is running," he said. "Ready to go?"

"Oh!" Myra looked at her feet. "We need boots!"

"I don't have any with me," I said. I didn't even own a pair of shoes suitable for hiking. I'd never been on a real hike. Sometimes Luanne and I walked the canal path on our lunch hour, but we just slipped sneakers on. It was flat and straight. Most of the stretch we walked on was paved. But here, with all the mountains surrounding us, I highly doubted that was the kind of hike I was in for.

"Holy crap!" Myra said, clapping her hand to her forehead. "I have your boots."

She tore off though the kitchen, and we heard her feet pound on the basement steps.

"Hey, Jess," Fish said, coming to kiss me. I turned my head so his kiss landed my cheek.

"Hey," I said, flatly. With Myra bound to come back any minute, I didn't want to start anything, but I didn't want him to think I was happy with him either.

"So," he said, "it's pretty nice out today. We should get some good views."

"Good," I said softly.

He watched me, trying hard to keep eye contact. I looked away, but I knew he was still staring. When he looked away, I looked at him. His face was soft and sad.

When I got back from the hike, I would look for a flight home. I had no right to fight with him, but I didn't want to spend a whole week feeling so awful.

We heard Myra's feet on the basement steps again.

"Look what I found!" she shouted, tearing across the kitchen, into the living room. She held up a pair of powder-blue hiking boots. They were hideous. "Remember right before graduation, when we all went hiking? You left these here. Grammie was going to give them to Goodwill about six times over, but I wouldn't let her."

She handed me the boots and pulled hers out of the closet. I sat on the couch to pull them on. I felt like Cinderella taking the shoe test.

I failed miserably. Jessie Morgan had markedly bigger feet than me. Better bigger than smaller. At least I could get my feet into the boots, even if it felt like there was room for about four pairs of thick socks in there too.

"I don't really have a jacket either. Just my blazer," I said, hoping that maybe Myra and Fish would go hiking without me.

"I have an extra jacket in the car," Fish said.

"Great!" Myra grabbed her camera bag. "We're all set."

"Great," I said, smiling at Myra, trying so hard to be upbeat, even though I didn't want to wear Jessie's ancient boots and Fish's jacket. His jacket probably smelled like him.

When we got out to Fish's truck, I ducked down and pretended I needed to retie my laces, so Myra would get in next to Fish and I could sit by the door. I didn't want to sit in the middle, with my leg touching his leg. I didn't want to think about what we had done.

"Where's Chip?" Myra asked.

"He's with my dad today. His nurse had to take the afternoon off, so I left Chip to take care of him."

I wondered if Chip was Fish's brother, until Myra said, "Chippy's such a good dog." It seemed crazy to me that a dog could take the place of a nurse, but I figured maybe Fish's dad just got lonely or something. I didn't know why he needed a nurse to begin with, Fish hadn't mentioned it. I wasn't sure how new the situation was, so I couldn't ask.

Myra fiddled with the radio and filled Fish in on the latest about her new clothing line. I looked out the window and took in all the storefronts as we drove back through Snoqualmie. I watched Fish when we drove right past the spot where I saw him with that woman. He didn't even react. I wasn't expecting him to break down and confess or anything, but maybe he'd twitch his eyebrows or something.

"You're so quiet, Jess!" Myra said. "What's up?"

"Oh," I said, "I think the jet lag is finally catching up with me."

"Did you guys eat lunch?" Fish asked.

"We had some PB and J," Myra said, laughing.

"My! You have to eat like a real person," Fish said. He gave me a look like he wanted me to back him up. I turned and looked out the window again. "You can't hike if you don't eat."

When we got to North Bend, he turned into the parking lot of a place called Taco Time.

We got out of the car. My feet were swimming in my boots. I felt like I might turn my ankle in the parking lot before we even started hiking. When we got inside, I handed Myra a twenty and said, "Just get me whatever you're having." I ran into the bathroom to find some paper towels to shove in my boots to keep my feet from slipping around. But of course they had hand dryers, so I had to go into a stall and cram heaping wads of toilet paper into my boots instead. It wasn't much help, but it was something.

"You okay?" Myra asked, when I came back. She handed me a to-go bag and a large soda. Fish only had a cup of coffee.

"Fine," I said, taking a sip of the soda. It was regular, not diet, and I wasn't used to how sweet real soda is. I always drank diet. Jessie, apparently, not so much.

"I can't believe I'm letting you guys eat tacos in my truck," Fish said, when we all climbed back in. "Robbie is going to have a heart attack." I'd managed to preserve my seat by the window. Myra was short. It made sense for her to sit in the middle.

"It's your truck," Myra said.

"Yeah," Fish said, shaking his head, "tell Robbie."

"Sure you're not hungry?" Myra said to Fish, opening up one of her little paper packages. Lettuce fell out into her lap, and she carefully picked it off her leg and threw it back in the bag.

"Unlike you," Fish said, "I keep food in my house. I had lunch before I left." He took a swig of his coffee and balanced it between his knees while he drove. He kept looking at me. I busied myself with unwrapping my tacos and pretended not to notice his glances.

Apparently, unlike me, Jessie Morgan liked her tacos extra spicy. Beads of sweat formed on my upper lip; I could feel my face turning red. My tongue was in so much pain that it almost went numb. I drank my soda and wished I could fish out the ice to hold in my mouth without raising suspicion. There was a packet of Tater Tot–like potato things in the bottom of the bag. I ate them slowly and methodically between bites of taco, to keep myself from openly weeping.

"I don't know how you eat spicy food like that," Myra said, shaking her head. "You must have an iron stomach or something."

"Yeah," I said, trying not to choke.

There were three tacos in the bag, but I could only make it through two. "You want?" I said, passing the last one over to Fish. I didn't want to talk to him, but there was no way I was getting that last taco down, and I didn't want to leave it in the car while we were hiking. The whole truck would smell.

"Sure," Fish said, reaching across Myra to take it from me. His smile was hopeful, like the taco was some sort of peace offering. It wasn't. I turned away again as soon as the taco was safely in his hand.

I knew I needed to pretend that the mountains were old hat, but they weren't. We were specks in a valley. Everything was bigger than I thought it could be. The clouds had cleared, and the sky was bright blue.

Fish turned onto a side street, and we followed a narrow road that twisted down into a ravine and then up again into a small development of deserted ski chalets. I started to feel sick to my stomach. I had been so worried about everyone finding out my identity that I hadn't thought about the fact that I was in a car with strangers in a remote location.

No one knew where I was. I hadn't told Luanne or Deagan or my mother or my boss. It was so stupid. Myra and Fish could be anyone. Maybe they knew all along that I wasn't Jessie. They could be conning me right back. Maybe this was all some kind of elaborate human trafficking plan, and they were going to sell me to a creepy old man in the woods. That's why no one had said anything about Fish's girlfriend. Fish spending the night with me was just part of the plan. My heart pounded and my stomach churned. I couldn't stop sweating.

We parked and crossed a footbridge. Myra pulled her camera out and ran back to take a few pictures of the vacant chalets, leaving me alone with Fish.

"God, Jess! Who the hell do you think you are?"

"Excuse me?" I said, looking around us, trying to figure out where I would go, how I could get away if I needed to. The boots were going to be a problem. I couldn't sprint off into the woods in boots that were two sizes too big.

"Why are you running cold on me already?" Fish said. "It took you like, what? Twelve hours? Unbelievable!"

He took a step toward me. I stepped back.

"I'm unbelievable?" I said. "I saw you with that woman today. It only took you like, what? Twelve hours." It was ridiculous that I was yelling at him, but I couldn't help it. I felt like a raw nerve.

"What woman?"

"Downtown. That blond lady, with the golden retriever."

"She's a client," he said, rubbing at the stubble on his chin with his index finger. "I was helping her with dog commands." His eyes were so kind. His face was so sweet. He might have been an adulterer, but my thoughts of him as a kingpin in a human trafficking ring were starting to deflate.

"What kind of doctor does that? I've heard of doctors doing house calls, but not street calls. You had your hands all over her."

I knew it wasn't fair, but Deagan had probably cheated on me, and my dad had cheated on my mom. The idea of being the other woman was more than I could handle. He was out on the street, pretending to be the perfect caring boyfriend to this lady, and she probably thought he was. She had absolutely no idea Fish had slept with me the night before. I was devastated for her. "How could you?"

"I'm not a doctor, Jessie," Fish said, shoving his hands in his pockets and rocking back and forth on the soles of his shoes. He smiled. "I train guide dogs."

"But you said you were premed in college."

"And then my dad had a stroke, and I felt like life was too short," he said, bumping my shoulder with his. I didn't back away this time. "There's no point in doing something if your heart isn't in it."

"So she really was a client?"

"Yes."

"I'm not the other woman?"

Fish took one hand out of his pocket, grabbed my hand, and pulled me toward him. "You could never be the other woman," he said, kissing me.

I kissed back.

And then we heard Myra's camera click. "Caught you!" she said, running back to us. "I knew it!"

❖

A river ran through the ravine, and the path looked down on it from steep heights. It seemed like there should be a guide rail or rope or fence. Myra and Fish hiked easily, navigating roots and rocks and slippery moss without even looking. With the terrain and my toilet-paper-filled boots, and the fact that I'd never really been hiking before, I worried I'd trip and tumble down into the raging river at any moment. I was so out of breath from trying to keep up with them that I could barely do more than listen and nod.

"That's why I dropped out of med school," Fish said. "I went into medicine because I wanted to help people. But when I took time off for my dad, I started training Chip to help around the house and I realized it was what I wanted to do. This way I can help people, but I still have time to build my house and be with my dad and work on the truck with Robbie."

Something skittered into the leaves next to the trail. I stifled a shriek.

Fish was too busy talking to notice. "Sometimes when an opportunity is in front of you, you're so busy asking if you're good enough for the challenge, you forget to ask if it's good enough for you, you know?"

"Yes," I said breathlessly.

"So now instead of spending my days in some medical building, under fluorescent lights, I trade time between the kennels and lifestyle training. I get to work outside. I get to train dogs. Give people mobility."

"That's amazing," I said, barely managing to squeak out the words. I hugged the inside of the path and tried my best to look confident, like I knew what I was doing.

"I'm so out of shape!" I said, clutching the stitch in my side when a particularly steep incline started to get the better of me. "Rochester is really flat. My legs aren't used to these hills anymore."

"Muscle memory," Fish said. "It'll all come back to you."

When we got to the edge of a waterfall, Fish helped me over slippery rocks and held my hand tightly, even after I was on sure footing again. I watched the way he tried to fight a smile, like he wasn't quite sure it was safe to let me know just how happy he was to be there with me.

Even though my lungs felt like they were about to give up, and my feet were throbbing, I was actually enjoying the hike. I loved the dampness of the air and the piney scent of the trees. I loved the way the moss was so green it almost seemed to glow. Myra nimbly made her way over a heap of rocks to get a picture of the rushing water, and I wished I could keep everything about that moment.

By the time we got back to Myra's house, the toilet paper in my boots was soaked and pilled up into little damp balls. My feet were red and blistered. I dumped the soggy wads of paper in the toilet and flushed it. When I put my loafers back on, my feet were so swollen they barely fit.

"Shoot!" Myra said, as I was walking down the stairs. She and Fish were sitting in the kitchen, and I could hear a coffeepot gurgling. Myra was looking at her cell phone.

"What's wrong?" I asked, joining them.

Myra put her phone down on the table. "I have to go to the store. There's an order that's supposed to come in tomorrow that's coming in today. Apparently the fulfillment company doesn't know the meaning of the word 'closed.'"

"I should really check on my dad anyway," Fish said. "Want to come with, Jess? I'm sure he'd love to see you."

"Sure," I said. As much as I knew it was probably best to limit the circle of people I met while I was pretending to be Jessie, I wanted to be with Fish. I wanted to know more about him.

"Great," Fish said. "You go do your store stuff, My, and we'll meet you back here later."

"Works for me," Myra said. She ran upstairs to change out of her hiking clothes. When she left the room, Fish reached over and kissed me.

"I don't think I'll ever quite get used to the fact that I can do that," he said, smoothing my hair behind my ear before he kissed me again.

We turned down a gravel road, and then drove for several minutes under a dark canopy of trees. There were no signs of civilization. I began to think I'd misunderstood and we were going hiking again, but when we finally neared the end of the road, I saw a big log cabin. There was a second-floor balcony and a grand stone staircase leading up to the front door from the driveway. Behind the main house was another house, framed out and partially completed. It looked a lot like the chalets we'd seen on our hike. There was a huge pile of rocks next to the foundation.

"I'm building that one for me," Fish said. "The fireplace is next."

"You're building it yourself?" That's what he'd meant earlier when he talked about having time to build his house. I'd assumed he meant time to hire a builder, pick out fixtures, and decide if the kitchen should have an island or a breakfast bar.

"With my own two hands," Fish said, taking his keys out of the ignition and tossing them from one hand to the other. "Robbie comes out and helps too. It's good guy time. Although, actually, Heather puts us to shame."

I loved the idea of all of them working together. Heather wielding a power drill and wearing a tool belt.

"Hey, Dad!" Fish called out, as he opened the front door.

An enormous German Shepherd came barreling down the stairs to the foyer in a black-and-tan blur. He jumped up, put his paws on my shoulders, and licked my face. He was almost as tall as me. It took all I had not to scream. I stumbled until my back hit the wall.

"Chip! Off!" Fish said firmly. "Sit!" Chip's butt hit the ground instantly. He wagged his tail along the floor and looked up at Fish.

"Chip's not a real guide dog," Fish said, running his hand along his face. "I swear I do a much better job with my guide dogs. But he started out as a pet. My dad got him when I went to school, to keep him from feeling like an empty nester. He spoiled the heck out of him. I didn't start training Chip until after the stroke."

"He's beautiful," I said. Chip looked at me with his big brown eyes, his tongue hanging out of his mouth. He almost looked like he was smiling.

"I can't believe you didn't freak out!" Fish said. "You always hated dogs."

"I'm older and wiser," I said, petting Chip. He leaned his head into my leg and looked up at me. I wanted to bury my face in his neck and tell him everything.

Before my parents got divorced, my dad brought home a Springer Spaniel. I woke up Christmas morning to a soft, sweet puppy wearing a big red bow around her neck, licking my face. It was like a dream come true. And then she peed on the carpet, and my mom started screaming and the puppy started shaking. But at least when I hid in my room, waiting for the shouting to stop, I had Brownie with me. I held her tight. We sat on the floor of my closet, and I let her chew on one of my socks.

We only had Brownie for about a week before my mom took her to the pound. And then there was more yelling when my dad came home from work and found out. I sat in my closet to wait it out alone, drawing pictures of Brownie by flashlight so I wouldn't forget what she looked like.

◆

"Gilbert! Is that you?" a wobbly, hoarse voice called from upstairs. There was a slight pause between each word, like it took him a moment to move on to the next one.

"Dad!" Fish shouted. "You'll never guess who's here!"

We walked up the stairs from the foyer to the living room, and as soon as our heads were at floor level, the voice said, "It's no one I recognize, but she sure is pretty."

My heart flip-flopped. I didn't know much about strokes. Maybe he wouldn't have recognized the real Jessie either.

He was a small man. He sat slightly crooked in a big chair made from branches. His feet rested on an ottoman, and his legs looked like bent twigs. He was holding a book in his lap with his forearm. His hand was contorted into a claw. He had thick gray hair combed neatly against his head and blue eyes like Fish's.

"Dad," Fish said, "it's Jessie Morgan. You remember Jessie."

He waved his hand at Fish. His fingers flapped against his palm. "Psh, there's nothing wrong with my memory. I'm not senile, Gilbert," he said. "Although I think you'd like that, wouldn't you? I couldn't nag you as much if I forgot to." His smile was high on one side and limp on the other but still bright and warm.

"Dad, it's Jessie," Fish said.

"Well, then," he said, "come over and say hello, Jessie." He leaned forward and patted the ottoman for me to sit down. The book fell off his lap. Chip ran over and pawed at it until he could get a grip on it with his mouth. He picked it up and nudged it back onto the edge of the chair.

"Wow," I said.

"I can't take books out of the library. Teeth marks," he said, laughing. "Here. Sit."

I wasn't sure if he was talking to me or the dog. I sat on the edge of the ottoman. Chip sat next to the chair.

"Hi, Mr. Foster," I said, thankful that I remembered Fish's last name from the reunion poster. I was shaking and hoped it wasn't visible. I kept my hands in the pockets of Fish's jacket until Chip put his head in my lap and I couldn't resist petting him.

"You're an adult," Mr. Foster said. "None of this 'mister' crap. You can call me Ernie." He patted my arm. His hand was stiff and knotted. "Where are your manners?" he said to Fish. He had an impish look in his eyes. Despite the fact that I worried he was on to me, I really liked him. "Offer her some tea."

"Jessie, would you like some tea?" Fish said, laughing.

"Sure," I said.

When Fish went into the kitchen, Ernie leaned in and said, "Are you responsible for the spring in his step?"

I felt my face get hot.

"I don't know," I said.

"Well, I hope so." He studied my face carefully. I was pretty sure if he suspected that I might be an impostor, he would have come out with it already. He didn't seem like someone who held much back.

He pointed behind me, and I turned around. We both watched Fish in the kitchen, filling the kettle, getting out mugs and tea bags. "He's a good man," Ernie said. "He's a good son." He cleared his throat. "He deserves to have a spring in his step." He shook his head. It was more like a wobble. "I'm not a fan of that Karen girl."

"Oh," I said, because I couldn't think of anything else to say.

Karen who was still in Florida. I knew the kids weren't Fish's. I knew she'd been friends with Jessie, but I didn't know much more about her.

"Don't look sad," Ernie said. "She's not competition. I think she just wishes she were."

I scratched Chip behind the ears. He made me feel calm.

"So where do you live?" Ernie asked me.

"Rochester," I said. "New York."

"Oh, you don't want to live there. Cold and snowy and far away from Gilbert."

"Dad," Fish called from the kitchen. "Are you forcing me on Jessie?"

"I like this one," Ernie said. "There's something about her."

"I like her too," Fish said, bringing a tray with tea, milk, and sugar into the living room. He set it down on the coffee table and set up a tray table next to Ernie.

"I think Chip's in love," Ernie said, gesturing to me.

Fish laughed. "It's just so funny to see you cuddling up to a dog like that, Jess."

Ernie winked at me. It made my pulse spike. Why would he be nice to me if he did know? Why would he be nice to me if he didn't? Jessie led Fish on for years. What kind of good parent would encourage their kid to go back for more? Fish deserved better than Jessie. Fish deserved better than me too.

"Damn," Fish said, looking out the window before he sat down with his tea. "It looks like it's going to rain. I want to put a tarp over the fireplace rocks so I don't have to wait for a sunny day to get them to dry out again."

"Do you want me to help you?" I asked.

"I can do it," Fish said. "But I bet my dad would love the company."

"Do you Scrabble?" Ernie asked.

"Do I play Scrabble?" I asked. "Like the board game?"

"It makes you sound more serious if you say it like it's a verb."

"Well, then, yes," I said. "I do Scrabble."

"Uh-oh," Fish said, grabbing his coat. "You don't know what you're in for. He's become a Scrabble pro in the last few years."

"Well," I said, "I'm no slouch." As an only child, there weren't many games I could play by myself, but Scrabble was one of them. I would switch from one set of tiles to the other on each turn. It wasn't the same challenge as playing with another person, but it was still a word game. It was less pathetic than when I tried to play Battleship alone.

Fish got the board and another tray table for us to play on before he left.

"You'll have to do the letters for me," Ernie said. "I'll give them to you and tell you where they go."

"I'm happy to," I said.

"I make a mess when I do it myself."

Ernie kept his tiles in the box top in his lap instead of on the small wooden stand. They were shielded by the table, so I couldn't see them.

I got to go first. I spelled out "honed."

"So what are you doing with yourself these days," Ernie asked, handing me a *J*. He pointed to the spot on the board where he wanted me to start and gave me the letters one by one.

"I'm an account executive at a PR firm," I said, laying his letters on the board carefully until I'd spelled out "jivey."

"I used to be in ad sales for the newspaper." He wobbled his head. "And I hated every minute of it."

It surprised me to think of Ernie in sales. He was wearing a thick wool sweater, sweatpants, and shearling slippers. He was short, like Fish, only a couple of inches taller than me if he were standing, I guessed. But he had broad shoulders and a square jaw, and I could picture him more easily as a carpenter or a fisherman than a salesman in a suit.

"It's so fake," he said. "You're always pretending to be excited about something you couldn't give a damn about. Exhausting! And at the end of the day, you haven't really done anything. All you have to show for yourself is a couple of squares in a newspaper, filled with ads for car insurance or business college."

"That's how I feel about my job," I said. "Most of the time. There are good days."

"I watch Gil," Ernie said, "and I wish I'd had the smarts to be like him. Even on a bad day at work, he's still changing someone's life."

We played and chatted. I boiled more water and filled our mugs again.

Fish came in wet and dirty and said he was going to take a quick shower.

"We're fine," Ernie said. Then he smiled at me. "I shouldn't answer for you. Are you fine?"

"I'm fine," I called out.

We were neck and neck in our game. I was just three points behind Ernie when he handed me his remaining letters, one by one, to spell out "quixotry." I wasn't entirely sure it was a word, but I was too polite to say so.

"Challenge me," he said, giving me his half smile. "I can tell you want to."

"I'm sure if you say it's a word . . ."

"Challenge me," he said. "It's more fun that way. The stakes are high! For the win!"

"Okay," I said. "I challenge you."

"Mean it!" he said, waving his fist at me.

"I CHALLENGE YOU!" I cried, waving my fist back at him. I was embarrassed as soon as I did it, but Ernie was thrilled.

"Wonderful!" he said, clapping the heels of his hands together.

Ernie pointed to the bookshelf. "Dictionary!"

I went over to look for the dictionary. Chip followed me, looking up at the shelf too, like he wanted me to know that he could step in and help if I needed it. In front of the dictionary was a picture of Fish in his graduation gown. He had one arm around Ernie, who was handsome and healthy, his smile straight, and his hand making rabbit ears behind Fish's head. Fish's other arm was around a woman with curly brown hair, big brown eyes, and a nervous smile. She wasn't looking at the camera. She was looking past it. She and Fish had the same nose, straight and narrow through the bridge. It was the day Fish worked up the nerve to tell Jessie he loved her. He must not have done it yet. The smile on his face was real. I wondered where his mother was. I hadn't heard him talk about her at all.

I grabbed the dictionary and brought it back to Ernie. Chip followed me and sat down at the side of Ernie's chair.

"Susan left me," Ernie said, gesturing toward the picture. "After the stroke. She couldn't handle it."

"I'm so sorry," I said.

"It's amazing," Ernie said, "that me and Susan—both cowards—could make a man like Gilbert. He never complains, even with all of this." He shook his hand.

"He's a good guy," I said.

Ernie's mouth crinkled into a strange smirk, and I worried for a moment that he might cry. Chip got up and solemnly licked Ernie's hand like he was trying to comfort him. Ernie took a deep breath and shook his hand up and down. "Read the word. Look it up," he said, when he could talk again.

I used the thumb imprint at the side of the book to find the Qs and flipped through the pages until I found it. "Quixotry," I read out loud. "Visionary schemes."

"See," he said. "It is a word." Then he laughed. "Actually, I wasn't a hundred percent sure."

I laughed too.

"It's nice to see Fish happy," Ernie said. "The old Jessie Morgan made him miserable."

"What do you mean?" I asked, feeling my heart beat in every single inch of my being.

He bumped his hand against the side of his nose, like the way people do to say they're in on your secret. Or maybe he was just referring to Jessie's supposed nose job. "I mean you're a new girl, and I like it."

I wished I had the courage to challenge Ernie again, to nail down exactly what he meant.

❖

"So," Fish said, when he drove me back to Myra's house, "I'm thirty-one years old and I live with my dad. Do you still like me?"

"I think I like you even more," I said.

There was a purple sedan in Myra's driveway, next to Myra's Honda.

"You coming in?" I asked, when he shifted the truck into park.

"No," he said. "Heather is here. I think you guys have some girl time ahead of you." He got out of the truck and ran around to open my door. "I promised Robbie I'd help him finish up a motor repair that's giving him trouble. And I can't dance to Janet Jackson to save my life."

He walked me to Myra's door and kissed me on the doorstep, just like the end of a date on a TV show. Myra must have seen us. She flashed the porch light.

She opened the door just enough to stick her head through. "Ooh," she said, and then shut the door again.

Fish laughed. "I'll see you tomorrow?" he asked.

"I hope so," I said. I watched him walk to his car and drive away before I opened the door to join Myra and Heather.

I had a sleepover party at my house once. Fourth grade. My parents were still together then. My mom was having a good streak. We made invitations for the party on the kitchen table, and she didn't even yell at me when I squeezed the tube too hard and got glitter glue everywhere. There was a spot of purple glitter that didn't get cleaned up, on the seat of the chair where I always sat. I never scratched it off. It was like a reminder that it had all really happened.

The biggest problem with having my mom for a mother was that when she wanted to pretend something hadn't happened the way it really had, she just acted as if the reality she wanted was true. So my memories were all twisted around varying levels of truth and lies. Things I actually remembered mixed with things my mother told me happened. Sometimes the lies were like looking through a piece of gauze, because I could still see behind them. But sometimes the truth was the gauze and the lies were like silhouettes. Sometimes I forgot which was which, and there were two versions of a story, but I couldn't remember which one to believe.

But I know I had a sleepover birthday party when I was in fourth grade, and I know we made invitations with purple glitter for every single girl in my class. And I know that at the party, around midnight, when we were supposed to be asleep but were waiting until the clock struck twelve to see what would happen if we said "Bloody Mary" into the mirror three times, my parents started fighting.

What began as hushed, sharp whispers turned into my mother's voice exploding from the bedroom, and my father yelling that he was tired of her bullshit. Some of the girls laughed, but most of them didn't, and in the green light from the VCR, I could see the horror on their faces. Tracy Witzleben pulled her sleeping bag over her head and cried.

On Monday no one made room for me or Tracy at any of the lunch tables. We got stuck sitting together at an empty table by the smelly garbage cans. We didn't talk. I'm pretty sure she hated me.

I didn't work up the nerve to have friends over again until the Four Amigos, in junior high school. But when things started to get bad with my mom, I knew how hard I needed to work to keep it a secret. I never had another birthday party. Drinks and dinner with Luanne don't count.

Even under the current circumstances, having a sleepover with Myra and Heather felt much safer than my fourth grade party. My mother was all the way across the country, for one thing.

Myra's house smelled warm and garlicky. Heather was in the kitchen cooking, and something sizzled loudly in a big wok. She used a pair of chopsticks instead of a spatula. The steam from the pan made her blond curls frizz around her face.

"What are you making?" I asked, walking into the kitchen.

"Pad see ew," she said, waving her chopsticks at me. "I found the hugest shrimp at the public market today. They're like fists!"

"I've never been particularly keen on eating my hand," Myra

said. She was sitting at the kitchen table, scissors at the ready, thumbing through a magazine, with pieces torn from the pages piled in front of her.

Heather gave her a look.

"What?" Myra said, laughing. "It smells amazing, but if you were going to write it as a menu item, 'fist-sized shrimp' wouldn't necessarily be the most compelling description."

"Are you opening a restaurant?" I asked.

"I wish!" Heather said. "It's a pipe dream. Robbie needs me at the store. And we don't have the kind of start-up funds lying around to make it happen."

"I keep telling her that she should get a job at a restaurant to start making the right connections," Myra said. She cut paper dolls out of the magazine scraps. A model from one magazine, a skirt from another. The beautiful blue sky, from a perfume ad, cut into a blouse.

"But who will do Robbie's books?" Heather said. She squirted oil into the pan, and the sizzle turned into a roar.

"They're called accountants," Myra said.

Heather held up her hand and gave Myra the finger over her shoulder.

"I'm just saying," Myra said, "you're talented. Don't let fear stop you. You need to think about what you'd do if you knew you couldn't fail."

"Well, that's stupid," Heather said. "Because, obviously, I'd fly." She piled noodles into three bowls and brought them over to us. Myra swept her paper dolls into a pile at the side of the table, to make room.

"You would?" I asked. "Because I think I'd swim the Atlantic."

"I don't know," Myra said. "Just because you wouldn't fail doesn't mean you wouldn't get really freaking cold."

"True," I said.

"I guess I'm just saying that it's a little different for you," Heather said to Myra. "And it's a bullshit mantra—'What would you do if you knew you wouldn't fail?'—the whole idea that passion counts for everything. Because it doesn't. Tons of people want to be fashion designers. They couldn't all be you. Tons of people want to be chefs. Some of them have to settle for being bookkeepers. If I'm doing the books and Robbie has a bad month, he doesn't have to pay me. If he hires an accountant or an employee, he loses the wiggle room. It's not the same as your business. You don't have a mortgage. You don't have a husband counting on you."

I worried it was about to get ugly. I wasn't sure it was necessarily the safest thing in the world to point out to a woman who'd just had a run-in with her married ex that she didn't have a husband. But Myra seemed to take it in the spirit in which it was intended. There was enough history, enough love built up, that they could be blunt. They could say the difficult things.

"I know," Myra said. "I do get it. It's just I think you're so talented that if you took the leap, you wouldn't fail. Not everyone can be a chef, but I honestly believe you could. Because this"—she pointed to her bowl with a chopstick—"is like the best food there ever was."

I nodded. It was. The noodles were super hot, with just the right amount of salty and sweet.

"And, you know," Myra said, "I'd tell you if I thought otherwise."

"Oh," Heather said, sighing. "You are such a pain in my ass."

She reached into Myra's bowl with her chopsticks and stole one of her shrimp. "Like fists, I tell you." She smiled a crazy big smile and Myra retaliated by stealing a shrimp from Heather's bowl.

I was quiet while I ate, focusing carefully on balancing bits of vegetables between my chopsticks. Luanne and I never had talks like this. We always skirted on the edge of trying not to offend each other. We really only scratched the surface. I wondered who I'd be if I'd had friends to say the hard stuff.

Myra insisted on doing the dishes. She wouldn't let me or Heather help. "Cooks and guests don't clean," she said, shaking her head.

Heather and I refilled Myra's huge green glass goblets with wine and sat out on the back steps.

"Where did you learn how to cook?"

"My mom taught me," Heather said, taking a sip of her wine. The goblet was so big it looked like she could drown in it. "She cooked so well, remember? I never bothered to learn. But then after I married Robbie . . ." She stopped and held her breath. Her face was pinched, her lips pressed together until they were almost white.

"Are you okay?"

She nodded, but she took a minute to collect herself, taking another sip of wine. "After I married Robbie, I had her teach me." She made a funny sound, like a cross between a gasp and a squeak. I thought she was going to tell me that her mom had died. I searched my brain for the right thing to say. My attachment to my parents wasn't the same as other people's. I didn't want them to die, but sometimes the idea of them simply not existing any-more calmed me. I'm sure that wasn't the way Heather felt about her mother. I'm sure her death left a hole, a space that couldn't be filled. I wondered what it was like to have the kind of mother who made life easier, who taught you how to cook. I couldn't imagine having a wonderful mother and losing her.

But then Heather burst into tears and said, "I wanted to be the kind of mom she is." She sobbed so hard that her wine sloshed over the edge of the goblet and splashed on the steps. I took the goblet from her and set it down next to me. I put my arm around her and hugged. I didn't know what else to do.

"We've been trying for a really long time," Heather said into my shoulder. Her voice was muffled and wet.

"I'm so sorry," I said.

She sniffed and pulled away, wiping her face with her hands. "Oh, I'm sorry." She took a few deep breaths. "You don't need me crying all over you."

"It's okay," I said. "It's really okay."

Heather laughed. "You spend high school being terrified of getting knocked up, you know?" She reached across me and grabbed her wine.

I nodded, but I was so far from knowing. In high school I'm not even sure I thought sex was a thing that actually happened. I didn't kiss anyone until I got to college. And even then it wasn't like it was a frequent occurrence.

"Now we're actually trying and it just never happens. I went to the doctor a couple of months ago." She looked like she was going to say something more but didn't. She put her wine down and picked at a splinter on the railing of the steps.

"Are you okay?"

"Yeah," she said. "Everything is fine."

"Well, that's good," I said. "Maybe it'll just happen when—"

"Do you think," she said, "since you're here . . ." Her voice trailed off. She pried the splinter loose.

I thought for a moment that she was going to ask for one of my eggs or wanted me to carry a child for them. I took a big gulp of wine.

"Do you think you could talk to Robbie?" she asked. "He listens to you. All my tests came back fine, so now Robbie is supposed to go, you know, give a sample." She smiled awkwardly. "But he won't." She used the pointier end of the splinter to poke at the pad of her opposite thumb, watching as her skin yielded to the pressure instead of breaking. "He's missed two appointments. He says he'll go, but then he doesn't."

"I don't know," I said. "I mean, it's been a long time since—"

"I know, I know!" Heather said. "But to Robbie . . ." She sighed. "To Robbie it hasn't. He still talks about you all the time. He still thinks about you."

It made me wonder what Heather thought of Jessie. What she was thinking about me now. The fact that she said that Robbie still felt close to Jessie made me feel like she didn't. Like there might be old wounds or bad feelings. I felt a twinge of rejection.

"I'll try," I said, desperately wanting to make up for everything Jessie Morgan had done.

"Thank you," Heather said, squeezing my arm.

"Hallelujah!" Myra sang from the kitchen in a fake operatic voice. "Hallelujah! Hallelujah!"

"Are you done with the dishes?" Heather called from the step.

"Righto," Myra said.

"Movie time!" Heather yelled, standing up.

"Right again!" Myra said.

We were all hanging out in the living room in our pajamas—mine borrowed from Myra—watching *The Breakfast Club* and eating popcorn with hot sauce and melted American cheese on it, reciting lines along with the movie, when we heard tapping on the window.

"What was that?" I asked.

Heather smiled.

"What?"

"Robbie mentioned he'd be stopping by. He said you guys had business to attend to."

We hiked along a narrow dirt trail. Robbie held the flashlight steady in front, and whenever there was a rock or a root in the path, he'd shine it behind him to show me so I could step around it. I was still in Myra's pajama pants and an extra Carhartt jacket Robbie had in his truck. It was heavy and lined with flannel, but it was so big on me that the damp, cool air snuck in all the gaps. It smelled like Calvin Klein cologne and gasoline.

There was a steep section with rocks. Robbie grabbed my hand to help me up.

"All right, there we go," he said, when I made it over the rock. He held on to my hand until he was sure I had stable footing. We were in a clearing. The clouds were thick, but in small clear pockets there were stars, and off in the distance we could see the lights from Seattle.

He turned the flashlight off, and we stood in silence, letting our eyes adjust.

"God," Robbie said, finally. "We snuck out here so much. I think I barely spent a night in my own bed in high school."

"Yeah," I said, worried suddenly that Jessie and Robbie had some kind of romantic thing going on that Heather didn't know about. I took a step away from him.

But then Robbie said, "You were my best friend. Best part of my life back then was sneaking out with you and lying here." He kicked his toe into the ground. "Staring at the stars, talking about stuff."

Robbie pulled a tattered box of cigarettes from the inside pocket of his jacket.

"I don't smoke," I said; then, correcting myself, "I quit. Heather says you did too."

"I did quit," Robbie said. "These are the last two cigarettes from the last box I ever bought. We smoked our first cigarettes here. I saved these. Hoped we could smoke our last ones together too." He pulled one out with his teeth and handed me the box.

I had never actually smoked a cigarette. I also felt like I was treading on something sacred. "I don't know if I should, Robbie."

"Come on," he said. "For me. For closure or something." He patted his pockets until he found his lighter. "I'm not sure I would have survived if it wasn't for you." I could hear the catch in his voice. "Just to have someone else know what it's like when your dad gets trashed and turns into a monster. It made things a little better, you know?"

"Yeah," I said. I did know what that was like. It was a strange kind of comfort to realize that I wasn't the only person in the world who grew up with Jekyll and Hyde for a parent. I'd given up so much to keep it a secret. It felt like my own private shame, but maybe there had been other people around me going through the same thing. Maybe if I hadn't been so desperate to cover it up, I would have seen them. I took the cigarette and handed the box back to Robbie. We sat on the ground. The grass was wet, but Robbie didn't seem to care, so I decided I didn't either.

"Remember the night you broke our window?"

The dampness from the grass seeped through my pajama pants. I leaned on one arm and pulled Robbie's jacket under my butt with the other so I wouldn't end up soaked.

Robbie put his arm around me. "I think my dad would have killed me if you hadn't thrown that rock. He was so out of control."

"I'm sorry you had to go through that," I said.

"He was so far gone. And I was the one who was ashamed of it. Like it was my fault." Robbie took a deep breath, and it came out uneven, ragged.

I reached up to hold the hand he'd rested on my shoulder. I understood that exact mix of shame and misplaced responsibility.

We'd had an assembly in school in ninth grade. The police came in and told us to "just say no" to drugs. They warned us of the dangers of underage drinking and drunk driving. But no one told me what to do about my mother.

I even asked my father once, on one of my few and far between weekends at his house. I couldn't make myself say the words about the wine bottles, the glasses of water that were not water. All I said was, "You know how she gets." I breathed deeply and whispered, "And sometimes she drives." They weren't words I could say at full volume.

My dad took a swig of his beer and said, "I couldn't control her when I was married to her. What makes you think I have a say now?"

In the filmstrip they'd showed us in the auditorium after the police left the stage, there was a small lump on the side of the road with a gray blanket draped over it. There were paramedics and flashing lights, and a broken tricycle. The person who drove drunk in the movie was a reckless teenage boy in a leather jacket, with slicked-back hair and a torn, yellowed undershirt. I'd been in the car with my mother when she'd been drinking. I'd held on tight to the door handle and bit the inside of my cheek when she slammed on the brakes at the very last minute to avoid hitting the car in front of us.

I remember how hard I cried when I finally worked up the nerve to say, "Dad, what if she kills someone?"

"Jenny," my father said, pinching the bridge of his nose with his thumb and forefinger, "you're worrying about people we don't even know," like it was the most ridiculous thing he'd ever heard.

I squeezed Robbie's hand hard and hoped he couldn't tell I was crying.

"Oh man," Robbie said, "all the times we snuck out here. Trading stories about what freaks we were. You saved my life." He took his arm back and pulled a handful of grass from the ground, throwing it away one blade at a time. "Remember when we tried to build a fort out of tree branches?" He laughed. "At, like, three in the morning."

"That didn't go well," I said. It was an easy guess. I wiped my eyes with the heels of my hands.

I thought about the nights alone with my mom when things were so bad that I would sit in my closet and try not to make a sound. I wanted her to forget I existed. I didn't want to give her a reason to come in and scream and break my things and tell me how sorry she was she ever had me. I didn't even want to exist anymore. I would have given anything for a Robbie, for failed attempts at fort building, for someone to hide with.

He lit his cigarette and then reached over and held the lighter out for me, shielding it with his hand. I sucked in, the way I'd seen smokers do, and the paper started to burn.

"I missed you, Jess. You're like my sister."

"I missed you too," I said, trying not to choke. In the strangest way, it was true. I missed out on having someone like Robbie in my life. I didn't know how to pick the right friends or the right boyfriends. I didn't know how to choose things for myself, because I couldn't trust anyone. I'd never learned how. But Jessie, she had Robbie. She had someone who loved her in the right way for the right reasons. She had a friend to be a freak with. If I had a friend like Robbie, I would have thrown that rock too. I would have fought for him. I would have had someone to fight for.

My lungs burned and my eyes filled with tears again.

We lay on our backs on the ground.

Robbie sucked hard on his cigarette, blowing smoke up to the stars. "God, these are stale," he said. "It's like smoking a basement."

"Yeah," I said, even though I had no idea what a cigarette was supposed to taste like. My head buzzed. The sky was big. Robbie scooched over so I could use his arm for a pillow, and his body heat kept me warm.

I'd always wanted a big brother. It's what I used to wish for when I lost an eyelash, or the clock said 11:11, or I threw a penny in the fountain at the mall, even though I knew it was an impossible wish. Lying there with Robbie made me feel safe the way I'd always imagined having a big brother would.

"Does your dad still drink?" I asked him.

"Yeah," Robbie said. "My mom left him. Finally. My brother won't talk to her. He took my dad's side. It broke her heart, but she's doing okay."

He sighed, and I felt his chest expand next to mine. "It's like she has to learn how to be a person again. She was a hostage for too long. My dad still lives in that house." He blew smoke out of his nose like a dragon. "I drive the long way home after work so I can pretend he isn't even there."

"My mom still drinks," I said. It was the first time I'd ever said it out loud.

"Jesus," Robbie said. "I didn't know your mom drank too. Your dad was bad enough for two parents."

I gasped but turned it into a cough and pretended it was smoke related. "I guess because he was worse, I didn't notice her problem, you know?" I didn't know if Jessie's mom was a drinker, I only knew that mine was. I'd never really talked about it before. I wanted to. I wanted to say the words out loud and have a witness.

"What about your dad?" Robbie asked.

I didn't want to make up more than I had to about Jessie's parents, so I said, "My father is irrelevant," because it was the truest thing I could think of to say. He was.

I hadn't even talked to my father since last Christmas, when we made stilted conversation over an artisanal cheese course at his girlfriend's favorite restaurant. I had to leave before the meal, to go to my mother's house, where she accosted me for choosing "that man" and his "chippie" over her. She didn't even have dinner for us. We ordered Chinese. She passed out by six thirty and called me a waste of genetic material when I tried to get her into bed. I gave up, threw an afghan over her on the couch, and tried to push her over on her side before I left.

When I got back to my apartment, Deagan called from Telluride to tell me how his mom had baked a full turkey in the chalet they'd rented. "Yeah," I told him, "we had turkey too. Christmas tradition." Deagan didn't notice that my voice was flat and dead, that there was no enthusiasm to be mustered. Part of me wanted him to ask what was wrong, but part of me was terrified that he would. I'd have to explain, and it would make me seem like one of those people with problems that needed to be whispered about.

He didn't ask.

When Deagan said good night, I hung up the phone and cried until the lady who lived upstairs pounded on the floor for me to shut up.

Robbie and I were quiet for a long time. Watching the stars. Watching our smoke circle up into the air.

"Last one ever," Robbie said, sitting up to stub out the end of his cigarette on the sole of his boot. "Right?"

"It's a pact," I said.

He took mine from me and stubbed it out too; then he put both butts in the box and put the box back in his pocket. "Ha, look at us being all responsible. Not littering." He pulled a blade of grass from the ground and started tying it in knots. "Where did all the time go? When did we grow up?"

"I don't know," I said, sitting up, leaning against him. "I thought it would be . . . different. To be this age."

"Me too," Robbie said, handing me the knotted blade of grass.

I remembered my promise to Heather.

"Heather says you don't want to go get your swimmers checked," I said. It occurred to me how weird it was to be talking about sperm with a stranger. Except that he didn't feel like a stranger anymore.

He didn't say anything. I heard him sniff. He dropped his head into his arms. His side shook against mine. I thought he was laughing for a second, and then I realized he was crying.

"Robbie?"

Nothing.

"Hey," I said, nudging his shoulder with mine. "Are you okay?"

"I can't," Robbie said. His voice was blurry and muffled.

"Why not?" I asked. "They give you porn. It's a free pass for porn, Robbers."

"What if it's me?" He looked at me and even in the dim light I could see how devastated he was. His cheeks were streaked with tears. "I don't want to know if it's me. If it's my fault."

"It wouldn't be your fault, Robbie," I said. "It's just the way things happen sometimes."

"But it's Heather. She was born to be a mother. She's the best wife," he said, and even through his tears he smiled when he said it. "How could I tell her that I can't give her a family?"

"I think," I said, "what she wants most is you."

"I don't know," Robbie said, wiping his eyes with the back of his hand. "I don't know if that's enough."

"It's not just about that, is it?" I asked, figuring he was probably feeling what I did when I thought about having kids. I realized for the first time that it's probably what every kid with a shitty parent fears most.

"No," Robbie said, shaking his head. "It isn't just about that."

"You're not your dad," I said. "You won't turn into him."

"What if it's inevitable? What if having me is what turned my dad into a monster."

"He had a choice. He could have gotten help." My mom could have gotten help. It was a devastating, liberating thought.

"I guess," Robbie said.

"It's hard to look at it like that, isn't it? Because if you can be a better parent than the ones you had, you have to face the fact that your parents had that choice too. If you're not fated to be an awful parent, they weren't either. And," I said, feeling my throat tighten, "it's easier to believe that we're all just fucked than it is to know that there are choices." I rubbed my hands together to try to get my fingers to warm up. "It hurts less to think they couldn't have done any better than they did, doesn't it?"

"How'd you get to be so smart, Jess?"

I laughed. "You guys are going to be great parents."

"I want to be," Robbie said.

"If you can't trust yourself yet, trust Heather," I said. "She won't let you fall short. She loves you too much. You're not your father, and Heather isn't your mother. Right?"

"Jess," Robbie said.

"Yeah?"

"Don't disappear again, okay?"

"Okay," I said, because I didn't want to. We lay back in the grass holding hands, staring up at the stars until the sky started to brighten again.

It was almost daylight by the time Robbie and I made the trek back to Myra's house. We snuck in. Heather and Myra were asleep on the couch, a head on each armrest, their feet tangled up in the middle. Robbie grabbed a quilt from the back of the rocking chair and sacked out on the floor next to Heather. I watched him kiss her cheek before he settled in. I pulled an afghan off the back of the love seat and curled up. I couldn't have slept more than three hours before my phone started buzzing. In my sleepy haze, I accidentally answered it instead of turning it off. "Hold on," I whispered into the receiver.

I could hear my mother saying, "Jenny? Jenny?" as I tiptoed through the kitchen and into the backyard. It was freezing outside. I didn't have shoes on.

"What?" I said into the phone, allowing my voice to sound ever so slightly irritated, even though I knew I'd pay for it.

"I don't like your tone," she said. Her voice was dangerous, wounded. I could picture the look on her face too clearly. The sharpness in her eyes, the softness of her cheek as it trembled with anger.

"It's still early here," I said. "I was sleeping."

"You haven't called me back in five days." She said it with the kind of accusatory inflection that other people would reserve for saying something like "You left me for dead on that desert island"

or "You mass-murdered a school bus full of nuns before you ran
over all those kittens."

"I'm on vacation."

"Well, I didn't realize you needed a vacation from your
mother."

I wanted to tell her that she was what I needed a vacation
from most of all. But instead I said, "I just need to go back to
sleep, Mom."

"Fine," she said, "but . . . ," and then she proceeded to tell me
about every slight or perceived slight she'd experienced in the past
five days: from the guy in the Cutlass Supreme who cut her off on
390 to the hairdresser who didn't seem to take enough time
bleaching her roots ("Like she was in a rush, Jenny! I mean, I had
an appointment!") to my dad's latest infraction that had something to do with not sending her an engagement announcement,
even though it would have sent her on a rampage of the "how dare
he rub my face in his marriage?" variety if he had. I stopped listening about ten minutes in. I sat on the back step, rested my face
against the splintery wood railing, and closed my eyes. I would
have just put it on speakerphone if there wasn't a risk of someone
coming outside and hearing her call me Jenny. My butt was freezing, and my body ached from only getting a few hours of sleep
curled up on a love seat. But hanging up wasn't an option. Hanging up was never an option. It started an explosion that took days,
if not weeks, to clean up. It set off a drinking binge. It made her
my problem on a greater scale than she already was. Phone calls
ended when she was ready for them to end, and not a moment
sooner.

Once, in college, I'd been so desperate to pee that I'd brought
my portable phone into the bathroom with me. I'd covered the

receiver while I went and was about to get away with it, when someone in the stall next to me flushed.

"Are you," she said, with heavy disgust in her voice, "in the bathroom? I raised you better than to talk on the phone in the bathroom!"

I made the mistake of saying, "You raised me better than to wet my pants."

The next day I got a call from her saying that she didn't think she could afford my tuition anymore and that it was hurtful to both her and my father that I had chosen a college with such high tuition, without giving a thought to her needs. She said she couldn't believe she had raised such an ungrateful daughter. Because I peed and I talked back.

Instead of realizing she was acting crazy, I believed I was an awful person for choosing an expensive school. The shame I felt clouded the fact that she'd been proud of me for getting into Ithaca. She'd loved bragging about it to everyone she came into contact with. I had gotten enough of a merit scholarship to take tuition down to the price of a state school. But because I'd hurt her feelings, suddenly my choice of college was a horrible, hateful act. I believed her, because I was nineteen and she was my mother. I spent the next two years dragging around mountains of guilt just for getting an education the way everyone had always told me I should.

But I wasn't nineteen anymore. And just because she was my mother, it didn't mean she had the right to control me or guilt me or make me feel bad about myself.

The people sleeping in Myra's living room were a family, not because of any genetic obligation, but because they loved each other. They made each other's lives better. They weren't a constant dead weight dragging everyone else down. It was a merit-based family. It counted so much more than the kind of family you just get stuck with.

I was never going to make my mother the person I needed her to be. I was never going to get what I wanted from a mother, no matter how many times I took her phone calls or cleaned her house and paid her bills and put her to bed when she was too drunk to walk upstairs by herself. Taking care of her had kept me from ever being part of a family of my own.

"Can you believe him? That he had the nerve to . . ." I heard her say, probably about my father. Yes or no wasn't the right answer. Neither one would get her to stop ranting. My role in these conversations was to mumble "mmhmm" at appropriate intervals, which was something I could practically do in my sleep now. But my feet were cold and my muscles were sore, my breath was making clouds in the air, and I didn't want to hear her list of grievances anymore. I hung up the phone without saying a word. And then I shut off my phone completely, so I couldn't hear her call back.

"Hey," Heather said.

I jumped.

"Sorry," she said, sitting down next to me. She smoothed my hair away from my face. "Are you okay? You seem upset."

"My mom called," I said. "I think I'm starting to realize that she's never going to be the mom I wish I had."

"I'm so sorry, honey."

"Yeah." I waved my hand like I was ushering the problem out of the way. "It's not even worth discussing."

"Karen's home," Heather said. "She wants to meet for lunch. And Robbie said he's fine without me for the morning, so why don't we go pretend to be tourists and then meet Karen and Myra at Portage Bay for Mexican."

"Works for me," I said. As much as I knew it was going to be challenging to pretend to not be a tourist, I was excited to get to see Seattle. Staying busy would help me keep my phone off.

"Beach, shopping, or Space Needle?" Heather asked, when we climbed into her purple Ford Escort to head into the city after Myra left for work.

"Beach," I said.

"Thank goodness. If you'd said Space Needle, I would have lost a little respect for you. There's a fun level of pretending to be tourists, and then there's snow globes in the gift shop."

"The beach sounds perfect."

"Great!" she said. "I haven't been to Carkeek in forever! And I could use a good walk." She patted her impossibly small waist.

"You look fantastic," I said.

"Yes, and there's a reason for that," she said. "I move. I hate the whole going-to-the-gym-in-spandex kind of exercise, so I just focus on making sure I'm always walking or hiking or stuff like that. I help Robbie move boxes at work." She flexed her arm to show me her bicep. It popped up like an apple.

"Nice!" I said.

"I was so sedentary in high school. Blah." She stuck her tongue out. "It helps that my husband is completely hyperactive."

On the ride to the park, Heather told me about the house she and Robbie hoped to build. "Right now we live in a glorified mobile home, but when Fish is done building his house, he's going to help Robbie start on ours."

"Like a barn raising," I said.

"Exactly," Heather said. She filled me in on her dream kitchen and the fire pit they'd build outside. "Robbie wants to build on some of Fish's dad's land. But I already feel like I'm married to two boys sometimes. I'm not sure I could handle Fish living right next door."

I laughed.

"I mean, I love Fish," she said, "but those boys are even more inseparable now than they were in high school."

When we got to Carkeek Park, we parked the car at a trail-head. Heather slung her little gray and pink messenger bag across her shoulder, and we were off.

We hiked along a creek. It was dark and damp. Lush ferns and moss everywhere. I didn't understand how we would find a beach when we were so clearly headed toward woods. Heather walked fast, and even though my legs were much longer than hers, I struggled to keep pace, so we didn't talk much. My feet were still bruised and blistered from the other day, and the mud made a mess of my loafers. Finally the path was drier, and there were little glimpses of water through the trees. We hiked down a steep dirt path, and then the ocean was right in front of us. We crossed a bridge over some train tracks and ended up on a gravel beach. "Oh," Heather said, taking a deep breath and sighing, "I always feel better when I'm around water."

She took off her shoes. "I know I'm going to regret this when my feet turn to icicles, but I love walking on beach rocks barefoot."

I took my shoes off too, happy for the chance to let my blisters breathe a little.

"Geez," Heather said, "what happened to your feet?"

"Hiking with Fish and Myra," I said. "Myra had my old hiking boots, but they don't fit like they used to."

"I know!" Heather said. "You shed your baby fat and nothing fits the same. I'm so sorry! If I'd known I would have just parked over here."

"No!" I said. "The walk was nice."

She put her foot next to mine. "That's so funny," she said. "I remember you teasing me about my little hardly there baby toe, but yours is like that too."

I curled my toes into the gravel. "I think it's just because they're so swollen," I said.

"I think," Heather said, "that it's karma. Let this be a lesson to you, Jessica." She smiled. "You make fun of stubby toes and you end up with them yourself." She picked up a rock and tossed it out toward the ocean. It didn't quite make it to the water.

We walked closer so she could try again. This time her rock went far, splashing into the water. My feet were freezing, but the cold numbed the pain. I picked up a rock and threw it. It made it about half as far as Heather's rock.

We walked around, picking up beach glass, poking long strips of seaweed with driftwood. We sat on a log and looked out at the water. "You know," Heather said, scratching a big *H* into the pebbly beach with a stick, "my parents are pretty great, but I've watched Robbie struggle with his. I know how much it hurts." Her lowercase *e* was round and bubbly. "It wouldn't be fair for me to sit here and say, 'But she's your mother,' because all I'd be doing is filling in the blanks of your mom with mine." Her *a* had a roof like a typewriter *a*. "I did that to Robbie for too long." She looked up at me. "What I do know is that when I finally stopped telling Robbie how people are supposed to feel about their parents and listened to how he actually felt, we started getting somewhere. It gave him permission to focus on the people who do matter. He wasn't putting so much time into the people who kept hurting him."

When she finished all the letters, she drew a heart and handed me the stick.

"You're right," I said. "I know you are. It's just hard to let go of the guilt." I drew a giant outlined J, and instead of writing the rest of my name, I filled it in with stripes and polka dots.

"Everyone you have in your life, everyone you give time and attention and love to, should deserve it. You deserve to be loved back, honey." She hugged me. "And if you're not, it's only human to want to take a break. Maybe she'll only ever make a change if you force her hand. Maybe she won't change at all, but you'll be moving forward and it will hurt less than it does now."

When the next wave hit, water filled in her name and my J and left them shimmering when the wave slipped back from the shore.

As we walked back to the car, Heather looked at her watch. "We still have almost two hours before lunch. Kayaking?"

I laughed, hoping she was joking.

"I mean, when was the last time we even went?" she said.

"I know! Right?" I said, and climbed into the passenger seat. Not only had I never been kayaking, but I was a terrible swimmer, which didn't make me all that keen to go out on open water.

Heather drove us to Portage Bay. The sun was looking like it might make an appearance, and it had started to warm up a little. We parked near a giant drawbridge and walked to the boat shop. Heather asked the guy behind the counter for two kayaks.

"Okay," he said, writing something on a piece of paper. "I'll need a credit card and a driver's license for each of you."

I had enough cash in my pocket to cover a rental, but I couldn't give him my driver's license. I pulled my wad of bills out. My head spun through possible excuses. But then Heather said, "Oh no! My treat. Put both on here." She slid her credit card across the counter and dug through her wallet for her license.

"Put your money away," Heather said, pushing my hand back toward my pocket. "My treat."

Normally I would have insisted on paying for myself, but I hoped if Heather paid, the guy wouldn't want my license. He filled out the forms and Heather signed them. Then he said, "And if I could just have your license." He pointed at me with his ball-point pen.

I smacked at my pockets like I was looking for it. In truth it was hidden in the lining of my suit jacket, which was wadded up in the bottom of my travel tote. I thought it was safer not to carry it on me. If I was caught with my credit card, I could say I'd gone to lunch with my friend Jenny and we'd accidentally taken the wrong cards after we split the bill. I'd worked out a great story about how we'd promised to pay each other's bills until I got back and we could switch again.

"I think I left it at Myra's house," I said.

Heather gave the guy a look. "I'll vouch for her," she said. "She won't steal the kayak. Promise. I've known her my whole life."

"All right," the guy said, smiling at Heather. He obviously thought she was cute. "You have an honest face," he told me. "I'll let it go this time. But you have to sign your insurance form."

I had to print out Jessica Morgan. But when I signed Jessie's name, I just wrote a *J* and then two squiggly lines. I know it didn't really make it any better, but I couldn't bring myself to actually sign her name, even though it was such a thin and ridiculous line to refuse to cross after all the vast gorges I'd been leaping over.

The guy handed us life vests and paddles and walked us down to the dock. He held the first kayak steady. Heather took her paddle, placed it along the back of the seat, and used her arms to help guide her seamlessly into the boat.

I tried to do the same, but I got one foot in and the boat shook and then my arms shook and I had visions of ending up in the water right next to the boat. I very inelegantly rolled myself back onto the dock.

"Is this your first time kayaking?" the guy asked.

"Oh, she's an old pro," Heather said.

The guy raised his eyebrows at me.

"I'm rusty," I said. "It's been like thirteen years."

"Okay," he said. "Well, I've got the kayak. It's going to move, but you have to trust that I've got a hold of it. It can't go too far."

I put my arms back on the paddle and just went for it. Both feet in one quick movement. The boat rocked back and forth, but I was in and everything was okay.

"All right," he said. "You're off." He pushed my boat away from the dock. Heather was already out of the slip and ready to go. I used the paddle to push off until I couldn't reach the dock anymore and had to rely on paddling.

I watched Heather carefully and did everything she did. Of course, while her paddles hit the water with a tiny *splish*, mine smacked the surface and sent water splashing everywhere.

"I guess it's not like riding a bike," Heather said, laughing. "But I'm sure it'll come back to you."

"I hope so," I said. "My arms aren't in the kind of shape they used to be."

Heather was fast. Even after I got the hang of it, I could tell she was only paddling at half capacity so I could keep up. My arms hurt and my shoulders ached, but every time she looked back, I'd smile. It was even starting to seem like something I might enjoy doing once I got stronger.

We paddled past houseboats and pointed out the ones we liked the best. But then a boat whizzed by us from a few yards away. Heather turned her kayak like she was turning around, so the pointy part was facing the wave. I tried to do the same, but I couldn't move fast enough, and before I knew it, the water hit the side of my boat and splashed into my lap.

"Oh!" Heather said, laughing. "That's got to be cold!"

She rode the wave out and then paddled toward me.

"Are you okay?"

"Yeah," I said, trying really hard not to cry. Jessie Morgan wouldn't cry over a little water. Of course, Jessie wouldn't have gotten doused to begin with.

"It's about time to go back anyway," Heather said. "Maybe they'll have a towel for you."

We ran into Myra on the walkway up to the café. "Why are you wet?" she asked.

"We went kayaking," Heather said.

"It's not like riding a bike," I said. "You do forget."

"She got caught in a wake." Heather fake pouted, like she felt sorry for me, but I could tell she was a little amused by the whole thing.

Myra laughed and opened the door for us. Karen was already waiting at the hostess station. I recognized her from her high school pictures. She was still pretty but thinner, harder, tired. "I just put our names in," she said, leaning in to kiss Heather's cheek and then Myra's. "I should have called ahead. There's a little bit of a wait." She kissed my cheek with as little fanfare as if she'd just seen me two weeks ago. "Hey, Jessie." She gave me a sharp look when she pulled away. It made me nervous. I wasn't sure if she was questioning my likeness to Jessie, but I was certain that this wasn't a warm, fuzzy, long-lost-friend reunion.

"Is Dylan better?" Heather asked.

"Yeah," Karen said, shoving her hands in the back pockets of her jeans. She was so thin, I found myself wondering how her skinny body ever fit a baby in it. "He's feeling better. He's just tired and crabby. My sister's watching him today, and Paige is back at school. Poor kid. She spent most of her vacation holed up in a hotel room." She made her hands into tight fists. "Oh, some days

I want to track down Travis and kick him in the nuts. It's ri-diculous, trying to be everything to those kids. And all the things he's missing." She looked at me and looked away when my eyes met hers. "I called him to see if he'd come to Paige's dance recital next month. You'd think I was asking him to give me a kidney."

"Well," Heather said, "Robbie and I will be there with the biggest bouquet of flowers that girl has ever seen."

When the waitress came to lead us to our table, Heather and Myra followed immediately. Karen brushed past me. "I don't be-lieve you," she hissed, under her breath. It was almost a relief, the idea of finally being caught, of finally giving it all up, but then she said, "Showing your face here. After what you did!"

I shivered. Everyone else walked away, and I stood there in shock for a second before Myra said, "Earth to Jessie!" and waved me over. I walked slowly. My feet did not want to take me to that table.

I got stuck sitting between Karen and Heather. Karen talked over me like I wasn't even there. Myra and Heather didn't seem to notice.

I was quiet through most of lunch. If Karen was going to tell the others whatever it was Jessie had done, I was pretty sure she would have already. It had to be a solid, locked-away secret for Karen to keep it all these years. But there was no point in pushing her buttons. With my mom, when I was walking around a mine-field, it was usually better to keep quiet. I was good at blending into the scenery when I needed to.

I ordered what Heather was having, because I didn't have the energy to look through the menu, and she'd ordered right before me. Karen showed Myra and Heather pictures from the trip, from the one day they spent at Disney, before Dylan got sick. I made vague efforts to crane my neck to see the pictures on her phone and pretend I was a part of the conversation. I was exhausted. My jeans were wet and getting tight. My thighs stung from the salt water. The lump in my throat felt like it could choke me. I hadn't had a good night's sleep in days. And even though Karen probably had every reason in the world for rejecting Jessie, and no reason to include me, it still felt shitty to be on the edge of their friendship.

I picked at my taquitos, sipped horchata, and focused on little things: the fraying tablecloth, the chip in Karen's burgundy nail polish, the condensation patterns on my glass. It was what I'd always done when I couldn't deal with what was in front of me. When my mother made me want to cry, I'd focus on the width of dark roots betraying her bottle-blond hair. It looked like I was paying attention, but in reality I was counting her grays.

"So that's it," Karen said, dropping her phone in her purse. "My glamorous vacation."

"Oh," Myra said, holding her hands over her chest. "I really wish you'd been at the reunion, Kar."

"You should have seen Jess and Robbie singing karaoke," Heather said, laughing.

"Yeah," Karen said, like she was completely and totally bored. "That must have been something."

She tried to give me another sharp look, but I busied myself by counting grains of rice on my plate and refused to make eye contact.

When we'd paid and the table was cleared, Myra rushed out

because her parking meter was about to expire. Heather snuck into the ladies' room, and Karen and I were left alone in front of the restaurant. I wished I'd asked Heather for her keys so I could wait in the car.

"I'll hand it to you," Karen said. "You've got balls. Sitting there like that, like nothing's happened. I never thought I'd see you again."

"Whatever," I said, trying to act like I wasn't afraid of her.

"The only reason I haven't told is that I know it'll hurt her more than it'll hurt you."

The door to the restaurant opened and Heather walked out. I studied Karen's face. Was Heather the 'her' Jessie had hurt?

Karen's sharp eyes gave me no clues.

"Ooh! It's so nice to see you guys catching up!" Heather said, standing between us and putting an arm on each of our shoulders. "I worried you wouldn't be back in time to see Jessie!"

"Yeah, that would have been terrible," Karen said.

Heather didn't pick up on her tone.

Heather had to go to work, so she dropped me off at Myra's. I used the Hide-A-Key by the mailbox to let myself in, like she'd told me to. I would have felt like I was trespassing even if I actually was Myra's old friend. My hands shook as I slipped the key into the lock.

I remembered that Myra said Jessie's portfolio pictures were in a box in the basement somewhere. I walked down the creaky stairs, whacking my head on the low doorframe. The basement was dark and damp, the walls were moldy cinderblock, and the beams were only a few inches above my head. The light from the tiny windows was bright enough for me to see a bare lightbulb with a pull chain in the middle of the room.

There was a mess of old furniture, Christmas decorations, fake flowers, skis, a rocking horse, a dress form. I worried I'd never find the box. I poked through a stack of boxes in the corner, but they were all filled with children's clothes. Snowsuits and hand-knit sweaters, mittens without mates, and a pair of Strawberry Short-cake roller skates that must have been Myra's. I had the very same ones in first grade. I knocked out my front tooth skating in the driveway. It took almost a year for the new one to grow in, and my mom never let me have another pair of roller skates.

Eventually I forgot that I was going through Myra's things. They could have been mine. Rubber jelly bracelets in every neon color imaginable. A plastic charm necklace with googly-eyed bears and bunnies, a whistle, a tennis racket, a sneaker, an abacus with rainbow-colored beads, a telephone with a spinning dial, and a harmonica that really worked. I had most of the same charms on my necklace.

Myra had a big stuffed Care Bear. Hers was Friend Bear. I'd had Wish Bear. I held his paw in my hand to help me fall asleep at night.

There was a box of Baby-Sitters Club and Sweet Valley High books. I wasn't allowed to read Sweet Valley High at the age when I actually wanted to, but I used my allowance to buy every Baby-Sitters book I could get my hands on. We both had Debbie Gibson tapes and black hats with brims and neon-colored CB ski jackets, even though I'd never been skiing. I'd always wanted an Easy-Bake Oven. Myra had one.

I looked through each box and was careful to put everything back the way I'd found it. There was no sign of Jessie's photos.

Then I noticed a set of shelves in the corner of the room. Each one was labeled with red plastic tape embossed with one of those old-fashioned dial label makers: Eddie, Marcie, Julian, Myra.

I think Eddie was Myra's father. She'd mentioned something about her dad retiring to Sedona. From what I'd pieced together from the photos around the house and things Myra said, Marcie was Myra's aunt. Julian was Myra's brother. He lived in San Francisco. Myra hadn't seen him since Grammie's funeral. They didn't even talk. When their parents got divorced, Julian sided with her mother and Myra sided with her father, and it broke up their whole family. I couldn't imagine having a big brother and not talking to him, because I'd so desperately wanted one my whole life. But maybe it was like what Heather had said about my mom—maybe I was projecting my idea of what a brother was onto Myra's brother. I didn't know Julian.

Eddie's shelf had a box of golf tees and a stack of Time-Life books on the Old West, a stuffed toy elephant, and shoe boxes that were labeled things like "Army Men," "Erector Set," and "Rubber Bands."

Marcie's shelf was full of dolls in boxes, with cellophane windows that let them peek through. Their plastic eyes wobbled in their faces when I touched the boxes.

Julian's shelf was empty. Myra's shelf was piled with shoe boxes: "Brooches," "Colored Pencils," "Bric-a-Brac," "Ribbons," "Sketches," "Smurfs." The one box that wasn't labeled was full of black-and-white photos of Myra, Jessie, Robbie, Fish, Heather, and Karen.

The first group of photos was of the gang in black and white. It looked like maybe they were taken in the high school auditorium. Hardwood floor. The background was a black curtain. They must have raided the costume closet. Robbie was wearing a feather boa, and Fish had a top hat perched on his head. Spotlights made sharp shadows. Jessie was in some of the pictures. She must have had a timer on her camera. The shots were high contrast, shadowy, film noir, and everyone but Heather played along, with longing stares, pensive looks. Heather gave the camera a great big smile. The dimples in her chubby cheeks made two big black spots on her face. There was one of Jessie and Robbie sucking in their cheeks, their faces pressed together. Their hands entwined and arms outstretched to the camera like they were doing a tango. Jessie wore a black hat with a fishnet veil covering one eye.

There was Myra, small and sad, alone on the stage, no costumes, no makeup, looking right into the camera. She must have trusted Jessie so much to look that vulnerable in front of her. I wondered what they talked about while Jessie photographed her.

The next group of photos was wrapped in a yellowing envelope and held together with a rubber band. They were a series of self-portraits. On the back of the envelope, there was a list in pencil. Jessie had taken the letters of her name and made new anagram names. Then she acted the names out like they were different people. Each photo had a name from the list written on the back.

Jasmine Gores was a Southern Belle with a flower behind her ear. Miss Jean Ogre wore a dirty lace dress like Miss Havisham. Anise Jogrems had dark lipstick painted on her lips and blew smoke at the camera. They were juvenile, cartoony ideas of who the people with these names would be, but the photos were striking.

Jessie's resolute stare, the defiance that radiated no matter who she was pretending to be, was unsettling. I wondered how anyone could believe I was her, because despite the fact that we had similar cheekbones, the same shape to our eyes, and the same skin tone, I didn't have that look. I didn't have that ability to shine through any persona I took on, to insist on who I am.

I heard a car door slam. I shoved the box back on the shelf and ran upstairs just in time to meet Fish as he walked in the door.

"Hey," he said, kissing me cautiously, like he still wasn't used to the fact that he could kiss me when he wanted to. "I have to bring a dog out to a client at the university. Do you want to come with me?"

We climbed into his truck. Waiting for us on the seat was a beautiful blond dog in a blue vest and a seatbelt harness. I was pretty sure he was the same dog I'd seen with Fish on Sunday.

"This is Matisse." The dog looked at Fish. Fish nodded to him, and Matisse turned to sniff my hand.

He was confident and quiet, the polar opposite of the frantic Golden Retriever my neighbors had when I was a kid. He let me pet him briefly, but then he turned his attention back to watching the road in front of us. Sitting next to him made me feel incredibly calm.

"Like the painter?" I asked.

"Yup," Fish said. "We were pretty sure he was going to be Anita's dog, so we gave him a painter's name."

"Why?" It seemed like a cruel choice to me.

"She's the head of the art department," Fish said.

"But she's blind," I blurted out, and then immediately wished I could catch the words and shove them back in my mouth. "I mean, I'm sure there are ways blind people experience art. I just thought . . ."

Fish said, "Anita isn't blind. She has seizures."

"Oh," I said, blushing. I was relieved that we'd clarified things before I met Anita and said something stupid in front of her. "How does a dog help with that?"

"Well," Fish said, "the hope is that Matisse will get to know

Anita so well he'll be able to detect the slight changes that can happen before a seizure, before Anita can even tell what's going on. But that's really going to depend on their relationship. Matisse's abilities to pick up on the signs and Anita's ability to pick up on Matisse's warnings are going to be key." Every time Fish said Matisse's name, the dog looked at him with full attention. "You can't train a dog to detect seizures. But we have worked with him on the usual guide dog obedience and behavior. He'll carry her medication and an emergency cell phone in his vest, so she can access them if she needs to call for help. He'll lick her face to try to keep her alert. Things like that."

Fish put his hand on Matisse's side to keep him stable as he made a sharp turn. "And also, just knowing that he's going to be there is an amazing comfort. It's so scary not knowing if or when another seizure is going to happen. So Matisse gives her some peace of mind."

"Wow," I said. "And you've trained him to do all of this?"

"Yeah," Fish said, smiling shyly. "Matisse lived with a family who volunteered to help raise him and train him until he was about a year old, and then I started working with him. Since Anita is local, we've been working together for a while. People who don't live close enough usually come out and stay for a week and go through our program, but Anita has been a part of the whole training process. This is the last little bit. I'm going to take Anita through her usual campus routes so we can troubleshoot and see if there are any issues with taking a dog in and out of the buildings where she works. We'll do a seizure drill in her office, and then Matisse gets to go home with her."

"So you work with him all this time and then you have to give him up?" I said.

Fish nodded. "That's always the best part and the hardest part. It's easier now. I've worked with so many dogs. And I'll just jump right into working with the next group of puppies. The first few dogs I worked with—it killed me when I had to hand them over." He glanced at Matisse. "But I'll get to check in with Anita and Matisse from time to time."

When we got to the campus, Fish drove to the art building and pulled into a space in the far corner of the parking lot. When Fish unbuckled the seatbelt harness and gave the okay, Matisse followed Fish out the driver's side door. Fish told him to sit, and then knelt down and pressed his forehead to Matisse's nose. I stood at the back of the truck, to give them a moment. I heard him say, "This is it, buddy. You be a good boy, okay?" and felt tears well up in my eyes. I used the corner of my sleeve to soak them up before Fish could see. I didn't want to be a big emotional mess when I was just a bystander. Fish probably needed someone to be strong and make him laugh when this was all over. He didn't need me getting weepy.

"All right," Fish said, getting up. "Okay, Matisse."

We walked to the art building together. Matisse watched Fish for direction and didn't pull on his leash or try to sniff any of the other people around us. It was obvious that he was working and took his work seriously.

"Hi, Matisse," Anita said, when we walked into her office. Matisse's tail wagged.

"Okay," Fish said, and dropped the leash. Matisse ran over to Anita and licked her face. "Anita, this is my friend Jessie. She's here just in case we need an extra set of hands."

"Great," Anita said, standing up from the piles of paperwork at her desk. She was wearing dark blue jeans and a worn blue work shirt that showed a history of her work in paint splatters. Her blond hair was piled high on top of her head in a messy bun. She wiped her hands on her jeans and said, "Nice to meet you, Jessie," shaking my hand. Her fingernails were stained with paint. It made me jealous. I wanted a life where it made sense for me to be messy like that.

"Nice to meet you," I said.

We went through a condensed version of Anita's day. I stood in for students or coworkers whenever needed, so Fish could direct Anita. It was the kind of thing that would normally make me feel awkward, but I was too fascinated watching them work to bother being self-conscious.

We put our heads together to brainstorm when a piece of furniture or the layout of a room posed a problem. We made sure there was a good spot for Matisse next to Anita in every classroom, conference room, and studio she spent time in.

When we walked into the graduate student studio, I gasped. Tall windows. Hardwood floors. The smell of paint and turpentine. "It's a gorgeous space!" I said. "This light!"

I had taken as many art classes as I could in college, squeezed in whenever I could. Senior year, I even emptied my bank account to take advanced painting so I could finish my minor in studio art. It put me over the credits covered by tuition, and there was no way either of my parents would have been supportive of me getting an art minor. Spending the afternoon in the studio, letting everything I'd ever felt come out on a canvas, was the happiest I'd ever been. Having that sense of purpose to create made everything else feel easier.

"Do you paint?" Anita asked.

"I did," I said. "I'd like to again. I minored in studio art in college. But then work got in the way after I graduated."

"What do you do now?" she asked.

"I'm in PR," I said.

"You could always go back," Anita said, with a mischievous
smile. "We like our MFA students to have a little life experience
under their belts. Having a PR background is a fabulous bonus. So
much of any artist's job these days is knowing how to get their
work out there."

"I didn't know you painted," Fish said.

"I started in college," I said nervously, trying to cover for the
slip. It felt like the biggest lie I'd told so far. I'd been painting for
as long as I could remember. The only time in my life when I
didn't paint was while I was with Deagan. It had been almost a
year since I'd sat in the dining area of my apartment, with the
windows open, and the paints set out in front of me waiting to
become something. Deagan complained about the smell of turpentine and the stains on my hands, and eventually it just seemed like
a hassle to paint. I lost the sense of joy I'd had about painting
when the whole time I was working I knew that Deagan would be
annoyed.

"Well," Fish said, "it makes sense. You always took such great
pictures."

"I'd love to see your slides," Anita said.

"I don't have any with me," I said, "but I do have a few pictures on my phone." I'd taken photos before I moved my paintings
into storage over the summer. I turned my phone on, ignoring the
voicemail notifications, and held it close while I scrolled through
the photos, just in case there was something incriminating in my

albums. I found the series of paintings I'd done for my final project at school and handed my phone to Anita. She scrolled through them with Fish looking over her shoulder.

"Wow, Jess," Fish said. "I had no idea!"

Thankfully the first picture after my paintings was just a photo of me and Luanne at the Lilac Festival. Nothing dangerous.

"It's hard to evaluate work on such a small screen, of course," Anita said, handing back my phone, "but I like your aesthetic. Have you considered an MFA?"

"Look at you," Fish said, elbowing her. "Always the recruiter."

"I haven't thought about it," I said. "But I'm reevaluating a lot of things right now."

"Well," Anita said, "I'm here if you have questions."

After we'd gone through the studio and brainstormed potential issues and ways to maneuver with Matisse around the easels and supplies, we were done with our tour of Anita's day. I left the room while they did the seizure drill in Anita's office. Anita seemed embarrassed to have to pretend to have a seizure, so I asked where the bathroom was and left them to work.

I walked down the hall and went back to the studio. I stared at the easels and the huge rolls of canvas. I studied the paint stains on the floorboards. I sat on a stool in the corner and closed my eyes and thought about the things I would paint, imagining the feel of paint on brush, brush on canvas, the way a tightly stretched canvas gives just a little. Whenever I'd pictured myself married to Deagan, something about it always felt fuzzy. I couldn't picture myself at Levi & Plato, getting promoted, having my own office. But I could picture myself in this studio, painting, so clearly. I felt like it was where I was supposed to be.

A student came in with a jar full of brushes and a big black portfolio. She had long brown hair twisted into a braid, and was wearing a shapeless green dress. She had earbuds in and hummed to herself.

"Oh shit!" she said, when she saw me. "Sorry! Sorry! You startled me. I was in my own little world."

"Me too," I said, and got up.

"Don't feel like you have to leave. I didn't mean to interrupt you."

"No," I said, "I was on my way out."

Fish and Anita were done with the drill when I got back to the office. They were both praising Matisse. "Good boy!" Anita said, beaming.

Fish had a sad, longing look on his face.

"We're going to give you a moment," Anita said to Fish, and hooked her arm into mine. When we got out into the hallway, she said, "Here's my card. Call me. And I mean it. I think your combination of art and business talents could bring a lot to the program."

When Fish and Matisse emerged from the studio, Fish's eyes were red. "Here you go," he said, handing the leash over to Anita.

Anita smiled. "You . . . ," she said, kissing Fish on the cheek and giving him a big hug. "You just gave me my life back." When she pulled away, she was crying too, which of course made me teary.

I held Fish's hand on the walk back to the parking lot. As soon as he was safely inside the truck, he leaned over and buried his head in my shoulder. "I guess I lied," he said. "It doesn't get that much easier. But it's the best thing I can do, you know?"

"I'm so proud of you," I said.

He sniffed really hard and then wiped his face with his sleeve.

He took a deep breath and started the truck. "You don't get to make fun of me for this, Jess."

"I wouldn't dream of it," I said.

"It's not exactly the most masculine thing ever, to go around crying about a dog."

"What I'm amazed by," I said, "is that you're willing to put yourself through this over and over again so you can help people. It's kind of hot." I smiled at him.

"You know," he said, smiling, "I think Myra is still at work."

"I don't know," I said. "I don't know if I can do it in Grammie's bed."

"Who needs a bed?" he said.

◆

We didn't even make it upstairs. Fish kissed me the second we walked into the living room. The curtains were open, so we stumbled into the kitchen, shedding clothes as we went. Fish picked me up and sat me on Myra's kitchen counter.

"This is so rude of us!" I said, jumping down and pulling him to the floor with me.

"When did you get polite?" Fish asked, laughing.

"People prepare food up there!"

Fish's whole body shook against mine as he laughed.

I unbuckled his belt and pulled it from his belt loops. The belt smacked against the floor with a loud crack. I hadn't meant for it to.

"Mmm," Fish said, kissing my neck. "You're still a little bit wild."

"Very," I said, biting at his bottom lip. It made sense to go with it.

"**Y**ou," Fish said, when we were lying breathless in a pile of clothes on the kitchen floor, "are—"

My phone rang. I'd forgotten I'd turned it back on. Thankfully, it was just Heather. I picked up.

"Is Fish with you?" she asked, instead of saying hi.

"Yeah," I said. "We're at Myra's."

"How did the dog drop-off go?"

"Good," I said. "Hard."

Fish laughed.

"I mean," I stammered, "I don't know how he does that over and over again."

Fish laughed again. He got up and ran to the bathroom.

"He's amazing, isn't he?" Heather said.

"Yeah," I said, sighing.

"Okay," Heather said. "Tell him we'll be over in five to do the thing. See you, sweetie!"

"What's the thing?" I asked, but she'd already hung up. "What's the thing?" I asked Fish when he came back.

"Was that Heather?"

"Yeah."

"Shit," he said, "we better get dressed. She's always earlier than she says she'll be."

"She said five minutes."

And then the front door opened. My shirt was crazy wrinkled. Fish handed me his sweater to cover it up.

"Hey, guys," Heather said.

"Are you decent?" Robbie called.

"Will you settle for immoral and horribly decadent?" Fish said, walking out of the kitchen to give me an extra second to button up.

I joined them in the living room. Heather had a big grocery bag in one hand and a random assortment of wooden and plastic mixing spoons in the other, like a bouquet.

"Ready to eat your feelings?" Heather handed each of us a carton of ice cream and a spoon. There were three cartons left over. We sat on the couch, put our feet on the coffee table, and opened the cartons.

"To Fish!" Heather said, and put her spoon out. Robbie and Fish clacked spoons with her, and I followed suit.

"Which one did you get, Jess?" Robbie asked.

I looked at the container. "Chocolate Fudge Brownie Fro Yo."

"Shoot," Heather said, taking the container away from me. "I didn't mean to get Fro Yo."

"It's fine," I said.

"No," Fish said, gravely. "It's not."

"It's too close to being healthy," Robbie said, shaking his head. "You can't eat your feelings with health food."

Heather reached into the bag and pulled out a carton of Cookie Dough ice cream. She double-checked the label before handing it to me. "Much better."

I opened the carton and dug in with my wooden spoon. Trying to get the ice cream into my mouth with the long handle was a challenge. Robbie, Heather, and Fish were pros. I didn't comment much, because I wasn't sure how old of a tradition it was. Talking didn't seem to be a part of eating our feelings anyway.

I was a quarter into my ice cream when Heather yelled, "Switch!" and everyone swapped cartons.

"Ew!" Robbie said, after taking a scoop of his new carton. "This one has fruit in it!"

"It's Cherry Garcia," Fish said.

"It's fruit," Robbie said, and swapped cartons with Fish.

"Hey," Fish said.

"Deal," Robbie said.

"I believe we're here for me," Fish said. "I don't think you get to steal my ice cream."

Robbie responded by opening his mouth and waving his tongue around, to show Fish the ice cream he'd just shoveled in.

"Eat your fruit, Fish," Robbie said. "It's good for you. Fiber. Helps you live long and prosper, man."

Fish leaned his head on Robbie's shoulder. "The longer I live, the longer you have to put up with me, dude."

"Good," Robbie said, and shoveled another heaping mixing spoon of ice cream into his face.

We heard Myra's car pull into the driveway. My heart skipped, the way it always did when I heard my mom's car as a kid. The sound of tires on gravel always made me feel like I was about to get in trouble.

"Oh my God," Myra said, as she walked in the door, "the flop sweat!" She lifted her arms and waved at her armpits. "I was so nervous taking about the details on the Blackberry line today! I'm glad we were ironing things out over the phone, because I could not control the sweating!"

She stopped and looked at us. "You're eating your feelings without me?"

"It's what you get for working late," Fish said, waving his spoon at her, dripping ice cream on Robbie's jeans.

"We're meeting Karen at Fish's in an hour," Heather said. "Fire pit. I got salmon and potatoes for hobo dinners. Robbie is going on a beer run if he can ever tear himself away from his Chunky Monkey."

"I believe that's *my* Chunky Monkey," Fish said.

"That's what that was?" Robbie said, moving away from Fish's leg. "I thought it was just a pen in your pocket."

"Robert Marcus Henry!" Heather yelled, but she was smiling.

"Oh my God!" Myra said, laughing. "You guys will never grow up, will you?"

"Not if I can help it." Robbie smiled.

"Okay, well, I'm going to go take a shower." Myra climbed the stairs.

"Cool," Robbie said. "We'll see you over at Fish's."

"Save me some Cookie Dough," Myra called from the top of the stairs.

"Not likely," Heather shouted back.

Robbie and Heather left to pick up the food and grab some beer, and Fish went home to get the fire started. I said I'd stay and wait for Myra, which bought me some time to go back to the basement and snoop through the photos. One thing I'd already learned about Myra was that she took really long showers, and then she took forever to get ready. I didn't even hear the water wheeze through the pipes when she turned the shower on until after everyone had eaten their fill of ice cream and was gone.

I walked down the stairs carefully, trying not to make too much noise, just in case Myra had crazy sonic hearing. I pulled the box off the shelf and opened it, skipping the pictures of Robbie, Heather, Karen, Myra, and Fish and going straight to the photos of Jessie. The anagram Jessies.

I let the rubber band hang on my wrist while I flipped through the pictures again, looking for clues. Jasmine Gores. I looked at Jessie's anagram alter ego in her floppy hat and lace shawl and wondered if I could pretend to be her too. How far had Jessie taken these characters? Was it just for the photographs? Did she ever go out into the world as Jane Rose Migs or Anise Jogrems? And then it occurred to me that maybe Jessie was pretending to be one of them now. Maybe that's how I would find her. It was one last straw to grasp at. Maybe Jasmine Gores or Miss Jean Ogre would show up and answer all my questions. I sat on the floor with the stack of pictures next to me and typed each name into the browser on my phone. My hands shook. If I knew where the real Jessie Morgan was, what I was doing would seem so much worse. But maybe if I found recent pictures of her online, what she'd done would somehow be obvious. Maybe there would be another clue. Something else I could learn to head off Karen's anger.

I went through every single one of the names on the pictures, and unless Jessie Morgan had found a way to morph herself into a six-foot-tall drag queen, I was shit out of luck. I turned off my phone.

The pipes shuddered when Myra finished her shower. I ran up the stairs before she came out of the bathroom and busied myself with cleaning up the sticky ice cream cartons in the living room.

"So," Myra said, running down the stairs, "since we're a little late, I thought we could drive over. If we drink too much, we can always stumble home and get the car tomorrow."

Her hair was still damp from her shower, but she had done her signature black winged eyeliner and was perfectly styled to go to a campfire. Dark blue jeans cuffed to midcalf, unlaced work boots with thick wool socks, and an apple-green sweater with big wooden buttons that looked like it had probably belonged to Grammie.

I was still wearing Fish's sweater, the jeans I'd bought at Myra's shop, and my loafers, which looked ridiculously fancy in this context. There was no way I was going to get my feet back into Jessie's hiking boots or my heels. I felt dowdy in comparison to Myra, but I liked the way Fish's sweater smelled like him and the way the wool scratched my chin.

"What's with the dirty rubber band?" Myra asked. "Trend I haven't heard about yet? Should I be stocking them?"

"Oh," I stammered, taking it off my wrist and dumping it in

one of the empty ice cream cartons I was throwing away. "I don't even know where it came from. I'm a rubber band klepto." I laughed.

"Rubber band klepto?" Myra looked amused.

I told myself that she had no reason to think the rubber band came from the photos downstairs.

"Yeah, you know how some people always swipe pens?" I said. I had no idea where the words spilling out of my mouth were coming from. "I'm like that with rubber bands. If I'm near one, it ends up on my wrist."

"Weirdo," Myra said. She helped me clear the rest of the ice cream mess. "Although, I met this woman who made these studded rubber bracelets. They were recycled bicycle tires. But maybe layers of rubber bands would work too." She nodded like she was trying to move the thought into a place in her head where she'd be able to find it later.

"**S**o what's the deal with you and Karen?" Myra asked when we got in her car to go to Fish's house.

"What do you mean?"

"I mean she never really seemed surprised that you left. She was . . ." Myra rested her right hand on the back of my seat while she backed out of the driveway, and held her thought until we were on the road " . . . smug about it. I always thought she knew something she wasn't telling us, or maybe she even knew where you were. She'd never say that she did or didn't. And she didn't seem happy to see you today."

"You noticed that too?" I said. "Heather didn't seem to notice. I thought I was losing it."

"Well, of course Heather didn't notice," Myra said, laughing. "She's Heather. She wants us all to love each other so much that she puts on blinders to everything else."

I played with a loose thread on Fish's sweater cuff.

Myra aimed the heat vents to blow hot air toward her and shook her hair out with her fingers to get it to dry faster. "So what does Karen have stuck up her butt?"

"To be completely honest," I said, looking at her, "I have no idea."

When we got to Fish's, they'd already started the bonfire. Fish's soon-to-be house was lit up with caged lightbulbs hanging from extension cords.

Robbie balanced on a log, drinking a beer and stoking the fire with a pitchfork. When we got out of the car, he waved the pitchfork in the air and howled at us.

Fish and Karen were sitting on another log near the fire. Karen had her hand on his shoulder and was showing him pictures on her phone. The screen lit up their faces. Fish was smiling, and the way Karen kept tossing her hair made me nervous.

"Hey, guys," Myra said.

"Hey," I said too.

Myra walked up to the house frame, so I did too. My instinct to avoid Karen outweighed my desire to see Fish.

Heather was in the future kitchen, using a piece of plywood laid across two saw horses as a table.

"Hey, girls!" she said, smiling. "Come help!"

She had big hunks of salmon, sliced potatoes and onions, pats of butter, and bunches of herbs laid out on plates in front of her.

"We're doing hobos. I have one more onion to chop, so if you want to set them up, that would be awesome."

"Sure," I said, even though I had no idea what a hobo was in this context.

"I don't want to touch the fish," Myra said.

"What, do I have cooties?" Fish said, walking up behind her, wiping his hands on her back. "Now you do too." Myra laughed and pretended to wipe Fish's cooties off her back in mock disgust.

Fish leaned in to kiss me on the cheek. When I turned around to hug him, I could see Karen, sitting by herself in the firelight, watching us.

"I'll touch the fish," I said to Myra, and I felt a thrill when I watched Fish blush.

"Okay," Myra said. "I'll do the rest."

Myra grabbed a box of aluminum foil from Heather's tote bag and started ripping off big sheets and stacking them at the end of the table.

I hooked my finger into Fish's hand. "How're you doing?" I asked him.

"Better," he said, smiling.

Myra worked fast, layering the onions, potatoes, and other ingredients.

"Okay, your turn," she said, and handed me the first packet.

I let go of Fish's hand and grabbed a slab of slimy salmon. I dropped it in the center of the foil, on top of all the other stuff. Then Fish folded the foil into a neat little packet while I held my slimy hand over the salmon plate and waited for Myra to finish the next one. Heather wore a pair of Fish's safety glasses to keep her from crying while she sliced the rest of the onions. I looked at all of them, at the fire, at the house frame lit up against the night, and felt a longing that hit me so sharply it made my eyes sting.

"I love that we're all together," Myra said, bumping shoulders with me. "The whole family."

I clenched my teeth to keep from crying. As much as I wanted it to be, I knew none of it was mine. Once the week was over, I'd never see them again. I didn't have a family.

"Are you okay?" Fish asked, putting his hand on my back.

"You know," I said carefully, trying to keep my tears in check, "those are strong onions."

"Go up to the big house and wash your face," Heather said. "Sometimes that's the only thing that will work."

I ran up the hill, pushed the front door open, and ran into the bathroom to wash my face with cool water. My mascara ran and my hair got wet. I washed my makeup off with hand soap and wiped under my eyes with toilet paper so I wouldn't get black smudges on the hand towel. My skin felt tight from the soap and my cheeks stung when the tears came on hard. I sat on the floor with my back against the tub and took deep breaths, trying to get myself under control.

I heard the door pop open, and Chip ambled into the room, pushing his big black nose into mine, licking my face with his great big tongue.

"Hey, buddy," I said. He nudged his nose into my armpit and pushed at my side. I felt crazy, but it seemed like he was trying to get me to stand up, so I did. He walked to the door and looked back at me until I followed him and then walked halfway down the hall and looked back until I met up with him. He led me into the living room.

"I thought that was you," Ernie said, from his armchair. I wondered if he'd sent Chip after me. "Are you okay? Sit."

"Onions," I said, sitting on the ottoman next to his feet.

"Did the onions call you names?" Ernie asked. "You look like you got your feelings trampled."

"It's hard," I said slowly, "when you know things can't be the way you want them to be." I knew I was saying too much, but I couldn't stop myself. I needed to confess to someone. I needed to give part of the weight of everything to someone else. "When you can't be who you wish you were."

"Nobody is ever who they want to be right off the bat. Sometimes we have to strip away who we thought we were. And that part really sucks."

"I'm not—" I said, looking Ernie in the eyes, pleading for him to really hear my confession, but he cut me off.

"You'll figure it out," he said, smoothing my hair away from my face with the side of his shaky hand.

I nodded and bit my lip to keep from crying again.

"You're a smart girl. It will all be okay."

"Do you want to come outside?" I asked. "I could help you."

"No," Ernie said. "But could you help me move to the chair over by the window? I love watching all your faces in the firelight."

I lent Ernie my arm to help him stand. Chip followed us closely, like he was ready to step in and help if I needed it.

"Maybe you could send Heather to bring me some food when it's ready?" he asked.

"Of course," I said.

When I went back outside, they were all seated around the campfire. Heather poked at the foil packets with a long stick, turning them to make sure both sides cooked evenly.

Fish patted the log next to him, and I sat down. He put his arm around me, and I snuggled into his chest, determined to soak it all up while it lasted. "Your dad put in his order for dinner," I said. Karen was staring at me. I tried to ignore her and keep my face turned away.

"You're so sweet to check on him," Fish said, kissing me.

"Who the hell are you?" Karen shouted. The way the firelight cast shadows on her sharp brow and bony cheeks made her scowl even more ominous.

I looked at her, trying to think of something to say, but I was too stunned to form words.

"You and Fish?" she said, standing up and walking over to me. "Do you still think he's a sad little puppy dog? Do you still think he's pathetic? You used to joke about the way he followed you around all the time." She let out a sad, sick laugh. "We made bets on whether you could get him to do things for you. And now you're kissing him? You're, like, together now?"

She looked at Fish. "Do you remember all the times you did her homework? That was a calculated thing. She wasn't a damsel in distress. She was playing you."

Fish's arm stiffened, but he kept it around my shoulder.

Karen stood up on the log in front of me. Her voice was so loud that everyone could hear. "And you're all chummy with Heather? You used to call her Half-Wit Heather. You used to laugh about her behind her back."

I couldn't even look at Heather

"Stop," I said softly. "Please."

"And the best part," she said, spitting out the words. "You and Myra are BFFs now? Does she know you broke up her parents' marriage?"

I shook my head. "I don't know what you're talking about," I said, hoping the fact that I really didn't know would show on my face and make her stop. That maybe she'd think she was wrong about whatever it was that had happened.

"You slept with her father, you fucking whore." Karen's eyes were bright and shining.

Myra gasped and clapped her hand over her mouth.

My throat tightened. I couldn't breathe. The smoke from the fire made my lungs burn.

"I caught you. Right before graduation. You saw me." She pointed at me. Tears streamed down her face. "Don't pretend like you didn't. Like you don't know what I'm talking about. You saw me, and you just kept at it. Like you loved getting caught. And now you're here, and I'm supposed to keep your secrets when you're flaunting it in my face?"

Myra ran up the hill and into the house.

"Myra!" Fish called. He got up and followed her, slamming the door behind him. I started to get up, to follow him, but Karen grabbed my shoulder and pushed me back down. I thought she was going to hit me. I squeezed my eyes shut.

"Karen!" Robbie said sharply. "Enough." He put his arm around Heather and they walked up to the house together.

"I'm not—" I started to say.

"You're not anything," Karen said. And then she walked away too.

❧

I ran back to Myra's house. The shock of the pavement shot sparks through my shins. All I could feel were the sparks, the burning in my lungs, a stitch clenching my side in its claws. I kept running like every monster I'd ever imagined had come out from under the bed to chase me.

I let myself in with the Hide-A-Key, shoved all my stuff in my bags, and used the phone in the kitchen to call the Salish Lodge to reserve a room and arrange for the shuttle to pick me up.

Before I left, I took Fish's sweater off. I let myself smell it one more time and then I folded it carefully and left it on the coffee table.

Then I ran down to the basement and took Jessie's photo box. I couldn't help myself.

I walked to the end of the street to meet the shuttle, in case anyone came back to look for me, so I wouldn't have to see them and they wouldn't have to see me. I don't think anyone came after me anyway.

I lay in bed in the hotel room, staring at the television. There was a nature show on about a mama bear and her cub. She nudged his furry little butt over logs and rocks and taught him how to catch fish and which berries were good to eat. She was gentle and attentive and anytime he wandered off, all he had to do was cry out for her and she'd find him. It broke my heart. I flipped the channels, but my brain was in overload. I couldn't make sense of anything on the screen, and eventually I got tired of holding the remote. I rolled over and buried my head in the pillow and cried until I thought I might suffocate. My head throbbed.

Someone on the TV said, "The great thing about this product? It's all about what isn't there. No germs! No bacteria! No—"

And then I had a thought. A brilliant, crazy thought that got me out of bed. I dug through my bags until I found the box of Jessie's pictures.

This time I looked at the list she'd scribbled on the back of the envelope. I lined up the photos in the order of the names. It wasn't about the pictures that were there. It was about the pictures that were missing.

Jessie used the pictures as her portfolio for school. Maybe the ones in the box were the outtakes. The ones she didn't use. So the best anagram portrait was the one she'd sent. The one that wasn't there. I laid them out on the bed. All the faces of Jessie stared back at me. I matched each picture to a name on the envelope.

The only names without pictures were Ms. Rease Jigno and Maree Jigsons. I pulled out my laptop and searched for Rease. There were no results. But Maree Jigsons was on Facebook. Her profile picture was a dark silhouette of a person on the beach at sunset. There was no light on her face, but it had to be Jessie. Maree Jigsons wasn't a real name.

Since we weren't friends, I could only see the very basic details of her profile. She lived in Portland. She was a University of Oregon alum. She worked at a place called Morgan Studios. I found the website. Morgan Studios was a photography studio that appeared to specialize in portraits. It was owned by J. E. Morgan, but her bio only said that she was a University of Oregon alum and had studied abroad for a year after college as an assistant to a photographer I'd never heard of. She hadn't posted a picture with her bio.

It wasn't an airtight cover, but it's not like she was in the witness-protection program. She just didn't want to be found by her high school friends. There were enough J. E. Morgans in the world for her to stay lost. And her friends had stopped looking for her a long time ago. One of the girls I worked with used her mother's maiden name on Facebook instead of her real last name, because she didn't want her ex-boyfriend looking her up. It had to be more than coincidence linking Maree Jigsons to a photographer named J. E. Morgan.

I called down to the front desk. "I'm going to need to rent a car in the morning," I said. "Can you help me with that?"

I watched her through the window for a long time. Morgan Studios had a small seating area and a reception desk in the storefront. Larger-than-life-sized portraits hung on the walls: A grandmother. A biker with a furry chest wearing a leather vest. A baby crying. A businessman with a spot the size of a tennis ball on his tie.

She walked around straightening magazines, threw an empty paper cup from a side table into the trash can behind the desk. She looked up at the portraits and studied them for a moment before walking over to straighten the one of the baby. She did look like me. Sort of. She was taller. She had more curves and honey-brown hair, with a few well-placed blond streaks, that fell in curls past her shoulders. She wore a plain black T-shirt, a gray cotton scarf wrapped loosely around her neck several times, and tall black boots, with tons of buckles, over ripped, faded jeans. She didn't see me standing in the doorway outside, watching her through the glass. She was in her own world.

Jessie drummed on the desk. I wondered what song she had stuck in her head. I wondered if we actually had anything in common.

I waited for her to look up or notice me, but she didn't. I finally worked up the courage to walk in. She looked up when the bell on the door jingled.

"I don't do weddings," she said, her voice was throaty and

scratched. "I shoot babies, kids, portraits, corporate stuff, and other events. I even do bat mitzvahs."

She smiled. "I don't *shoot* babies," she said, as if she thought that's why I looked like I was about to go into shock. "I photograph them." She hadn't gotten a nose job. She had a thin gold hoop that curled into her nostril. Her smile was closemouthed but reckless. The wild look in her eyes and the matter-of-fact tone to her voice seemed to say that she'd done it all and seen it all, and, yes, it was fantastic. I could see why she'd gotten away with so much when she was younger.

There wasn't a good way to lead into what I had to tell her. There was nothing I could say to soften it. It wasn't like I could ask about her portrait rates and then casually say, "By the way, I'm a Jessie Morgan impersonator."

"So," I said, taking a deep breath. "I've been pretending to be you. I went to your high school reunion." I handed her the photo box.

Her eyes widened. She took the box from me. Her hands were shaking. She gripped the box tightly to make them stop. Her knuckles turned white. Her lips tightened. She studied my face without saying anything.

"I fell into it," I said. "It wasn't planned. I was there for a conference, and Myra saw me and thought I was you."

She smiled. It seemed like she was trying very hard to keep her shock to herself. "Yeah, I can see it," she said, gesturing to my eyes. "In here. Maybe we have the same chin too." She hugged the box to her chest and drummed the sides of it with her fingers.

"I'm sorry," I said.

"Do they know?" she asked. Her voice was a raspy whisper. She cleared her throat. "That you're not me?" She looked past me, out the window, like she was trying to pretend she didn't really care about the answer. She blinked a few times.

"No, but Karen told them about the affair with Myra's dad."

"Shit," she said softly. There was a hint of weariness, like an acknowledgment that things eventually catch up with a person. She put the box on the desk. She started to open it, looked at me, and then put the lid back on.

"I'm so sorry," I said.

She was really quiet for a moment. She looked at her hands. "Well, I'm assuming Karen told everyone because she was being bitchy to you, right?"

"Yeah."

"At least she didn't let that bomb drop because she was mad at Myra. She thought she was hurting me. That's slightly better than if she was trying to hurt My. Right?" She pulled a pack of cigarettes from the desk drawer and gestured to me to follow her.

She was like the Pied Piper. It didn't even occur to me to do anything other than follow her. The fact that she hadn't really reacted much to my confession made me all the more fascinated. I think she knew that.

We walked through the studio, a big room with white walls and backdrops. With every step, the heels of her boots clacked against the floor. The buckles rattled. "With Karen," she said, calling back to me over her shoulder, "all you can hope for is lesser shades of bitchy."

She grabbed a leather jacket from a hook by the back door and put it on as she walked outside.

"It was going to come out eventually," she said, sitting down on the back stoop. She pulled a cigarette out and stuck it in her mouth. "Mmph?" She grunted and held the box out to me.

I shook my head.

She cackled. "You can't be my doppelgänger and not even smoke. It's ridiculous. That!" she said, waving the cigarette box at me. "That is how they should have known." She acted like she'd expected all along that there would be people out there who would want to be her. Like she'd seen it coming. The more we talked, the less I was sure if it was a ploy to hide her discomfort or sheer arrogance.

I decided not to tell her about me and Robbie and his last two cigarettes. I would keep that part for myself.

She lit her cigarette, took a deep drag, and blew smoke up to the sky. "I'm actually impressed Karen kept it a secret for so long. I assumed they already knew." She got quiet again. "How are they?" she whispered. She cleared her throat. "Are they good?" Her eyes sparkled when she asked.

I told her about Myra and her store, and Robbie and Heather, and how Karen had two kids. It was hard. Like I was giving them back to her. Like I would fade completely once I did.

"And Fish?" she asked.

I didn't want to tell her about Fish. He was the one I wanted to keep the most.

"He trains guide dogs," I said. "Mr. Foster had a stroke."

"Mr. Foster!" Jessie said, laughing. "That man hated me."

"Really?"

She didn't even react to the fact that he'd had a stroke.

"Yeah. I get it now. I used to see him as this bad guy for not wanting Fish to hang around me. But he just loves his kid. I have a little boy. I totally get it."

My jaw dropped.

"He's four," Jessie said. "God! He's not like Myra's half

brother or anything." She laughed. "He's only four. But if a girl like me ever strings Eddie along, I'll rip her to pieces." She stubbed her cigarette out on the stoop, leaving a black mark behind, and flicked it across the alley, making it someone else's problem.

We went back into the studio. She pulled a bottle of scotch out of the bottom drawer of her worktable. "My parents didn't give a shit. Fish was lucky to have a dad who hated me."

We sat on the floor, drinking from paper cups. I stopped after a few sips. She did not. I looked around at all the photography equipment. Everything looked shiny and new. There was a row of camera cases on one counter and an enormous computer monitor on a desk in the corner. She was doing well for herself.

"Did you really climb out the bathroom window after Fish told you he loved you?" I asked.

Jessie caught herself just before she spit a mouthful of booze. She swallowed with a loud gulp. "No! No!" She shook her head and laughed. "I said I had to go to the bathroom, but I really just went to the parking lot and drove away."

"Yeah," I said, thinking of Fish in his graduation gown, heartbroken. "That's totally different."

"Hey, Fake Jessie," she said, pointing her finger at me. "I don't think you get to judge."

"True," I said.

"What was I supposed to do? I was sleeping with my best friend's father. Fish was telling me he loved me. Myra's mother threatened to tell Myra and my parents if she ever had to even look at me again." She sniffed and wiped her nose with her hand. "I'd already made all the bad decisions. It's not like I could fix anything. I didn't crawl out the bathroom window, but if that was the only way out? I would have freaking crawled through the sewer if I had to. I was a caged animal."

We talked for almost two hours. Every time I thought I hated her, she won me over again by saying something that was kind or smart or showed the slightest hint of vulnerability. And it all fit. She was Jessie *Fucking* Morgan. She was exactly the kind of person who would have stolen her dad's credit card and checked into a hotel, worn a tube top and a miniskirt to give a debate speech, sang karaoke even though she had a terrible voice, and thrown a rock through Robbie's window. She was exactly the kind of person who would leave everyone behind. It made sense.

"You could come back with me," I said. I don't know if I wanted her to say she would or she wouldn't. I don't know what I wanted to happen.

"If screwing Myra's dad was the worst of what I'd done," Jessie said, "I might be able to go back and see them again. But I fucked everything up and then I jumped ship." She had tears in her eyes. Her nostrils flared. "I can't make up for that. They gave me every-thing that was solid in my life. I never even said good-bye." She wiped her cheek with the back of her hand and wiped her hand on her jeans.

"Maybe you can talk to them. Fix things. They're such good people."

"They're such good people," she said, laughing. "I fucking know they're good people." She pointed a finger at me. "You don't have to tell me they're good people. I fucking know."

I felt like I should be afraid of her, but I wasn't. I felt sorry for her.

She stretched her legs out in front of her and rolled her feet back and forth, the buckles of her boots clanged against the beat-up hardwood floor. "They even tried to find me. Myra sent me an e-mail asking if I was her 'dear friend Jessie Morgan from Mount Si,' and I never wrote her back. I can't fix that. And it wasn't a one-time thing with Myra's dad. It was six months of nights."

"God!" I said, before I could stop myself.

"Oh," she said, nodding. "Yeah, you didn't know that part, did you? Six months. She's never going to forgive me. It will always be a failing situation."

"But you were a kid. An adult took advantage of you. Maybe Myra will understand that."

"You know . . . ," Jessie said, pulling the box of cigarettes from the pocket of her jacket. "You know . . ." Her voice trailed off. She took a cigarette out and lit it, even though we were inside. She blew smoke at the ceiling. "Oh, don't even start with me, Fake Jessie. Just don't."

"Jenny."

"Whatever. It's not like you know. It's not like you were there." She was quiet for a long time, smoking. Staring into space. I didn't know what to say, so I just sat next to her, watching the smoke curl into the air and disappear.

"But do me a favor," she said finally, as if we were still midconversation. "If you see them again, tell them I'm sorry." She stubbed her cigarette butt out on the bottom of her boot, ashes falling to the floor. "I love them. It's just that I'm not the same Jessie anymore, and I really can't go back."

When we walked out of the studio, I noticed, on the wall, a framed picture from that shoot she did in high school. Karen, Robbie, Heather, Myra, and Fish standing in a line, smushing their faces together. Jessie wasn't in the picture.

drove all the way back to Mount Si and tried to find my way to McCleary's. Myra had pointed it out when we drove past. It was Wednesday night. They would be there. They had to be there. Myra talked about how they spent every Thursday at McCleary's Pub. Tuesday was movie night. Sunday was breakfast. Thursday was drinks and bar food.

I made a few wrong turns, but then I found it. Just off the main strip of downtown Mount Si. Fish's truck, Heather's purple car, Myra's old Honda—all lined up in the gravel parking lot. I parked next to Fish.

They didn't notice me when I walked in the bar. I already had tears in my eyes. My legs were shaking. I hadn't eaten much all day, which was adding to my feet feeling less than stable on the dusty, warped floorboards. I stood in the corner by the door and watched them.

Karen was nowhere to be seen. I hoped she was home with her kids. Myra was trying to get Robbie to eat a piece of celery from a plate of wings. She had it pressed against his lips, and he was shaking his head like a baby trying to avoid a mouthful of peas. Heather's face was bright red from laughing so hard. Fish stood up and tried to pry Robbie's mouth open. But then he saw me and stopped. He stood up straight. His smile faded. Myra and Heather turned to look at what he'd seen. Their smiles disappeared too.

Robbie took the opportunity to grab the celery away from

Myra, but then he realized why they'd stopped. "You're back," he said.

I walked over, each step taking more strength than the last.

"Well," Robbie said, "out with it," like he just wanted everything settled so he could move on.

"I'm so sorry," I said.

"No," Myra said. "I'm sorry. I'm not okay with so much of this. With the lying. With the things you said. But it was a long time ago. And my father—" Her voice cracked. "I'm so sorry he took advantage of you. I can't believe how—"

"Don't you dare apologize to her!" Karen said, storming across the bar from the ladies' room. "She was eighteen. She knew what she was doing. It's not like she was some sad little wallflower who didn't know any better. She's a predator and a liar. She's a total whore. "

"Karen!" Fish said sharply.

"Listen, please!" I was shocked my voice even existed anymore. "I'm not—"

"You are," Karen said. "You broke up Myra's family."

"It's more complicated than that," Myra said. "It's not a black and white—"

"Bullshit," Karen said. "You don't fuck your friend's dad. I don't care how complicated things are."

"I didn't," I said.

"I SAW YOU!" Karen yelled. The bar was mostly empty, but the few scraggly looking guys in the corner turned to stare.

"No," I said. I was shaking badly. My teeth chattered. "You saw Jessie."

They stared at me blankly. Except for Karen, who gasped and clapped her hand over her mouth. "Oh my God," she said softly, her eyes getting wide. She stared at my face. "Oh my God." She pointed at me.

"What?" Heather said.

"I'm not Jessie," I said softly.

"What?" Robbie said, laughing. "Jess?"

Myra stared at me. She rested her hand on her nose.

I couldn't even look at Fish. He was still standing behind Robbie. I couldn't bring my eyes to meet his.

"I'm not Jessie Morgan," I said. "I was here for a conference and Myra saw me in the elevator and I just—" I sobbed.

They all stared at me. No one said a word for a long time. Finally Myra said, "How could you?"

"I needed a friend." It was so sad and sick and gross. I wanted to leave, but I felt like I owed them as much of an explanation as they wanted from me. I didn't deserve to be comfortable. I didn't deserve to run away.

"I let you stay in my house!" Myra covered her face with her hands, but her big brown eyes showed in the vees between her fingers. "I stayed in your room at the lodge. We took you hiking. I told you . . . everything."

It was stupid, but I'd had this image in my head that they would all be mad at Jessie and then I'd say, "Surprise! I'm not Jessie," and suddenly they'd be so happy that I wasn't the person they were mad at, the fact that I was an impostor wouldn't be such a biggie. But, of course, they all looked horrified and hurt and like I was the most grotesque monster they'd ever seen. Except for Karen. She had a smirk on her face, and she clenched her hands into fists. I worried, again, that she might punch me.

Finally Heather said, "So who are you?" Her big blue eyes were filled with tears.

I know I said things. Words came out of my mouth. I offered some semblance of an explanation, but even as I was talking, all I could think about was how it wasn't enough. There was no excuse. There was no good explanation. I wanted to start with my fourth grade birthday party and tell them about every single moment that ever made me want to be somebody else. I wanted to make them understand that it was easier to figure out who Jessie was than to figure out who I am. But those were words they didn't need. It wasn't their job to hear them.

After I gave them the basic stats on Jenny Shaw, I said, "I'm so sorry," and it felt like the tiniest, most pathetic little speck. Like a grain of sand.

"I found Jessie," I said. "She's in Portland. I went to see her. She's sorry too."

None of them would look at me. "I know," I said, "that this isn't going to make sense, that it isn't going to seem right, but being here, with you, who I've been as Jessie"—I wiped my eyes—"is the truest part of me. You guys don't know how lucky you are. You don't know how important you are. You're superheroes. You saved each other. I wanted you to save me too. I wanted to belong to you. To know what it felt like to have friends like you."

There was nothing else I could say. The tears were coming too hard, and Karen still looked like she might hit me. So I ran out to the parking lot.

I dropped my keys when I tried to open the door of my rental car, and when I bent down to pick them up, I saw Fish standing outside, under the overhang, watching me.

"I'm not Jessie," I said, walking back to him, "but I have never felt this way about anyone before. I kept pretending I was her, because I have never wanted to be with someone so much. Being

with you is the most right I've ever felt. Just being around you"—
I tried to hold back a sob—"makes everything better."

He had tears in his eyes. I could see the muscles in his jaw tighten.

"I know what I did was so wrong," I said. "And I know you might think I'm a stranger now, but I'm not. You know me. You know who I am. I promise you, it wasn't fake. Some of it might not have been true, but none of it was fake. Who I really am is someone who thinks you are the best person I've ever met. I am someone who doesn't want to let you go."

There were tears dripping from my chin. He reached out and wiped them away with his sleeve. He studied my face, and I thought for a second that he might kiss me. He didn't.

He shoved his hands in his pockets and sighed. "I know you want me to say something," he said softly, "but I can't. I don't know what to say." He looked at the door to the bar and back at me. "I think you should probably leave."

I nodded, my throat too choked with tears to talk. I turned and walked away. When I got to the car, I looked back to see if he was still there, but he'd already gone inside.

took a cab home from the Rochester airport. It was late and dark and cold. The cab driver talked on his cell phone to his wife or girlfriend. "One more fare and then I'll be home, sweetheart," he said. He actually called her sweetheart, and it made me feel horribly lonely. All I was going home to was a cat, and he didn't even like me.

When I got into my apartment, there was mail stacked up just inside the door and the suitcase I'd left in Deagan's car was waiting for me at the end of the hallway, his set of keys to my apartment balanced on top. I looked for a note, but there wasn't one. Mr. Snuffleupagus eyed me warily, perched on my desk. He had food in his bowl, but my leaving him for a week was enough of an injustice to earn me the cold shoulder.

I sorted through the mail. The notice for my lease renewal was in the stack. I thought I'd be moving in with Deagan. It was something I'd planned on. And even though I wasn't moving in with him, I didn't want to sign away another year. I needed something new. I didn't want to keep trying to be someone I wasn't.

I turned the TV on and stretched out on the couch to watch *Family Ties* reruns. Eventually Snuffy gave up his standoff and cuddled up with me.

I woke up to the sound of a key in the door to my apartment. I sat up on the couch. "Who's there?" I called. My heart was pounding.

"I'm glad you're alive," Luanne said, storming into the living room. "It'll make it more satisfying to kill you."

"What?" I said, rubbing my eyes, feeling my mascara stick to my hand.

"How hard is it to return a fucking phone call? Send a text? Something!" She looked like she hadn't slept. Her hair was a rat's nest, and she was wearing an oversized Ithaca Bombers sweatshirt. I'd never seen Luanne in a sweatshirt before.

"Oh," I said, realizing my phone was still off. At first it was a conscious thing. My phone felt like a ticking time bomb. I didn't want to know what hateful messages lurked in my voicemail. Then I didn't want to know what messages weren't there. I didn't want to know for sure that Fish hadn't called. That Myra and Heather and Robbie hadn't either. I didn't want to deal with any of it. And then I just sort of forgot that I had a phone. It was easier than I ever would have thought. I'd spent so much time with my phone fused to my hand, dealing with clients, updating Twitter accounts. But the silence, the time with my thoughts, the time to read magazines in the airport and sketch pictures on cocktail napkins on the plane, the time to just be with myself, was calming. It was a luxury I hadn't been ready to give it up. "My phone wasn't on."

"Where were you?"

"At the spa," I said.

"Bullshit," she said. "I called the spa when you didn't pick up your cell phone, after I called eighty million times. After I locked myself out of your apartment and the complex manager wouldn't let me back in to feed your damn cat."

"How'd you get in?"

"Deagan," she said. "I had to call Deagan to have him come

over and let me in." She gestured to my suitcase, still standing in the hallway.

"I'm sorry," I said.

"Where were you?" she said.

I didn't want to explain, but I didn't want to lie anymore. I told her everything.

"You're joking, right?" she said. "Who does that?" She had a panicked look on her face, like she was scared of me. Like I might suddenly morph into a horrible, slimy beast. It's not like I had thought she'd be accepting and understanding, but I didn't expect her to look at me with such disgust.

"I didn't want to be myself anymore. I wanted to be Jessie. I wanted to have friends like that. I wanted to have that kind of life."

"You have me," she said.

"It's so conditional," I said. "With you, with Deagan, with my mother."

"Don't group me in with them," she said. "That's completely unfair. I'm the one who's here. I'm the one who's calling hotels and hospitals and trying to figure out where the fuck you are when you won't answer your damn phone. Don't you dare put me in the same category as your mother."

"I just mean that we're not friends the way we pretend we are. We're not. I don't even think we said two words to each other in college. We never would have kept in touch if you hadn't moved to Rochester."

"But I did."

"And you acted like we were dear old friends, and I let you because I really needed a dear old friend. But sometimes I'm not sure you even like me. You compete with me. You love to take me down a peg. You love to comment on every little thing I do—everything I don't do the way you would. You're my friend as long as I never ever upstage you. It's not the same thing."

"Well," she said, staring at the ceiling, "well, at least I don't run around like a freak pretending to be someone I'm not." She slammed her copy of my keys down on my desk and walked out.

I hauled myself off the couch and climbed into bed, dragging Mr. Snuffs with me under protest. I stayed there for most of the day, not quite asleep, not quite awake, listening to the sounds of my upstairs neighbor's evening routine: vacuum, run the dishwasher, take a shower, and then the trumpets from the CBS *Evening News*. She never had friends over. I never heard two voices, two sets of footsteps. And for the first time, I wondered about her instead of just being annoyed by her. I wondered if she was happy in her routine. I wondered if she'd ever dreamed of anything more.

I got up, grabbed a jacket and my car keys, and left to go to my storage space so I could pick up my paints and paintings.

❦

I stayed up all night painting. I started with a painting of the clearing, the way the sky looked when Robbie and I were smoking. The clouds and the little spots that were clear, where the stars shone through. I painted the bonfire. I painted Fish's house frame and spent the longest time mixing the right color for the yellow glow from the lightbulbs. I painted the living room in Grammie's house and the couch we sat on when we ate our feelings and Myra's store with the gorgeous chandelier. I tried to capture every detail of all the places I'd been to with Jessie's friends, but I couldn't bring myself to paint them, to capture their faces. They weren't mine.

I sketched out the chandelier from Myra's store again and

played with the shapes until I turned it into a big ornate A with crystals that trailed down to form a C below it, and then I worked out different ways to spell the rest of Aberly Cadaberly. I settled on a swooping script like a signature, and painted the logo on a canvas board. I didn't know if I'd ever get up the courage to send it to her, but painting it made me feel like maybe I'd have the chance to talk to her again someday.

Monday morning sucked. I'd spent the weekend painting and I was still on Seattle time, so when my alarm went off, it felt like it was really three a.m. All my clean work clothes were still in the suitcase Deagan left, which was still sitting exactly where he'd left it. They exploded all over the floor when I unzipped the case. And every single piece of clothing, from pantyhose to underwear, was completely and totally wrinkled. I hung the clothes I wanted to wear in the bathroom while I showered, but it didn't do much to relax the wrinkles.

I was so tired that I could barely keep my eyes open while I tried to iron my blouse, and I rammed the hot iron into myself, leaving a thin, angry red line across my belly.

My fingernails were still stained from painting, but I didn't notice until I was in the car on my way to work. I ran my nails over my teeth to try to get the paint out from underneath them, but it didn't do any good and I was left with the base, musky taste of pthalo green in my mouth.

I made it to work on time, but I should have gotten in early. On time basically counted as late in the realm of associate account executives.

Someone had unloaded a case of Ivolushun on my desk. Candy-colored bottles of cheap booze littered every free inch. There were piles and piles of memos and faxes and reports. My voicemail was full, and I didn't even bother to turn my computer on. I didn't want to know about the e-mail situation.

I went to get myself a cup of coffee. Luanne stared at me from her cubicle, but when I gave her a weak smile, she looked away.

As soon as I got back to my desk, mug full and ready to sort through all the piles, my phone rang.

"Jenny, it's Monica. Can you come in here for a sec?" She had her metered work tone in effect, so I couldn't tell if it was good news or bad news or something completely inconsequential.

I hung up the phone and took the biggest swig of coffee I could manage, before dashing down the hall to Monica's office.

Monica leaned against the front of her desk with her arms crossed and her long legs stretched in front of her. I had heard rumors that she'd modeled when she was younger, and I believed them. She knew how imposing she was. She knew how to make someone feel less put together, less shiny, less pretty without even saying a word.

"Oh," she said, with the slightest hint of surprise on her face when I sat down. "That haircut is an improvement. You look nice."

"Thank you," I said, wondering what her thoughts had been on my hair before the cut.

"I heard from my friend Olga that you missed the last day of meetings." She crossed one slender ankle over the other, flashing the red sole of her shoe. I wondered if she ever got airplane bloat. "Is there a good reason for this?"

I shook my head. "There really wasn't anything worthwhile happening in those meetings."

She raised an eyebrow at me. I realized there wasn't a point in being anything other than honest, not about my extracurricular activities, of course, but about the conference. I sighed. "It was just people talking about concepts without ever saying anything practical. Throwing out big ideas and making umbrella statements with no thought of implementation. I mean, really, how much time can you spend making keyword clouds on the dry-erase board and call it working? I'm so sick of all of it! No one is really accomplishing anything!" I realized, as soon as I stopped talking, that I'd gone one step too far. I waited for the nerves to kick in, but they didn't. The truth of the matter was that I didn't care anymore.

I expected some sort of reprimand. Penance. Grunt work on the Ivolushun account or making a clippings report for one of Luanne's clients.

Instead she just looked at me with what appeared to be genuine concern and said, "Jenny, do you think you're in the wrong line of work?"

"Yes," I said calmly. "I really do."

"You could be the best at this if you wanted to be."

"Maybe being good at something doesn't matter if your heart isn't in it," I said.

She nodded.

"Why don't we consider this my notice," I said.

"Can you stay through the Ivolushun launch?"

"Sure," I said. I didn't want to. The last thing I felt like doing was pimping an alcoholic energy drink that tasted like rancid cough syrup. But I needed the time and the paychecks to figure out what should come next. And I'd agreed to take the account to begin with. I needed to follow through, not for the boneheads at Ivolushun, but for Monica.

"Thank you, Jenny," she said, smiling a very tired smile.

I got up and walked out of her office. I took a deep breath when I got past her door. I'd actually made the decision I'd desperately wanted to make.

Ilooked for other grad programs. I really did. I researched and submitted and applied. I studied work by various instructors. I called former professors for recommendations. I sent slides. I had phone interviews. But in the end, the best program for me was in Seattle. I loved the work the students were producing. I'd written a paper on one of the painting and drawing professor's thesis projects when I was at Ithaca, and I couldn't let go of the idea of being his student.

I painted at night, after work, in the makeshift studio space I cleared for myself in the dining area of my apartment, and dreamed of the way the light streamed through the windows in the grad student studio. I finally gave myself permission to go for what I wanted with everything I had, and everything else fell in line behind my goal. I only had three weeks until the application deadline.

I left work at five every day, leaving the other associate account executives to play the "who leaves last?" game. My work didn't suffer for not putting in the correct amount of overtime penance. Caring less made me more productive. I got as much done in an eight-hour day as I used to in ten or twelve hours. I picked up dinner at Wegmans on my way back to my apartment, and stayed up until well past midnight, painting. On weekends, I ate cereal and ordered pizza. I slept in my paint-covered clothes, and worked with more focus than I ever had before. I had four canvases going at once. A break from one painting meant it was time to work on the next. I worked so hard that I didn't have the energy to fight all the fears and insecurities I carried with me. I poured them into painting. I felt like a raw nerve. I didn't hold anything back.

I got my portfolio together and finished my application just before the University of Washington deadline, running to the post office on my lunch break so I could get my package postmarked at the very last possible minute. I was nervous when I handed the envelope over to the man behind the counter. My hands shook. Sweat beaded up on my lip. I worried that he might think I was handing him some sort of mail bomb.

When I got home from work that night, I found Anita's business card and dialed the number. I sat on my kitchen counter and swung my legs nervously while I waited for her to pick up the phone. I felt like my heart might burst.

"Hello?"

"Hi, this is Gilbert's friend Jessie Morgan."

"Yes," Anita said. "I remember you! I'm so glad you called."

"Only, I'm not actually Jessie Morgan." I explained about Myra and the class reunion, Deagan and my mom. She asked questions. I answered them. I told her about purple glitter and broken glasses and how painting was the only thing that ever made me feel right. I confessed more than I probably should have. I thought it would put me out of the running, but I had to be honest. I couldn't start the next part of my life with any lingering lies. I had to face up to being myself.

"So," Anita said, "I'd really like to see you do a series of paintings about identity. I think you'll have an interesting perspective."

"You don't think I'm crazy?" I asked, picking at a chip in the laminate countertop, exposing the plywood underneath it.

"Honey," she said, laughing, "if you'd had a normal life, you wouldn't paint. Perfectly happy, well-balanced people don't spend all their time trying to examine life or capture moments. They live." She sighed. "I mean, you don't have to be a tortured artist or anything, and I don't get the feeling you are. Good art comes from people who have been knocked around by life, made some bad choices, nursed hurt feelings. We're all a little nutty here. We've just learned to use it to our advantage. What doesn't kill us gives us superpowers, right? And I think that's what you're doing. You're using your paintings to make sense of your world. I saw it in the work you showed me, and I'd like to see more of it."

I told her I had submitted my application and was in the process of quitting my job. She said I wouldn't be able to start classes until the next semester, but there was an open spot as a research assistant that they wanted to fill before that.

"We're hoping to create a better focus on the effect of social media in art," she told me. "I can't say anything for sure yet, of course, but it seems like your perspective could be very useful."

When I hung up the phone, I closed my eyes and pictured what my life could be. A tiny apartment walking distance from the school, late nights drinking tea and poring over art history texts, a huge studio to paint in. Instead of exercising in the dark little gym in my apartment complex, I could jog out to the beach at Carkeek Park. Maybe I'd even learn to kayak.

The day before the Ivolushun launch, Monica called me into her office.

"Are you still leaving us," she asked, "after this is all over?"

"Yeah," I said. "I think I'm moving to Seattle. It's not a hundred percent certain yet, but I'm hoping it all works out." It felt nice to be honest with her and not feel like I had to scramble to tell her what she wanted to hear.

"What's in Seattle? Another agency?"

"MFA program, in studio art. Painting."

"You paint?" she said, raising her eyebrows. She gave me one of her dazzling smiles. "No chance I could move you over to art direction in the ad department, is there?"

I smiled.

"Listen," she said, sitting down in the chair next to me, like we were friends having a chat. "I get it." She rubbed her fingers against her left temple. "I was on track to be a psychologist. I was employing some of the right interests—it just wasn't the right channel. And then, when you find it, you can't stay on the same path. This isn't your channel. I get it." She laughed. "I want to chain your leg to your desk, but . . . "

"Really?"

"You're surprised by this? Why do you think I sent you to Seattle? You're my workhorse. The best and the brightest. Low drama, high productivity." She shook her head. "You have a knack for telling the client exactly what they want to hear. It's killing me to lose you, but I do get it."

"Thank you," I said, blinking hard, worried I might cry. It reminded me of what Anita said: "What doesn't kill us gives us superpowers." Of course I was good at telling clients exactly what they wanted to hear. I was raised to tell everyone what they wanted to hear and then scramble to make good on it as best I could. It just wasn't the right channel for me anymore.

"Can you give me another week?" she asked.

"Yeah," I said.

"I'm going to hand your accounts over to Luanne, and I'd like you to get her up to speed."

I hesitated.

"I've noticed you two aren't exactly chatty lately. Fix that, okay?" She raised an eyebrow and tried to look stern, but I think it was a personal suggestion more than a professional request.

"Yeah," I said.

"Good," she said, reaching her hand out to shake mine. "I wish you good things, Jenny."

"Thank you," I said, "for everything. I've learned so much from you." And it was true. As much as the scramble to keep Monica happy had worn me down sometimes, it had also forced me to up my game.

"Use it well," she said, and I think maybe, just maybe, she was fighting tears too.

When I got back to my desk, the phone was ringing.

"Hey," the voice said, "Jenny?"

"Yeah."

"It's Robbie."

"Really?"

"Well, uh, actually, I'm a Robbie impersonator." He laughed.

I didn't know what to say. "Um," I stalled.

"Too soon to joke? It's too soon, isn't it?" He sounded genuinely embarrassed.

"It's fine, Robbie," I said. "I wasn't expecting to hear from you."

"I remembered where you said you worked. I hope it's okay that I called."

"Of course it is." I wanted to say more, to tell him how much the time I'd spent with him meant to me, but I didn't know why he was calling. I didn't want to scare him off.

"So, okay, I guess this is weird, because I haven't actually known you since I was in diapers. But, uh . . ." He took a deep breath. I held mine. "I got my swimmers checked. The numbers are low, but not so low that it's never going to happen for us."

"Oh my gosh!" I yelped, clapping my hand over my mouth. The intern in the cubicle next to me poked his head up and gave me the evil eye. You didn't have to have worked at Levi & Plato long to know that Monica did not allow personal calls. Technically, I should have told Robbie I'd call him back later, but I was leaving anyway. It hardly mattered. "That's wonderful," I said in a low whisper.

"Is it weird that I wanted to tell you?" Robbie's voice was sweet and soft. I could picture him standing there, phone to his ear, scratching at the stubble on his chin.

"I think I've forfeited the right to decide what's weird." I thought about the stars. I remembered how safe I felt. "I'm glad you called."

"You know," he said, "I get why you did it—how it could be easier to be someone else. I know you didn't do it to hurt anyone."

"Thank you," I said. I drew the sliver of a moon on my desk blotter with my pen, leaving it empty and shading in the sky around it with a blue ballpoint.

"Jessie would never have talked to me like that. And she was never much for listening. I mean, there are things about Jessie that I loved, that I always will, but she wasn't . . . She wasn't always a very good friend."

"Really?" I said. "Because you guys were so happy to see me—her."

"Jessie rarely listened. She always did what she wanted to do, no matter what everyone else needed, but, man, if you were okay with being along for the ride, it was a freaking fun ride. We all miss her, but I think we all wanted her to be more like you. Maybe you're a better Jessie than Jessie." He sighed.

"She's certainly a presence," I said.

"So how is she?"

"She's doing well," I said. "She has a son. He's four. She has her own photo studio. She looks—I mean, I don't know her otherwise, but she looks good."

"Really?" he said, and there was this spark of interest in his voice. Even though I knew I had no right to, I felt a twinge of jealousy. But then he said, "How are you?"

I told him about the MFA program, and that I'd given notice at my job. As I talked, I drew the ground and the grass and me and Robbie and the smoke from our cigarettes curling into the sky.

"Am I crazy to do this?" I asked. "Are you all going to think I'm some sort of psycho stalker if I move to Seattle?"

"I won't. Karen might," he said. "But I don't think anyone's in the Karen fan club right now."

"It's not Karen's fault," I said.

"She kept Jessie's secrets. And then she was so set on hurting you, or Jessie, or whoever, that she didn't think about how she would hurt us. It's like you're not the only one who pretended to be someone they weren't."

"I'm sorry," I said.

"I know," he said, his voice brightening. "I'm still glad I met you. I never would have if you weren't a crazy Jessie impersonator." He laughed. "Plus there's a place near the UDub campus that has karaoke on Wednesdays. No one else ever wants to do karaoke with me."

Luanne was sitting at the bar at Good Luck with her Thursday night Manhattan. "Hey," I said. I stood next to her and waited for her to say something, but she didn't. I thought maybe she didn't want to talk to me, but then she called the bartender over and ordered a Manhattan for me too.

I don't actually like Manhattans, but details like that never seemed to matter to Luanne.

"You didn't even tell me you quit," she said, when I sat down next to her.

"You weren't talking to me. What was I supposed to do, send you a memo?"

"So Monica said you're moving to Seattle?"

"Yeah."

She pursed her lips and gave me a hard stare. "I don't think I understand this lifestyle choice. Am I supposed to call you Jessie now?"

"I'm not Jessie Morgan," I said. "I know that. Everyone knows that. And I'm not moving to Seattle to be her. I'm just trying to figure out who Jenny Shaw is."

"Don't talk about yourself in the third person," Luanne said, picking the cherry out of her martini glass with the little red plastic sword. "It's creepy."

"I'm just trying to figure out who I am," I said. "And I'm sorry that I hurt you."

"I never tried to keep you from being who you are. I wasn't, like, trying to stunt your growth." She curled a strand of hair around her finger and let it go.

"I know. I never stuck up for myself. I never insisted on who I was or what I needed from our friendship. And I know that's not your fault."

She sighed and stared into her glass. It seemed like she was annoyed that I was there, infringing on her ritual. I hadn't touched my Manhattan.

"You can have it if you want," I said, standing up and tucking a ten under the foot of the glass.

"Will I ever see you again?" she asked, her eyes suddenly filled with tears.

"Do you want to?" I honestly believed that she didn't. I was only trying to talk to her because I told Monica I would. I thought Luanne would just want me gone.

"Of course," she said. "I love you. You're my best friend. And I tried to be yours. I really did."

I wrapped my arms around her and rested my chin on her head. "I love you too, Lu."

"This doesn't mean I'm helping you move. I just got my nails done."

"I'm not moving for a few more weeks at least."

"Yeah," she said, laughing. "Same excuse then too."

"Come visit me," I said.

"Really?"

"Yeah. But no backhanded compliments allowed, okay?"

"Okay," she said. "But you have to call me on my shit. Push back. I won't punch you or anything." She smiled and stabbed at the cherry in my drink. "At least, I'm not likely to."

"Fine," I said. "It's a deal."

"Deal." She spun around on her barstool and hugged me. "When I visit, can we both take on aliases and talk to strangers?"

"Screw you," I said, laughing.

"Oh, right back at you, kiddo," she said, and planted a big, lipsticky kiss on my cheek.

I sat down next to her again and ordered myself a soda.

"So," she said, wrapping her cherry stems in a bar napkin, "you didn't get back together with Deagan, did you?"

"No," I said, stirring the ice around in my soda with my straw.

"Oh! Good! I worried you would." Her eyes were wide and she scrambled for more words, like she was trying so hard to say the right things. "I mean, it would be easy to, you know? Not just for you. For anyone. To fall back into old patterns." She swiveled to face me, planting her feet on the bottom rungs of my barstool. "Do you miss him?"

"Not as much as I thought I would," I said.

"Good," she said. "Because there's no point in being with any-one who's too stupid to realize that they should want to be with you."

The letter offering me the position as Anita's assistant arrived a few days later. I stuck it to my refrigerator with a magnet from the pizza place. Every time I walked into the kitchen and saw it, I flushed with pride and my stomach wobbled like I was looking down from a great height. I was taking a leap, changing the things I could change, leaving behind the things that I couldn't.

As soon as I sent in the paperwork to accept the job, I started weeding through my possessions and getting rid of things. I didn't want to live with ghosts anymore. My dishes were from my parents' bridal registry. My couch and love seat were hand-me-downs my dad gave me when one of his "chippies" redecorated his condo. Deagan bought me the coffee table for my birthday. I'd always meant for the wing chair to end up in his living room.

I packed it all up carefully and arranged to have Volunteers of America come pick it up. Someone who didn't know they were relics of failed relationships would be happy to have these things, but I didn't want reminders of hurt in my new life. I wanted to start fresh.

I kept only what I could fit in my Jeep, only the things that felt like they were really mine: my paints and paintings, some of my clothes, a sketchbook from Ithaca, my Bombers beer stein, the fancy vacuum cleaner I splurged on when I got my first paycheck, Snuffy's kitty condo.

I packed Deagan's things in one of the booze boxes I'd

snagged from the liquor store. Most of it wasn't really stuff he
needed anyway: the extra toothbrush he kept at my place, a contact lens case, the pair of scratched-up glasses he only wore when
he was desperate, slippers with unraveling stitches, a worn-out
sweatshirt. When he'd brought these things over, it felt monu-
mental, like a leap in a new direction, but I realized when the box
was sitting on the passenger seat on the way to his apartment that
he'd left behind things he could spare anyway. Plus if he'd really
wanted any of it, he could have taken it back when he left my
suitcase. But I didn't want the responsibility of throwing his stuff
away. I guess I also wanted to say good-bye.

The fact that we were done, that Deagan left me for someone
else, didn't negate the fact that for a very long time I had thought
of him as the person I was going to marry. I was really leaving.
There'd be no running into him at Wegmans or hearing how he
was doing from one of his friends when I saw them at the Public
Market. We wouldn't keep in touch. This was an honest-to-
goodness end, and I needed to be a grown-up about it and face it
head-on. I needed to say the right things and then say good-bye.

"**W**ow, Jen," **Deagan** said, "your hair looks great." He took the box from me and shifted awkwardly from one foot to the other, giving me a sheepish smile. It was all very civilized.

I guess part of me had wanted him to open the door and grab me and kiss me with a passion he'd never had before and tell me that Faye was just a horrible, stupid phase that made him realize how wrong he'd really been. I didn't want him back. I only wanted the upper hand. It was the natural breakup wish, to be the dumper, not the dumpee, to preserve a little more dignity. But Deagan looked good. Happy. And from the little I knew about Faye, she seemed like the right person for him. She didn't even mind the horrible foot smell of the indoor volleyball courts. I wasn't the right person for Deagan, and he wasn't the right one for me.

"Thanks," I said. "So, um, I'm moving and I wanted to drop this off before I leave."

"New apartment moving or moving moving?"

"Seattle," I said. "Moving moving."

"Wow," he said, shifting the box from one hip to the other. "Do you want to come in? I just made coffee."

"Sure," I said. "Thanks."

He stepped aside and let me in. It was odd to be in his apartment and not picture it as the place I'd be living someday, to feel like a guest all of a sudden.

He poured our coffee. He put mine in the mug I always liked best—the handmade one from People's Pottery—but I wasn't sure if it was on purpose or it was just the mug he grabbed.

"I shouldn't have broken up with you like that. I'm sorry," he said.

"Yeah."

We sat side by side on the stools at his kitchen counter.

"I know it's probably not important," he said, looking into his coffee cup, "but I didn't cheat on you."

"Oh," I said, taking a deep breath. My eyes stung. "That actually is important." I looked at him. "I thought—you canceled the spa reservation like a month before and I thought—"

"I canceled because I knew I needed to end things. I knew it wasn't fair to feel like . . ." He looked at me and looked away again quickly. "Then every time I saw you, I wasn't sure. I'd change my mind."

I scratched at a bubble in the glaze on the mug.

"But I didn't even tell Faye how I felt until after," he said. "I waited until after we broke up."

"You mean after you dumped me at the airport and drove off with my luggage," I said.

He gave me a horrified look. "I'm so sorry."

I smiled at him. "I want to be mad at you for all of it—to hold on to the idea that you're this bad guy—but I think I just need to get over it and move on." It was easier to talk sitting next to him, to just say things out into the kitchen in general. I didn't have to make eye contact. I didn't want to. It was easier to say the hard stuff. "I wish you'd been honest about who you are and what you want, but I wasn't honest either. I don't even think I knew what I wanted. I think I was just grasping for all the things I thought

I should want. Who I thought I should be." I took a sip of coffee. It was terrible. He always made his coffee too weak.

"So, did you get a job in Seattle?" he asked. He was kicking his foot on the rung of the stool and it occurred to me that he was nervous.

I wasn't. I felt calm.

"I'm going back to school," I said.

"Marketing?"

"Painting." I smiled.

"Really?" He looked at me like maybe I was someone he hadn't actually met before.

"Yeah," I said.

"I remember you used to paint. Why did you stop?"

"You hated the way the paint smelled."

We were both quiet for a while.

"I had no idea," he said finally, his forehead wrinkled up.

"Hey," I said, "I should have told you to suck it up. I was so scared of losing you that I put all my energy into trying to be who I thought you wanted." I laughed. "That's really stupid, isn't it?" I wrapped my hands around the coffee mug to warm them. "We're not right for each other. And that's okay."

"Maybe I have no right to say this, Jen, but I'm really proud of you."

"Thanks," I said. I used my ankle to stop him from kicking the rung of his stool.

He smiled.

We finished our coffee. I hugged him good-bye. He kissed my cheek. After he shut the door behind me, I walked down the hallway, choking back tears. The next good-bye would be even harder.

Driving up to my mother's house, my breathing got shallow and my palms broke out in sweat. I'd spent every day of grade school with the same dizzying nausea taking over my stomach as I rode the school bus home, worried about the state she'd be in when I walked through the door.

We hadn't talked since I hung up on her. When I finally turned my phone back on, I'd expected a long string of messages from her, but there was only one. All it said was, "Apparently we were cut off." I tried calling her back, but she wouldn't pick up the phone. After a week I gave up. I didn't really want her to answer anyway. I didn't want to talk to her. It was easier not to. Maybe I should have been worried, but she'd cut me off like this before. It was the price for hurting her pride.

I used my key and let myself in through the front door. The air was greasy, tinged with the sour smell of sweated-out booze and stale cigarette smoke. There were piles of newspapers stacked on the coffee table and empty takeout cartons strewn across the kitchen counter. I hoped she'd had food delivered. I shuddered to think of her driving across town to the Chinese place.

"Hi, honey, is that you?" she called, in her saccharine happy mom voice. There was an edge to it, darkness. I knew I was walking on eggshells.

She sat at the kitchen table in her nightgown, poring over the latest issue of *Entertainment Weekly*. She was gaunt through her face, but her eyes were puffy. Her faded blond hair was dry and frizzy and had a wide swath of dark roots peppered with gray. The fill line on her acrylic nails was halfway to her fingertips, and the polish was chipped.

She turned her cheek to me, expecting me to kiss it. I didn't.

"What did you do to your hair?" she said, gesturing to her own. "It ages you."

"So, I came to tell you I'm moving to Seattle," I said, ignoring her. "I'm going to art school."

"What about Deagan?" she said. "Surely he's not going to leave his job."

"We broke up." I cleared a stack of magazines and mail off my chair at the table, hung my purse over the back, and sat down. "I got into an MFA program for painting. And I have a job as a research assistant." I looked down. There was still a speck of purple glitter on my chair. "I'll be working for the head of the department." I felt pathetic for telling her, for even wanting her to know, like some little puppy dog hoping for a pat on the head. I knew I'd never get it, but I held my breath for her answer anyway, hoping that something would be different.

"I can't believe you let Deagan get away," she said. She got up and bent over the stove to light her cigarette on the burner.

"You didn't even like Deagan," I said, scratching at the glitter with my fingernail until it was gone.

"He came from a good family." She sat down again, taking a drag of her cigarette, blowing the smoke in my direction. She never used to smoke in front of me.

"I don't want to talk about Deagan," I said softly, but loud enough.

She acted like she hadn't heard me. "And it's not like you're getting any younger." Her voice was bitchy and aloof, but I saw her cheek tremble. "I guess I'm never going to have grandchildren. You should have tried harder to keep him."

I didn't say anything. I looked around the kitchen at the stacks of newspapers and food-stained takeout menus. Wine bottles filled the space next to the sink, from weeks of missing the recycling pickup. Empty liquor bottles always went directly in the trash so no one would see them.

I looked at the woman sitting in front of me and thought about all the things I'd always wanted from her. I wanted her to be a mama bear teaching me to fish in the river, nudging me over logs and rocks. But she wasn't. She couldn't be. She didn't know how to hug me and tell me everything was going to be okay. She didn't know how to love me through all her hurt.

I stood up and walked around the kitchen, collecting half-empty Chinese food containers that smelled like they were at least a few days old. I dumped them in a plastic grocery bag along with the pile of condiment packets and questionably clean plastic utensils that littered the counter, saving a chopstick so I could poke it down the garbage disposal to check for silverware. I pulled out a fork and an earring, and then I ran the water and flicked the switch to get rid of the random detritus that had collected, probably since the last time I had been there and run the garbage disposal.

"Have you eaten today?" I asked, opening the fridge. There was a carton of eggs four months past their date, a bottle of ketchup, an empty carton of milk, and an assortment of decaying vegetables in the crisper that were so far gone it was impossible to tell what they had been.

"I'm not hungry," she said, smiling weakly. She liked the attention. She liked forcing me into this role where I had to feed her like she was a petulant child, clean her messes, calm her fears.

"You need to eat," I said. "Do you want me to order something?"

"I'm fine," she said. "I have to watch my figure." She patted her hip with her bony hand. I wondered who she thought she was watching her figure for. She looked so frail and feeble.

I grabbed the protein bar I kept in my purse for emergencies and placed it on the table next to her. "At least eat this," I said. "Please."

I picked up the array of mugs and glasses that formed the perimeter of her place at the table like a fort to obstruct her view of the seats that were empty. I balanced them in the crook of my arm, against my chest, and grabbed more with pinched fingers. She held her hand over the mug closest to her to keep me from taking it. I walked carefully to the dishwasher and stacked the glasses in the top rack one by one.

I thought about calling Anita, telling her I'd have to stay.

I set the dishwasher to run and sat down at the table. The protein bar lay unopened next to her. She flipped the pages in her magazine too quickly to be reading anything. My throat tightened. Her eyebrow twitched.

"I don't know how you think you're going to survive a grad program in art," she said, her voice a soft slur, her eyes shooting daggers. "Your paintings are always so self-conscious." She stared me down, waiting to watch the wound bleed. "You should have stayed with Deagan. I mean, I'm just worried what will happen to you when you can't make money with your little art projects." She placed her hand over her heart, like she was playing the part of a concerned parent in a community play. Her eyes sparkled. She lived for this. When she fought with my father, she used to glow. "I finally threw out those creepy girls in your room."

"What creepy girls?" I asked, but my heartbeat sped up. I knew.

"All those hideous portraits you had taped to the walls. The tape took the paint off with it. I'm going to have to repaint the whole room."

I thought about the way I'd painted Scout's face with the right amount of defiance, Jo March looked wise, and Emma had the kindest eyes. I'd painted them so carefully. I used to lie in bed and look at them and think about what it would be like to have Anne as my kindred spirit friend. I showed Jane Eyre to my art teacher after class. He'd encouraged me to apply to art schools. My portraits weren't hideous or creepy. She did it as payback for hanging up the phone. "You threw them away?" I said, blinking. I wished I could hide my hurt. She fed off of it.

She took a long drink from her mug. "I couldn't stand looking at them anymore. I don't know how you're going to make a living. No one will hire you to paint a hideous portrait. No one would want to look like one of those creepy girls."

"You're drunk," I said.

Her eyebrow twitched. Her face turned bright red. "You've always been an ungrateful bitch." She spit the words out. "I gave up my life for you. My career, my marriage. Such a waste! I wasted my life on you, Jenny." She said my name like it was the most trivial word in the world.

I stood up and grabbed my purse off the chair.

"You're drunk," I said again, trying not to yell, tears choking my voice. I wanted to say more, to find the right words to make her better. I wanted her to say she was sorry. I wanted her to be sorry. I still wanted her to be a mama bear. She couldn't.

"I can't fix you," I said, sobbing. I wiped my face with my sleeve. "I really, really wanted to, Mom, but you have to fix your-self. And if you won't, I can't be here anymore. You broke my heart. You keep breaking it. And I can't let you."

She didn't say anything. She didn't look at me. She clicked her nails together, flipped the page of her magazine, and pretended to be completely absorbed in a story about Brad and Angelina. I didn't exist.

"Call me if you're ever ready to get help," I said, squeezing her shoulder gently. "I'll help you find a program."

◆

I went out through the garage. I opened the door to her car and sat in the passenger seat.

On my last day of high school, my mother picked me up and we went to the movies in the middle of the afternoon. She'd been having a good week. We saw *Moulin Rouge*. We shared a big bucket of popcorn and a Diet Coke, and I watched her eyes light up each time she recognized one of the songs they were singing. She seemed lighter, softer—happy. We hadn't been to the movies in such a long time.

On the way home, we heard "Roxanne" on the radio and sang along at the top of our lungs. When we got back to the house, the song was only halfway through, so we sat in the garage with the music blaring, singing together like it was the performance of our lives. I remember thinking that maybe after that everything would be okay. Maybe she was better. She was wearing a red sweater set that I'd bought her for Mother's Day. She had blush on her cheeks and her lipstick had all but worn off. She looked so pretty. I remember thinking that maybe she was finally better.

I reached up and turned the dome light on to drain the battery. I closed the door behind me quietly when I left.

I drove to Wegmans, called the police from a pay phone, and gave them her license plate number. "Please watch for her," I said, my heart pounding in my throat. "She drives drunk sometimes." I felt like a traitor, but it was all I could do. I couldn't make her happy. I couldn't make her stop. She was never going to be the person I wanted her to be, and I couldn't give up any more of my life to keep her in maintenance mode.

◆

When I got home, I found Yarah on Facebook and sent her a request.

She wrote back a few minutes later: "My dear old friend! How happy I am to find you!" I responded: "I loved being an eight-legged sea creature with you," and she knew exactly what I meant.

The drive across country with Mr. Snuffleupagus was brutal. Snuffy cried in his crate and vomited every couple of hours, filling the car with the smell of cat food and stomach acid. There was too much time to think and too much time to worry that I was making some sort of colossal mistake. I spent my nights in crappy motel rooms, watching home-makeover shows, eating vending-machine burritos, and trying to get Snuffy to use the little travel litter box, instead of the motel carpet. So driving up to the apartment complex and seeing Robbie waiting in the parking lot for me, leaning against his truck, made all the difference. It made it less scary. I stopped doubting that I was making a colossally dumb decision. Even if I had nothing else, I had a friend, the kind who knew my deepest, darkest secrets and liked me anyway.

"Jenneroo!" he said, giving me a great big hug. "It's good to see you."

Heather didn't come, but she sent cookies. "I think she'll come around, you know?" he said, putting the container on the kitchen counter. "And she knows you're my friend. She knows how you get me." He leaned against the counter. "Plus a woman in her condition shouldn't really be lifting boxes."

"Wait! What?" I said, clapping my hand over my mouth. "Robbie! Wow!" I hugged him and gave him a big kiss on the cheek. "You're going to be the best dad, Robbers."

We blasted Meat Loaf and sang along while I hung my clothes

in the closet and Robbie inflated my air mattress. I'd have to go furniture shopping, but I wanted to wait until I knew what I wanted my apartment to look like. I wanted to give myself some time as a blank slate.

We finished unloading all my boxes. Snuffy was settled on a windowsill, glaring at us.

"Can I buy you a beer, Robbers?" I asked.

"I quit," Robbie said. "I'm not going to be like my dad." He smiled wide enough for the gap before his incisor to show. "But I could go for a milkshake."

"So, we're not going to have our last drinks together too?" I said, laughing.

"When my kid gets married," Robbie said, laughing. "You and me. We'll go out to the field and drink champagne and toast to Jessie Morgan, wherever she is."

"Deal," I said.

"So, be honest. Was that your first cigarette?" He was grinning ear to ear.

"Yeah," I said.

"I should have known," Robbie said. "You coughed way too much."

The next day, I stopped at Myra's store to give back the Jessie dress.

"Hey," Nancy said, when I walked in. She smiled, but it was the way you might smile at someone who just got released from the loony bin. Kind but cautious. Myra must have told her.

"I don't feel like I can keep this," I said, pushing the dress across the counter. "I know I wore it, so it's not like something you can sell, but I just feel like Myra should have it back."

She took the dress from me.

"And I think I should pay for it," I said.

"Nonsense," she said. "We can still use it for display. Myra wouldn't want you to pay for it. But if you want to shop, we appreciate your business."

I stayed for a while, trying on clothes. I was hoping Myra would show up, but she didn't.

I didn't have to get dressed up anymore. I didn't have to dress for anyone but me. I bought a fabulous pair of corduroy pants, a gray sweater knitted from recycled yarn, an organic cotton flannel shirt, and a necklace with a tiny octopus charm to replace the necklace Deagan had given me.

I paid and was halfway to the door when I remembered the other reason I'd come in.

"Nancy," I said, pulling the canvas board with the sign design out of my messenger bag, "can you give this to Myra?"

"Oh my God!" Nancy said, holding her hand over her mouth. "It's perfect. She'll love it."

I wasn't ready to go back to my empty apartment just yet, so I went next door to the coffee shop to get a latte.

I had my order and was ready to leave when I heard someone call, "Jenny?" And this time I was sure she said Jenny.

Myra was sitting at a table in the corner, with a huge cup of coffee, a mess of papers, and a calculator.

She got up and hugged me. It was probably obvious to anyone watching that we both felt awkward about it, but I was happy she saw me and didn't want to hide. I had been in my own little world. I would have walked right past her if she hadn't said something.

"Do you have a second?" she asked. She waved her hand in the direction of the chair across from her and gathered up the papers into a stack as she sat down again. "I have to do receipts over here," she said. "If I'm in the store, I just want to play with the clothes. Plus, see that guy over there?" She pointed to a good-looking man with curly brown hair, sitting at a table in the corner, typing on a laptop. "He's the owner, the one I told you about. He's always here." She smiled and raised her eyebrows.

I loved that she was confiding in me, even just the smallest bit, but I knew I shouldn't get my hopes up. "I brought the dress back," I said.

"You didn't have to."

"It felt like the right thing to do." I stared at my coffee cup because it was hard to look at Myra.

"I've thought about it a lot," Myra said. "I should have known, I guess. You're nothing like Jessie."

I thought it was an insult. Angry words. But when I looked up, she was smiling.

"And don't think that I don't love Jessie. Because I do. But Jessie being Jessie was way more drama than you pretending to be her. She always stirred up trouble. She had to. She couldn't keep her life simple, and if there was, like, the slightest hint of calm, she'd pick an epic fight with Robbie or tell me Karen said something mean about me behind my back. It was all drama, all the time. It was exciting when we were fifteen, but if she hadn't disappeared, I think we would have drifted apart anyway."

I picked at the seam on the cardboard sleeve of my coffee cup. I didn't know what to say.

"We talked," Myra said. "She called me. And, you know, she's Jessie. She said she was sorry and all of that, but it was, like, her grand statement to me. And it was all about protecting her boundaries and how she didn't want to feel like she ever had to come back here. She didn't want to feel like she owed it to anyone to be her old self." Myra shook her head. "That's Jessie. And I will always love her for the things in my life that I never would have had the courage to do if it weren't for her, for getting me to live outside my comfort zone. But even the way she pushed us to do things—all of that—I think every single moment of it was for her. So she could have partners in crime. So she could feel less alone. Not because she was being a good friend. It's easy to look back and fix it all in my head and say, 'Wow, Jessie was really trying to make me more brave,' and I did that when you were here. Your version of Jessie made me rewrite the real one. I believed you because that's who I wanted Jessie to be." She laughed. "And let's face it—I had no reason to think you weren't! I mean, who pretends to be someone else?"

"I know," I said, laughing. "Right?"

"It's weird, because I know you and I don't know you. And I think I probably don't know you more than I know you. That's a lot of knows. But, I mean, I can't just jump in and be your long-lost friend. And I think I'm still processing all of it. I'm still trying to figure out how I feel. So I guess what I'm saying is that maybe the door is shut right now, but it's not locked. Does that make sense?"

"Yeah," I said. "It does."

"I do, however, have to tell you," she said, smacking the table, "Blackberry loved my stuff and they want two more seasons from me, and a resort line."

"Really?" I said. "That's incredible!"

We talked for a little while longer. I told her about saying good-bye to Deagan and my mother, and about the series of paintings I'd been working on. "I'm not doing it to stalk you or anything. In fact, I tried really hard to find a program somewhere else. But it's just the right place for me."

"I'm really glad," Myra said, "that you're figuring out who you are. I think I know you enough to know that you're going to find a great person in there. You're going to find someone you want to be."

◆

A few weeks later, I drove past Myra's store on my way to the DMV to get my Washington State driver's license. Her old sign had been replaced by the one I designed. The mannequin in the front window was wearing the Jessie dress.

"**S**o," Luanne said—I could hear her slurp her coffee over the phone—"have you gone grunge yet?"

It was our new tradition. Once a week, when Monica left for her weekly nail appointment, Luanne would take a coffee break and call me from the office. I'd be just getting up and having my first cup. It was still a little weird between us but getting better. We didn't want the same things anymore. I didn't trigger her competitive side. She wanted to be my friend. That counted for something. As did her attempt to understand why anyone would want to quit a decent-paying job to go back to school, live on a research assistant's stipend, spend time around "germy college kids," and live in a studio apartment.

"Not entirely grunge," I said, "but I did buy a flannel shirt."

"No! Really?" she said, sounding slightly exasperated.

"Deal with it," I said. "It's not the end of the world."

She told me about Monica's latest meltdown, and I told her about the new painting I was working on. It was a self-portrait. I was trying to paint the most honest picture of myself that I could. "Zits and all," I said.

"Why?" Luanne said. "It's a painting. You can paint yourself with better hair and clear skin."

"I have great hair," I said. "And I think it's time that I face myself, you know?"

"Just promise me that you'll face yourself in something that isn't flannel."

"I make no promises," I said.

After we hung up, I bundled up and walked over to the studio. It was actually sunny in Seattle. The air was crisp and clean. My feet felt firm on the sidewalk. My legs felt strong.

I let myself into the studio, breathing in the smell of oil paint, watching the dust moats swirl in the light as I walked over to my painting: a canvas so big I'd have never been able to work on it in the confines of a tiny apartment. My self-portrait was larger than life-size. It let me examine every freckle and flaw, the curve of my chin, the slightly sad angle of my eyes. It let me see myself.

I wet down my brush, wiping the excess water on my thigh, adding a stripe of leftover pigment, a flash of pink, to the history of my work jeans. Then I began mixing my paints for the afternoon. I hummed to myself while I turned yellow into orange and blue into green.

I heard footsteps but I didn't turn around, trying to cling to the vision in my head and the feeling I had when I was alone with my paints.

"Hey," a voice said. "I was just checking in with Matisse, and Anita told me you might be here." I turned around and saw the person I'd missed the most.

"Hi, Gilbert," I said.

"Hi, Jenny."

He smiled, his blue eyes crinkling at the corners, and put his hand out to shake mine. "It's nice to meet you," he said.

Acknowledgments

To everyone who read *Stay*, recommended it to friends, tweeted and blogged about it, and came to book tour events, you made this book possible and I cannot thank you enough.

A gigantic thank-you to my editor, Denise Roy, for giving me the courage to take this story to the places it needed to go. Working on this book with you has been a wonderful experience. Thanks also to Phil Budnick, Kate Napolitano, Milena Brown, Lavina Lee, Jaya Miceli, and everyone at Plume for giving this book such a great home.

To my fabulous agent, Elisabeth Weed, thank you for your help, patience, and support. This book would not have flourished without you. Huge thanks to Dana Borowitz at United Talent Agency and Stephanie Sun at Weed Literary.

Michele Larkin, thank you for tirelessly sharing your beauty, brains, and bountiful common sense. You are the sister I always wished for.

Oh, Neil Gordon, you guru of storytelling! Thank you for being such an awesome friend and teacher. You are the bees cliché.

Joan Pedzich, thank you for lending your amazing talents as a reader and writer, and for loving my characters as much as I do. I don't know what I'd do without you.

Claire Cook, thank you for being such a gracious friend and mentor. I am so grateful for your wisdom and kind words.

Erika Imranyi, thank you for the spark that started it all.

Rainbow Rowell, oh goodness, I appreciate you! Thank you for all of your brilliant advice.

Evan Dawson, thank you for your support and for the fabulous conversations.

Sarah Playtis, you are circles and sea creatures and everything wonderful.

So much thanks and love to Melanie Krebs, Jennifer DeVille, Julie Smith, Brenda Kirkwood, Rainbow Heinrichs, Lisa Malin, Michele Christiano, Erin and Ted Jackle, Carol Kirkwood, Marty Herezniak, Deb VanderBilt, Dash Hegeman, Carolyn Bennett, Kristin Dezen, Nick Tebrake, Chris Sutton, Armanda Zardzewiala, and Andi Winterfield.

Mindae Kadous, thank you so much for your enthusiastic support and for being you.

One of the greatest gifts of being a writer is getting to know other writers. I am so grateful for the members of the Fiction Writers Co-op, and also Shawn Klomparens, Amy Hatvany, M. J. Rose, Beth Hoffman, Matthew Aaron Goodman, Beth Harbison, Susan Elizabeth Phillips, Melissa Senate, Sarah Strohmeyer, Julie Buxbaum, Allison Winn Scotch, Alison Pace, Sarah Pekkanen, Caprice Crane, Jen Lancaster, and Alice Bradley.

A huge thank-you to Christy Cain and her amazing team, especially Michael Miller, Linda and Roger Bryant, Rebecca Budinger-Mulhearn, and to the glorious gang at Titles Over Tea. Erica Caldwell and Terri Marchese, thank you for your support, hospitality, and amazing book recommendations.

Thank you to Katie at the Planet Dog Foundation for helping me with my research on service dogs. Thank you also to Wooftown Rescue, Mostly Shepherds, and GSRCNY.

Thank you to everyone at the Greenists, especially Courtney Craig and Mickey Dye, for being great green friends.

To my fellow Tuskers, I spent a great deal of time while writing this book thinking about what my life would have been like if I hadn't had such wonderful friends. I'm so thankful that I got to grow up with you. Special thanks and so much love to Katherine and the Robs (especially Russell), Sohini, Danna, Laura, Lauri, Lauren, Larry, Missy, Ellen, Bryan, Sabrina, and Zeni.

To John Cuk, thank you again for being an incredible teacher. Our chat was enormously helpful at just the right time.

A huge thank-you to the Larkins and the Ashbys for your unending encouragement. I'm sure if you've met my in-laws, Doug and Terry, you've heard about my books. I feel very lucky to be a Larkin.

Jeremy, thank you for being my home no matter where we go. I love you more than everything. And, of course, thank you to my trusty dogs, Argo and Stella, and the cat, even though she hates me.

Also available from Plume

978-0-452-29712-8

www.allielarkin.com

Plume
An imprint of Penguin Group (USA)
www.penguin.com